LORI WICK

Wings OF THE *Morning*

HARVEST HOUSE PUBLISHERS
EUGENE, OREGON

All Scripture quotations are taken from the King James Version of the Bible.

Cover by Terry Dugan Design, Minneapolis, Minnesota

WINGS OF THE MORNING
Copyright © 1994 by Lori Wick
Published by Harvest House Publishers
Eugene, Oregon 97402
www.harvesthousepublishers.com

Library of Congress Cataloging-in-Publication Data
Wick, Lori.
  Wings of the morning / Lori Wick.
    p. cm.
  ISBN-13: 978-0-7369-1321-8
  ISBN-10: 0-7369-1321-1
  1. Man-woman relationships—Maine—Fiction. 2. Women merchant seamen—Maine—
Fiction. 3. Ship captains—Maine—Fiction. I. Title. II. Series: Wick, Lori. Kensington chron-
icles.
PS3573.1237W56   1994
813'.54—dc20   93-23531
                                                                            CIP

3657014 10/07

Printed in the United States of America

07 08 09 10 11 12 13 / BC / 15 14 13 12 11 10 9 8

For my brothers- and sisters-in-law:
Jeff and Ann Wick,
Darrell and Jane Kolstad,
Chris and Margaret Arenas, and
John and Cheryl Wick.
You fill a place in my heart and life
that no one else could fill.
God bless you all.

About the Author

LORI WICK is one of the most versatile Christian fiction writers in the market today. Her works include pioneer fiction, a series set in Victorian England, and contemporary novels. Lori's books (more than 3.9 million copies in print) continue to delight readers and top the Christian bestselling fiction list. Lori and her husband, Bob, live in Wisconsin with "the three coolest kids in the world."

The Kensington Chronicles

DURING THE NINETEENTH CENTURY, the palace at Kensington represented the noble heritage of Britain's young queen and the simple elegance of a never-to-be-forgotten era. The Victorian Age was the pinnacle of England's dreams, a time of sweeping adventure and gentle love. It is during this time, when hope was bright with promise, that this series is set.

Prologue

MAINE COASTLINE
1828

THE TWO LITTLE BOYS RAN up the sandy beach, fiercely brandishing their sticks as swords. As the older boy at the rear drew close, the smaller boy dashed up into the rocks to escape. He turned and shouted to his brother from his lofty position.

"It's my turn to be Clancy for a while. You can be the pirate."

"No, I'm bigger, and that makes me a better Clancy."

"But you're always Clancy," the younger boy complained.

"That's because he always wins," his brother told him logically.

The younger boy flopped down on the rock, his "sword" lying forgotten at his side. His brother climbed up to join him, their gazes stretching out over the Atlantic Ocean.

"Do you suppose Clancy really did all those things we hear about, the races and stashing the ship's hold with gold and jewels?"

"Of course," the older boy spoke with assurance, although he had no proof. "He was the best sailor in all the world."

"His ship," the younger lad had caught the fever now.

"Please tell me about his ship."

The older boy's chest swelled. "None faster in all the Atlantic. Why, his ship was the fastest ship in all the *world*."

The younger boy let out a gusty sigh, as his gaze went to the sea once again.

"Do you suppose he's still alive?"

"Alive? Don't be ridiculous," his brother scoffed. "Why, he'd probably be over a hundred years old if he were alive today!"

The younger boy looked so crestfallen, the older boy took pity on him.

"It doesn't matter. We know he was the greatest sailor to ever live. It's enough to know that he was born and raised in Maine and that there will never be another Clancy..."

❧ ❧ ❧

"What's this, Papa?" the tiny moppet in the tub asked her attentive father.

He tickled her tummy before answering. "Why, that's your navel, Smokey."

The small three-year-old giggled and stood, dripping wet, to leave the tub. Her father, Clancy Simmons, was waiting with a piece of toweling. He wrapped her snugly and took the chair by the stove in his cabin, placing Smokey in his lap to keep her warm.

"I have five toes, Papa," she told him proudly, as she examined the foot that protruded from the edge of the towel.

"You forgot a foot," Clancy told her. "You have ten toes."

"Do you have ten toes?" Smokey wanted to know. Her huge, smokey gray eyes stared with rapt attention into his bearded face.

"Indeed, I do. It's how God made all of us."

They chatted away, and within minutes Smokey was in her nightgown and back in her father's lap. The warmth of the stove and the gentle rocking of the ship lulled her to sleep just moments later. Clancy was standing over her bunk, watching her still form, when his first mate, Darsey, joined him.

Darsey stood quietly watching the bent, graying head of his captain and wondered at his thoughts.

"It's hard to believe she'll be four this summer," Clancy spoke softly.

"Aye, Captain," Darsey agreed. "My sister says they grow up before your eyes, but that it happens so fast you still feel as though it's been a magician's trick."

"Vicky would have loved her to distraction," Clancy went on softly. His mate had no reply.

"Well, now," Clancy spoke bracingly after a short pause, obviously needing to pull his mind away from painful times. "Here I am getting all soppy and putting Smokey in a wedding dress when she's barely out of wet drawers. I've got my God, my ship, my men, and years to enjoy my daughter. I would ask for nothing more…"

❦ ❦ ❦

"I'm not asking you, Smokey; I'm telling you. Mr. Tucker *is* joining us this voyage, and you *are* going to study with him."

"I don't need this Mr. Tucker. I like studying with Darsey." Her small arms were folded across her thin chest, and her small chin was tilted aggressively.

"You're eight years old, Smokey—" Clancy's voice was gentle, "long past the time you should know how to read and cipher. You've got Darsey wrapped around your finger, and whenever you don't feel the need to study, you talk your way out of it. It will be different with Mr. Tucker."

Smokey made no reply, and Clancy sternly held her eyes with his own. He expected her to yield at any time and admit that she needed training, but if anything her chin rose yet again, and Clancy knew that stern measures were needed.

"You'll not set foot in the galley, climb on the rigging, or spend more than two hours on deck each day until you can read two pages to me from a book."

All arrogance deserted Smokey, and her small shoulders drooped. Darsey had joined them to speak to the captain, but stayed silent when he heard Clancy's ultimatum.

"Do you mean that?" Smokey asked, her voice small.

"I'm afraid I do," Clancy's voice was kind. "Your schooling is important, and I love you too much to ignore it."

"All right," Smokey spoke after just a moment, her chin tilted once again, this time with determination. "I'll study with Mr. Tucker. I'll learn to read and write and do my numbers. You just see if I don't!"

Both men watched her walk away, one with admiration and one consumed with worry.

"Doesn't it bother you, Captain," Darsey asked, "that with Smokey you don't take her toys away, but instead forbid her to climb in the rigging?"

Clancy laughed and clapped the younger man on the back. "Darsey, you're a young man, much too young to be such a worrier. She's never cared for dolls. And as you can see, my words did the trick. She'll learn to read, and that's what I wanted."

Clancy, well satisfied with the passage of events, went on his way. Darsey, wanting to trust his legendary captain, continued with his work...

❀ ❀ ❀

"You're Clancy," Smokey said to her father in a mixture of awe and chagrin. "*The* Clancy."

Clancy, knowing this would happen someday, sighed deeply and waited for her to go on.

"I've been reading this old journal, the one I picked up in the bookstand while we were in port. People think you're a legend."

Clancy reached for the contents of his daughter's hands and quietly studied the pages.

"Smokey," he began after a moment of silence, hoping none of his men would need him just now, "people love to create heroes and worship the legends of their own imaginations. They also love to exaggerate," he added softly.

"What do you mean?" Smokey's sweet, ten-year-old face studied her father intently.

"I mean that the escapades I've pulled have been stretched until they are of monumental proportions. Why, to do all of the things they claim Clancy has done, I'd have to be 200 years old."

"But you have done some great things, haven't you?"

"Yes, I have," he admitted honestly. "I've always sailed fast ships, and in my younger days I would never pass up a wager or a dare. My father taught me well, and I've sailed into port more than once with a holdful of valuables, sometimes worth a small fortune. But there was no magic in it. I work hard, and I'm a man who keeps my word. Put simply, the merchants trust me. I deliver, and quickly I might add. When something special comes their way, they send word to me.

"And don't forget that I was named after my father. He was a sailor too, not as foolhardy as I've been at times, but a sailor nevertheless. The name Clancy has been on the seas far longer than my 60 years."

Smokey stared at her father as though seeing him for the first time. The look did not please the older man.

"I'm still your father, Smokey." Clancy spoke with his heart in his eyes. "I'm still the man who loves you to distraction. I've never wanted to be a hero or a legend to you, just a good father, bringing you up God's way."

Smokey moved from her chair then, her young arms going around his neck. They embraced, and the young girl's anxious thoughts melted away. It mattered not what they said about him, truth or fiction. He was the most wonderful father a girl could have. His words had eliminated all doubts and fears.

❧ ❧ ❧

"I'm afraid, Papa," Smokey cried from her bunk as the waves tossed their craft as though it were a toy, high and low over the sea.

"There's nothing to fear, Smokey," the older man's face was calm as he sat on the edge of her bunk and took her in his arms. "You were only nine when you trusted Christ to save you from your sins, and now you must trust Him again in this storm. If our ship is going down, then it's His time."

A moment passed, and Smokey began to pray out loud as she had done so many times before. When she finished talking to the Lord, Clancy added his own prayers with quiet confidence. When he had finished, he waited for the question. She asked it every time there was a storm, and Clancy could never deny her.

"Will you tell me about Mama?"

"She loved you," Clancy told her without preamble. "And she wanted you for years. We weren't married until I was nearly 40, and she thought she'd always be a spinster schoolmarm, without a husband or children of her own."

"But you came along," Smokey prodded him.

"That's right, and it was love at first sight. She gave notice to the school board, and we were married that summer. We both assumed we would have children right away, but it wasn't to be. We waited years, and had actually given up. Then God gifted us with you."

"And you named me after Mama."

"That's right. She didn't want it, but I love the name Victoria, so she gave in."

"Then she died," Smokey added on a soft, somber note.

"Yes. It was God's time, and I know she's with Him." Clancy's voice was equally quiet. "She wasn't a young woman, and her body just seemed so worn out after the birth. She had an elderly aunt and a sister who offered to take you, but I wouldn't leave you. I knew your place was with me. If only your mother could see you now. Twelve years old." Clancy didn't realize until that moment that she'd finally fallen asleep. The storm still raged without, but Smokey was now in dreamland.

Clancy rose, balancing himself with the ease of an experienced sailor and repeated softly to himself once again, "If only she could see you now..."

❦ ❦ ❦

"When can I see her?"

"Be patient. You're supposed to have developed some patience at your age."

"You make me sound ancient."

"Sixteen," Clancy stated with a twinkle in his eye. "Most girls are married and raising a family at your age."

"I'd be all for that, if he wanted to live aboard ship."

Clancy laughed, but Smokey didn't hear him. She'd finally spotted the other ship, and Clancy stood back and watched the look of delight on her face.

"Oh, Papa," she breathed in soft reverence as she gazed at the neat, sparkling ship floating opposite them. "She's beautiful. What's her name?"

"The *Aramis*."

"Are you really going to buy her?" Smokey had yet to look at her father as she talked.

"I already have."

These words were enough to bring Smokey's head around. She gave a whoop of delight over the look on his face. Her arms came around him for a quick hug before she dashed to the railing for a better look at their new ship. Darsey was already there.

"Isn't she something, Darsey? I'm going to sail her someday."

Darsey ruffled her dark cap of curls with real affection. "A little thing like you? Why, you can't even see over the wheel," he teased her.

"Just you wait," Smokey teased right back. "I'll be tall enough—someday I'll be a regular giant…"

★ ★ ★

"You said I'd be taller," Smokey good-naturedly told her father the morning of her eighteenth birthday.

Clancy smiled and kissed her brow. "Happy birthday, Smokey."

Smokey smiled in return, and Clancy studied her for a moment.

"You're not really bothered by your size, are you?"

Smokey shrugged. "Sometimes. I don't really care to look like a little girl my whole life."

Clancy slowly shook his head. His eyes took in the huge gray eyes in a heart-shaped face, the mass of shining black waves that fell from her head, and her slim form, knowing how shapely it was beneath her baggy, practical garments.

"You might not be very big, but you don't look like a little girl. If you don't believe me, ask Russell."

Smokey grinned. Russell was the son of another sea captain. He was two years younger than Smokey and quite in love with her. She had no interest in him beyond that of a friend, but it was nice to be reminded that she was attractive in someone's eyes, even if she never dressed in a feminine way.

Dresses and skirts were simply not sensible aboard ship, and there were times when Smokey didn't feel the least bit like a woman. Of course, to give up the boy's garb would mean to give up her jobs aboard ship—no climbing the rigging, no fencing on deck with Darsey, and no helping when coming into port or casting off.

"I've a surprise gift for you." Clancy cut into Smokey's wayward thoughts, and she glanced around the room.

"Where is it?"

"On deck," Clancy spoke as he led the way out of the room. Up on deck, he stopped by the wheel. He turned and looked expectantly at his daughter, but Smokey saw nothing out of the ordinary. The only thing on deck that wasn't normally there was a wooden box, about 18 inches high and sitting right in front of the wheel. Smokey put a foot out to touch it.

"It won't shift. I had Darsey nail it down," her father said.

"Why?"

"Because that's your birthday present."

Smokey could only stare at him and then at the box. When she raised her eyes once again, Clancy continued.

"If you're going to captain this ship on our next voyage, you have to be able to see over the wheel."

"I'm going to captain?" Smokey asked, not quite able to believe her ears.

"That's right. I've word that there's a load of perfect wool to be had in Australia. If you want it, you'll have to go after it."

"And you?"

"I'll serve as mate and take orders with everyone else."

Smokey's grin nearly split her face. She rose on tiptoe and kissed his cheek before turning to speak to "her" men.

"Lay up stores," she told them. "We're headed out, and it'll be a long time before we're home…"

❀ ❀ ❀

"Do you ever wish we could stay here longer, Smokey? I mean live here and have a real home?"

Smokey stared at her father across their small parlor in disbelief. He was 70 now, but had changed little. Smokey never thought of him as old.

"I've never known anything but the sea, Papa. I realize 20 is not very old, but we've never really tried to make this a home, and I much prefer my cabin on the *Aramis* to my room in this house."

"You're sure?"

"I'm sure," she told him with a loving smile.

"What about after I'm gone?" Clancy went on, surprising her again.

Realizing how little they'd spoken of this, Smokey hesitated. "Well, I don't expect to have to face that for a good 20 years, so I guess I won't worry about it now."

Clancy nodded and watched as his lovely daughter went back to her writing.

She's never had anyone but me and the crew, he thought to himself as he studied her bent head. *I'll have to bring it up again sometime. We can't pretend I'll be here forever. And when I go, then what will she do?...*

      ❦ ❦ ❦

"What will I do, Darsey?" Smokey asked, as her father's carefully wrapped body was lowered into the Atlantic waves on August 16, 1848.

"He was 73, and had a wonderful, full life, but I've had him for all my 23 years, and I don't know what I'll do without him."

Darsey silently weighed his choices. To coddle her right now would make matters worse, but he fully believed that she needed to grieve her father. He decided that for the moment at least, she needed to buck up. Her grief could come later.

"I'll tell you what you'll do," Darsey's voice was stern. "You'll captain the *Aramis* just as he taught you."

Smokey looked at him in surprise and saw that the entire crew was standing by, 25 officers and men, their eyes not on the waters that had swallowed her father, but fastened on her. Smokey turned completely to face them, and as she did so, Darsey moved to stand with the men. A moment passed, and the bos'n stepped forward, his posture and voice holding perfect respect.

"What are your orders, Captain?"

She couldn't have been more surprised than if he had thrown something at her. She studied their faces, and as her eyes met those of each man, he removed his cap in a gesture of fealty. Smokey fought the tears that threatened to choke her and spoke when she could.

"I've a yearning for southern waters," she told them softly, her voice gaining momentum with every word. "Ready yourselves, men, and set sail."

"Aye, aye, Captain" was all she heard, her every word their command. She watched as they moved to their positions. Her own gaze went back to sea.

"You can do this," Smokey whispered to herself, "and you can do it well, thanks to your papa." She prayed then, asking God for guidance and wisdom. In so doing, she gained her first glimpse of what her father had felt all these years—the duty, the responsibility to his men, and even the loneliness in going on without someone you love.

Darsey surreptitiously watched his new captain from his place behind the wheel. He was praying also. Smokey might have been surprised to learn that his prayers were not for her as a captain, but for her as a woman. He asked God to bring a special man into her life. Someone who would love her enough not to be intimidated by her position. Someone who would see her for the extraordinary woman that she was.

Darsey understood more than any of her men what a superb captain she was. He believed, however, that she would make an even finer wife and mother.

WINGS *of the* MORNING

One

KENNEBUNK, MAINE
JULY 9, 1850

AMID THE CROWD OF WELL-WISHERS, Jennifer Pemberton stood next to her husband and studied the bride. She was as lovely a bride as any girl could hope to be, her eyes sparkling with happiness over the day's events. Jennifer was reminded of the way she had felt at her own wedding just the year before.

Hundreds of people were attending today's celebration, since the groom's father was a man of some influence in the area. Jennifer's attention strayed for a moment, and her eyes caught sight of another woman in the crowd. She looked pale and somewhat overwhelmed, and Jennifer wondered if she wasn't as much a stranger in these surroundings as she herself was.

Wearing a dreadful brown dress that did nothing for her, the woman, she observed, was quite petite in both height and build. Her hair was blue-black and shiny, but pulled back tightly into an unbecoming bun at the back of her head.

Jennifer wasn't sure what prompted her, maybe it was the almost fearful way the woman held herself, but she felt compelled to seek her out. After touching her spouse's arm, she moved a few yards away to stand beside her.

"Friend of the bride or groom?" Jennifer's voice was very kind, and the other woman, after starting slightly, looked like she had been thrown a lifeline.

"I guess the groom," she admitted in a hesitant voice. "My father was a merchant sailor, and we've had dealings with Carleton Shipping for years."

"*Was* a merchant sailor?" Jennifer prompted gently.

"Yes. He died two years ago. I run the business now."

Jennifer again heard the hesitancy in her voice, but couldn't place the reason. She took her to mean that someone sailed her father's ship or ships, and she did the book work.

"By the way," Jennifer spoke again, finally remembering her manners, "I'm Jennifer Pemberton."

"Victoria Simmons," she supplied, giving Jennifer her first real smile. Jennifer was so surprised at the way it transformed her features that for a moment she said nothing.

Why, she's lovely! she thought to herself. *The drab color of her dress and her severe hairstyle are hiding a lovely flower amid weeds.*

"Are *you* a friend of the bride?" Victoria wanted to know, feeling strangely at home with this woman who was watching her so intently.

"No. I'm in the same position you are, or I should say, we are. My husband does business with Carleton Shipping. I've never even met Ben Carleton, but Tate—that's my husband—knows him. Until today I'd never seen the bride or groom. What are their names again?"

"Steve and Bridget," Victoria replied.

"Oh, that's right."

Both women watched as the newlyweds made their way toward the door. Once they were out of view, Jennifer turned to find Tate headed toward them.

"Oh, here comes my husband. Tate," she spoke when he stopped beside her, "this is Victoria Simmons. Victoria, this is my husband, Tate Pemberton."

"It's nice to meet you, Victoria."

"Thank you. It's nice to meet you also." Victoria couldn't have been more sincere, but she was suddenly out of words as she stood before this tall, striking couple. A moment of silence fell until another couple approached, and Victoria found herself just outside their circle. After watching a minute with some regret as the other four visited with careless ease, she turned and walked away. It was going to take more than two hours to get home on the stagecoach, and she knew she had best get going.

She was a block away from the church when she heard a man calling her name. She didn't know anyone in this part of Kennebunk, so for a moment or two she ignored him. The voice was insistent, however, and Victoria finally turned. Tate Pemberton was rushing up the street, a look of profound relief covering his face.

"Jennifer nearly panicked when she couldn't find you. She thought we'd lost you for good. We have our carriage. May we offer you a ride home?"

"Thank you, Tate," she told him sincerely, thinking this was the nicest gesture she'd experienced in a long time. "And please thank Jennifer for me, but I live on the other side of Kennebunk, nearly to Kennebunkport, and I'm sure that's out of your way. I'm going to take the stage."

"We live in Kennebunkport, so your home must be right on the way," Tate told her with surprised pleasure as he took her arm and began to lead her back up the street. Tate asked her exactly where she lived, and when Victoria explained, Tate nodded decisively.

From down the street Victoria spotted Jennifer standing outside the church, looking anxiously in their direction. Even from a distance, Victoria could see her smile as they neared.

"I thought we'd lost you, and we had so little time to get acquainted," Jennifer told her sincerely, still wondering what it was about Victoria Simmons that attracted her.

"I appreciate your offer, but are you sure it's not a bother? I came on the stage, and it's really no trouble."

"You're right on our way," Tate supplied as the coach appeared. He ushered the ladies inside. Within moments they were headed down the road toward home, the women sharing one side of the coach and Tate across from them.

"I really appreciate this, Jennifer," Victoria began, but the other woman cut her off.

"Please call me Jen or Jenny. All my friends do. We're glad to give you a lift. The stage can be so crowded and stuffy."

Victoria smiled at her, and Jenny was again amazed by the change in her. Jenny would have been surprised to learn that Victoria smiled because, compared to some of the cabins she had occupied in her life, the stage felt huge.

"Jen tells me you're in shipping," Tate mentioned at that moment.

"Yes, I am. It's not a large business, but we're never without work."

"How many ships do you own, Victoria?"

"Just one," she told him.

"I might know your captain," Tate leaned forward slightly, frank interest covering his handsome face. "What's his name?"

"Do you always go by your full name?" Jenny asked, choosing that moment to interrupt her husband. "Or do your friends call you Vicky?"

"Actually," Victoria turned to Jenny, since Tate didn't look at all upset over the interruption, "my nickname is Smokey."

"Smokey?" Jenny was surprised.

"It's her smokey gray eyes, Jen," Tate said with satisfaction.

"That's right," the smaller woman told him with a smile. "That, along with the fact that when I was a baby, my father used to say I would get so angry he thought smoke might come from my ears."

The Pembertons enjoyed this, laughing at the vision. The conversation moved to many avenues in the next two hours, and with only one brief stop, Smokey was home a little ahead of the stage. She thanked the Pembertons for the ride and made her way into the house, a rambling, somewhat ram-shackle two-story that had been home since her father died.

Smokey lived with her first mate, Darsey, and his widowed sister, Willa, who were both still up and settled in the small parlor when she came in. Smokey took a chair by the open window, and they looked at her expectantly.

"How was the wedding?" Willa wanted to know.

"It was nice."

"It didn't give you any ideas, did it?" Willa's look was hopeful.

Smokey laughed. "What was I supposed to do, grab the first man I saw and make it a double ceremony?"

"That's not what I meant, and you know it," Willa told her with a stern look that could not mask the fact that she wanted to laugh at Smokey's words.

"Who brought you home?" Darsey questioned her.

"The Pembertons. They live just beyond Little Fishing Rock, and when we met after the wedding, they offered me a ride."

"Old Saul Pemberton? I thought he passed away more than a year ago." Darsey frowned in thought.

"It wasn't Saul, but his son, Tate, and Tate's wife, Jenny. Jenny's maiden name was Knight." Smokey fell silent for a moment.

"You should have seen her dress," she said almost dream-ily.

"The bride's?" Willa assumed, hoping the wedding had started Smokey thinking about having a family after all.

"No," Smokey's voice was still soft. "Jen Pemberton's. It was beautiful. Makes me wish I had taken your advice, Willa, and gotten myself some new clothes."

"Well," the older woman said almost indignantly. "There's nothing stopping you from getting some now."

"Yes, there is," Smokey replied matter-of-factly. She stood and stretched, hiding an expansive yawn behind her hand. "We sail for Wales in two days. What would I do with a fancy dress aboard ship? Goodnight, Willa." Smokey kissed the older woman's cheek and then moved toward Darsey.

"Goodnight, Dars," she said after she'd kissed him also.

"Sleep well, lass," he told her and watched her lovingly as she left the room.

Willa waited only until she heard the floorboards creaking upstairs before she lit into her brother.

"Honestly, Darsey, you've got more pull with that girl than anyone! You could have said something—put in a word or two!"

"About what?" the man asked in genuine confusion.

"Her clothes!"

"What's wrong with her clothes?" Darsey frowned in puzzlement. "She's always clean and well pressed."

Willa snorted in disgust. "I'm not talking about that. *I* wear clothes that are more stylish than hers. Most of her clothes look like widow's weeds. It's not as if she can't afford something new." Willa's emotions were high, but Darsey was calmly logical.

"Be that as it may," he told her, "it's just like Smokey said. What would she do with a bunch of frills on board ship?"

"Well, she's not going to sail forever," Willa said petulantly and rocked a little harder in her chair, all the while frowning in her brother's direction.

Darsey, who had entertained this thought on more than one occasion, suddenly had nothing more to say.

It was growing dark so Tate and Jenny had decided not to tarry at Smokey's small house in the country. Still, she was the main topic of conversation as they continued their ride home.

"Isn't she the sweetest thing, Tate?"

"Indeed she is," he answered as he moved across the coach to sit next to his wife. "There's something fascinating about her. She's such a mixture of confidence and vulnerability."

"I was surprised at her age when she first told us, but then as I watched her, I saw that she certainly isn't a child."

"Well, 25 isn't what you'd call old."

"No, but when we were at the wedding, I'd have said she was closer to my 20. Then as we talked, I realized she has almost a worldly look about her. Not worldly really," Jenny immediately contradicted herself. "But her eyes seem older than the rest of her, if you know what I mean."

Tate silently digested this. "You know," he said finally, "we did an awful lot of talking, and other than finding out that she shares our faith in Christ, we really didn't learn much about her."

"Do you suppose that was deliberate on her part?"

"No, I think she genuinely liked us, but I just get the impression that she hasn't many friends."

"Oh, Tate!" Jenny was struck with what she considered a wonderful idea. "Go back in a few days and invite her to come for a visit. I know we would have such fun, and something tells me she would love staying in a house that was right on the sea. It would be such a change for her after living inland."

Tate agreed wholeheartedly, and in three days' time the coach took him back to Smokey's house. Smokey wasn't there, however; the door was answered by a woman. Tate assumed her to be the woman named Willa, about whom Smokey had spoken.

Willa told Tate that Smokey was away and wasn't expected back for quite some time. Jennifer, he knew, would be very disappointed.

Two

MOROCCO
ONE MONTH LATER

"YOU DON'T HAVE TO SAY IT, YUSUF. I can tell by the look on your face that Smoke has been here. Is the whole load gone?"

"I am sorry, Captain, yes," the old man's grin belied his words. His smile was infectious, however, and Captain Dallas Knight grinned grudgingly in return.

"How does he do it?"

Yusuf's grin widened to rival the size of his thick waist. "The ship," he said, and Dallas' eyes narrowed in thought. "I am not saying Smoke is not good captain. But the ship is fast. Maybe even fastest." The captain nodded, catching the other man's meaning, even amid the broken English.

Dallas had gotten word concerning a load of tea in Tangier. Since he had been in Spain, he'd set sail almost immediately, but as usual, a ship called the *Aramis*, and a captain known only as Smoke, beat him to it. It was a continuation of the familiar pattern of the last two years, but that was no comfort. His business was suffering as a result.

Dallas appeared to study the toe of his boot, his mind miles away. *You wouldn't think that in an ocean the size of the Atlantic, one ship could cause me such trouble.*

It was all too true. To Dallas it seemed that the *Aramis*, or rather her captain, had no rules. The ship did not seem to be governed by time or wind. The *Zephyr*, Dallas' ship, had been on the losing end of the expertise of the *Aramis'* captain on many occasions. It never seemed to fail—if word aired that merchandise of great value was up for grabs, the captain and crew of the *Aramis* did the grabbing.

Dallas finally thanked Yusuf and returned to his ship. Within minutes they were underway. He had one other stop. Some miles down the coast, in Casablanca, a load of sugar awaited him. From there, he was forced to admit, he had no other leads.

"My immediate plans? Why would he ask such a thing?" Smokey frowned at Darsey where he stood framed in her cabin doorway.

"I think he's unhappy that you won't deal with him directly, but I think what he really wants is to get a look at Smoke."

"Well, I don't deal that way. Tell him we'll take our business elsewhere."

Darsey, although tempted to argue, nodded and left, leaving the door open. Within minutes Smokey heard the voice of the merchant apologizing profusely. Smokey had not been making idle threats, she never did, but the man had obviously been bluffing over what he was willing to pay.

It would be so much simpler to handle some of these exchanges myself, Smokey thought to herself. Darsey had told her on many occasions over the last year that she no longer needed to conceal her identity; maybe now was the time to listen to him.

Smokey put her quill down, rose from the desk, and moved to the cabin door. Seconds later she walked calmly across the

deck to where Darsey stood dickering with the most successful merchant in Greece.

Her men on deck stopped what they were doing at the
sight of her. As was her custom, she was dressed in black knee-
high boots, dark, baggy trousers and a long, full overshirt that
completely hid her figure from neck to knee. Her hair, as
usual, was completely concealed under a knit cap, pulled
down to the bottom of her ears.

Smokey came forward, knowing that she had stopped the
merchant in his tracks. She also knew that even though she
was dressed like a boy, her face and hands would give her
away. The skin of her cheeks was as smooth as a baby's, and her
hands, although work-roughened, were slim, with long fingers and fine-boned wrists. She looked like a cabin boy, but
she moved and spoke like a woman in command.

"Is there some problem, Mr. Brennan?" Smokey addressed
Darsey properly as she stopped beside the two men.

"Yes, Captain. Nikos feels the price is a bit steep," Darsey
told her and tried not to laugh at the stunned look on Nikos'
face.

"What did you have in mind, Nikos?" the young captain
asked solicitously, although her voice held a hint of steel.

"You are Smoke?" the man nearly stammered.

"My friends call me Smokey," she told him, "but you may
address me as Captain Simmons. Now please tell me, what
price did you have in mind?"

The man's eyes flicked down the front of Smokey, but he
quickly raised his face to hers when Darsey made a sound in
the back of his throat.

Smokey sighed and reached for her hat. With the movement of her hand, a fall of black hair came down over her
shoulders and back. The merchant blinked, and Smokey discovered great relief in having her identity revealed.

"Now that you know for certain," she spoke dryly, "let us
get down to business. Do you pay my price, or do we sail?"

"I'll pay," he said without hesitation, a gleam of respect, as
well as something else, entering his eyes.

Smokey allowed Darsey to handle the transaction from that point, and the unloading proceeded shortly. She watched from the deck as the Greek merchant left the ship and then gestured wildly to some sailors on the dock. Seeing the word spread was like watching ants running around a mound— Smoke was a woman! Smokey could almost hear them.

The *Aramis* finished her business in Greece and made four more stops in the next week. Each and every time, Smokey handled the negotiations and let herself be seen, and although she did not remove her hat again, the truth was being brought to light.

She was amazed at how quickly the word passed. The whole business began to wear on her, and she finally told her crew to head for home. Twenty days later they were back in port, and Darsey and Smokey headed to Willa's.

Smokey was rescued from the usual letdown of leaving her ship by the arrival of a letter from Jenny Pemberton. She invited Smokey to come for a visit at her soonest possible convenience, and to stay for an indefinite period of time. Smokey sent an immediate note of acceptance, with plans to leave for Kennebunkport in three days' time.

Three

"DO YOU THINK SHE'LL BE HERE this morning or this afternoon?" Jenny asked Tate for the second time that morning.

Tate chuckled and kissed her cheek. He had finished with breakfast and needed to be out the door.

"I think she'll be here by noon."

"Why do you think that?" Jenny's face was a mask of confusion.

Tate shouted with laughter. "Honey, you asked me what I thought, so I just made a guess."

"Oh, Tate," Jenny laughed. "Go to work so I can fret in peace."

Tate kissed her again, this time on the mouth, and moved toward the door. Jenny watched him go and then did just as she'd predicted.

"I thought you were headed to the Pembertons' today," Darsey commented to Smokey when the breakfast dishes were cleared and she had made no move to leave the table.

"I am, but I didn't say when, and it will be an embarrassment if they're not expecting me for lunch."

"Go on with you, Smokey!" Willa put in. She never failed to see to every need when Darsey and Smokey were in port, but she took care of them in a stern, yet loving way. "If you were going to be an inconvenience in any way, they wouldn't have asked you."

Smokey hesitated and Darsey rose. "Come on, I'll take you over."

"Why do you suppose she asked me, Darsey?"

Darsey paused on his way to the door and turned to look at her. *Because she sees what I see—a vulnerable, lonely young woman who makes your heart ache just to look at her.*

"She asked you," Darsey finally spoke out loud, "because you've been praying for a friend, and God has decided to provide one."

Darsey hoped she wouldn't press him further, because he knew he couldn't take it. She was so rarely insecure, but when she was, all Darsey wanted to do was sit down and weep. He was relieved to see Smokey nod so he could turn back to the door.

The subject was not raised on the way to the Pembertons', but Darsey knew that Smokey was having second thoughts about the visit. He was determined to get her there, however, so conversation was brief.

Once they had arrived, he sent Smokey to the front door with a kiss and a wish that she have a good time. He silently hoped she would stay for a month, partly because she needed the fellowship, and partly because he was getting too old to be roaming the sea.

When Smokey knocked, a servant answered the front door of the Pemberton home, a huge house that sat right on the Atlantic. She was greeted cordially, but felt her palms sweat as she stepped across the threshold and into the entryway. Smokey didn't know houses like this existed.

From her place by the door, Smokey looked as far as the open doors would allow. She could see what looked to be a library, a huge parlor, and possibly another smaller parlor. Windows directly opposite the foyer, on the east side of the house, gave her a splendid view of the sea.

She was tempted to walk to them and look out, but kept her place and continued to gaze around her. She was still studying the smoothly painted walls and light oak flooring when Jenny called her name and approached.

"You're here," Jenny said with a grin after she'd given her a quick, impetuous hug. "I'm so glad you could come," she told Smokey sincerely, as she slipped her arm within Smokey's and led her toward the parlor. "You can ask Tate if you like, but I've been literally pacing the floor watching for you. I'd have come to the door myself, but I was needed in the kitchen."

The mention of the kitchen reminded Smokey that she had been uncertain as to when to come. "I wasn't sure if I should come before or after lunch...I mean, if you would be prepared to have me for lunch." Smokey stopped when Jenny chuckled.

"Our cook is a dream. She can have a banquet on the table with just a few hours' notice. I assure you, you would have been welcome whenever you arrived."

Jenny wasted no time in making Smokey comfortable. She gave her an immediate tour of the entire house, and Smokey was more awestruck than before. The kitchen and dining rooms were immense and sparkling clean. The room off the foyer that Smokey had taken to be a second parlor was in fact a music room. Next to this was a sun room, with more windows looking out to the east.

The stairs were wide and carpeted as they led Smokey and Jenny to the second floor, which had nine large bedrooms. The two young women ended their tour in what was to be Smokey's bedroom during her visit. After showing her around the vast room, Jenny left her to freshen up.

A maid had put her few things away, and Smokey didn't know quite what to do with herself. Her men always took care of her on ship, but that was their job. Somehow this felt decadent. At Willa's, or aboard the *Aramis*, she had more jobs waiting for her attention than the hours of the day allowed.

Smokey circled the room slowly and stopped by the window. It was a huge piece of glass covered with sheer, lacy curtains. Captivated, Smokey touched them almost reverently. They were so unlike anything she had at home or on shipboard. Suddenly Smokey realized the curtain was hiding a spectacular view.

Moving gently, she pulled the curtain aside to display a sweeping panorama of the Atlantic. Smokey stared as though mesmerized. Living inland from the port at Kennebunk didn't give her daily views of the sea when she was at home. Why, it was almost like being aboard ship!

Suddenly Smokey found herself wondering whether she would ever sail again if she owned a house on the sea. Such a thought had never occurred to her, and she immediately felt upset at the idea. Before her thoughts could run rampant, however, she remembered she did *not* have a house like this and probably never would. Her business was a tremendous success, so she could easily have afforded to buy a home of her own, but the idea of living alone did not appeal to her in the least.

Her next thought, that of asking Willa to move, made her laugh out loud. Dynamite couldn't shift Willa from the house where she had raised all five of her children. The idea was so outrageous that Smokey couldn't hold her chuckles. She was still giggling when a maid knocked at the door and entered. She had hot water and clean towels for Smokey, who had just barely had time to school her features.

Tate placed a soft kiss on the back of his wife's neck when she asked him to button the back of her dinner gown. She and

Tate were in the habit of dressing for dinner and sharing the day's events as they did so. All Jenny's talk on this evening was of Smokey. They had shared a lovely afternoon together, and Jenny told Tate that although Smokey was still a bit hesitant with her, they were making progress.

"She seems so young and lost at times, and she looks at the house and furniture as though she's never seen anything like them before."

"So you feel sorry for her," Tate murmured softly. To his surprise, Jenny chuckled.

"No, I don't. I feel sorry for me. Something tells me that I haven't even scratched the surface of the real Smokey. And that if she ever opens up, I might just find myself in over my head. If only I can make her see..."

"See what?" Tate questioned when Jenny hesitated.

"That I really want to be her friend, a friend she can trust. I want her to like me so much that I hurt. I don't want to smother her, but I want her to see my friendship as genuine, and I—" Jenny stopped and shrugged helplessly. "Did that make any sense?"

"Yes. In your brief time together, you've come to care deeply for her, and you want her to care in return."

Jenny's sigh was one of relief over his understanding as they made their way to the door. They were in the dining room when Smokey came to the door. She paused on the threshold, her face a mask of dismay.

"What is it, Smokey?"

"I should have changed my dress." Smokey's cheeks had turned red with humiliation upon spotting her hostess' lovely frock. Jenny, horrified that she had been so thoughtless, found herself helplessly tongue-tied. Smokey stood stiffly on the threshold, wishing she could vanish, but Tate rescued them both.

"Please don't mind us, Smokey," he said. "Jenny's family is much more relaxed, but my family is used to dressing for dinner and we've fallen into the habit. We're really not snobs."

The cross-eyed look on Tate's face was so comical that Smokey immediately relaxed. They took their seats, and dinner was served. It was a sumptuous feast of beef, sage dressing, fresh turnip greens, and mince pie. Smokey ate her fill.

Jenny and Tate had decided they would not press Smokey in any way to share about herself, but as they ate and the conversation flowed, they learned little things.

"You don't have to leave right away, do you, Smokey? I mean, we were hoping you could stay for a few weeks," Jenny commented after the soup.

"I don't really have anything pressing right now. I didn't tell Darsey when I would need to be picked up because I wasn't sure."

Smokey realized that they weren't going to give her the third degree and she was thankful, but she could also see that she needed to explain about Darsey.

"Darsey was my father's first mate, and he still works for me. He's always been like a second father to me, and especially now that my father is gone. Willa, the woman I told you about, is his sister. We live with her when we're home." Not until after Smokey uttered the words did she realize that statement would need yet another explanation, but just then they were interrupted. A maid arrived and told them Buck was there to see them.

"Oh, thank you, Polly," Jenny told her before turning to Smokey. "Buck is my brother, and you're going to love him. Let's go into the parlor. I'll ask Polly to serve our coffee there."

Before Smokey could draw another breath, Tate had gently taken her arm and was leading her out of the room. She took a moment to conjure up what a person named Buck would look like, but as soon as she followed Jenny into the room, she could see that she couldn't be more wrong.

Engaging was the only word that would come to Smokey's mind, and that was before Buck had uttered a word. He was a small man, slightly taller than Smokey but shorter than his sister, and petite in build. His small frame and exact manner caused several names to jump to mind, but Buck certainly wasn't one of them.

"Hello, Buck," Jenny greeted him warmly. After kissing his sister, Buck dropped somewhat dramatically onto the sofa.

"I've decided to propose to her, Jen, but if she says no, then I'll wish that I had given her more time. On the other hand, if she says yes, I'll wish that I'd asked sooner."

Smokey, who sat on the small settee Tate had led her toward, stared at Jenny's brother. He had thrown his head back and said all of this with his eyes on the ceiling. Smokey looked to Tate then, who winked audaciously before turning to speak to his brother-in-law.

"Come now, Buck, I'm sure she'll have you. How could she resist?" Not realizing how serious Buck was, Tate wanted to tease him from his somber mood.

"I don't know. She was very quiet tonight."

"We have company, Buck," Jen said softly when it seemed he would lie there for some time. Jen could see that her brother was serious, and she wanted to listen, but she realized he must not have seen Smokey, for he would not want to share all of this in front of a stranger.

"Miss Victoria Simmons from Kennebunk is staying with us." Tate said this, having finally seen that Buck was truly feeling low.

His words did the trick. Without rising, Buck's head came up. His eyes narrowed and then widened upon spotting Smokey. An instant later he came off the sofa as though on strings and bowed low to his sister's guest.

"Excuse my lack of manners, my dear." The tone of Buck's voice was refined. "I am Rowland Knight, 'Buck' to friends and family alike."

Smokey watched in fascination as he came forward with all the manners of a gentleman at court, took her hand, and carefully kissed the back of it. Knowing her skin and nails were rough, Smokey squirmed with embarrassment, but the warm eyes Buck raised to hers made her relax in a moment.

Smokey found herself smiling hugely as Buck took a seat beside her.

"You know," he spoke to the room but never took his eyes off Smokey's perfect complexion and huge gray eyes. "If I wasn't in love with the widow Rittenhouse, I might fall in love with Victoria."

Smokey chuckled low in her throat, and because she sincerely liked him at first meeting, she teased him with a warm glimmer in her eye. "If you could change your affections that swiftly, Mr. Knight, I'm not sure I would have you."

Buck threw back his head and laughed in delight. Smokey glanced at her host and hostess and found them grinning also.

"I like you, Victoria," Buck told her bluntly.

"My friends call me Smokey," she told him.

"Smokey," Buck tried the name out loud. "It fits you."

"Thank you. I rather like it myself."

"Do you play cards?" he asked suddenly.

"Yes."

Tate and Jenny, who had sat quietly through the exchange, went into action. Within minutes the four of them were seated around a table. Jen was the first to deal, and then the cards went to Tate. By the time the deal got around to Smokey, she found herself more relaxed than she had been all evening. China cups and fine flatware were new to her, but cards, well, she'd been playing since she was a child. The lighthearted game, along with Buck's outrageous wit and easy smile, caused her to wish she lived much closer to Buck and the Pembertons.

Smokey missed the glances of her game partners as she allowed her gaze to roam the room. They noticed that she didn't even need to concentrate on the deck in her hands. She shuffled and dealt cards to them like a cardsharp. Everyone's eyes were dutifully back on their own cards by the time Smokey glanced back at them, but they all knew that they'd been given a glimmer of yet one more aspect that made up the person of Victoria "Smokey" Simmons.

Four

SMOKEY WAS UTTERLY SPELLBOUND with Jenny and Tate's small church—in particular, their pastor and his preaching. Smokey had spent so little time in church over the years that she had no idea a sermon could hold such meaning.

Clancy had spent many hours teaching his small daughter about God's Word, but he had also admitted to her many times that there were a great many things he didn't know about the Bible.

Smokey grew up on the stories of David and Goliath, Noah and the ark, and of course the birth, death, and resurrection of Jesus Christ. But Smokey didn't try to fool herself; she knew little about the Old or New Testament. She shared this with Jenny as they made their way home in the Pemberton buggy. Tate had business with one of the elders and would come later.

"I basically grew up on my father's ship. I don't remember being in port on Sundays, at least no more than a few times a year. There's so much I don't know."

"I'm glad you liked Pastor Chase, Smokey. He's a wonderful pastor; we feel so blessed to have him. Both Tate and I have learned a great deal from him in the last few years. You know," Jenny spoke excitedly now, "you don't live that far. Even when you go home, you could come over here for Sundays and plan on spending the day with us."

"Thank you, Jen." Smokey was so moved she fell silent. She also realized she was going to have to tell Jenny at some point that she was not usually in Maine on Sundays, that in fact she was usually not in Maine at all. As Smokey thought on this, the ride continued in silence.

After lunch Smokey went to her room for a while and found herself poring over her Bible. Pastor Chase had preached from the book of James, and Smokey wanted to read every chapter. She never got beyond the first, where she read verses that spoke to her of how often she needed to turn to God, and how He provides in ways she hadn't thought possible.

No one had ever told Smokey that she could ask God for wisdom, nor had she ever taken the time to search out God's truths for herself. In her job she had so many responsibilities. Too often she found herself going on her own and simply hoping for the best. It was like a gift to learn that she could turn to God, knowing that in His love, He was waiting to give her aid.

Life at the Pembertons' on Sundays was lazy and relaxed, and after Smokey had read the first chapter, she fell asleep on her bed as she prayed.

"My parents moved to South Carolina three years ago for my mother's health. They come to see us every other Christmas, and we sail down in the early summer to see them. My sister moved with them, but as you see, Buck and I still live here in Maine, as does Dolly," Jenny told Smokey over afternoon tea.

"Dolly is your sister?" Smokey asked.

"No, Dolly is another brother. Buck is the oldest, then Dolly, and then me. My sister's name is Shirley; she's the youngest."

Smokey's smile never wavered, but she didn't really hear the last statement. She was too busy trying to push down the images that rose up at the name "Dolly." Buck was a small man with a soft air about him, so did that mean a man named Dolly would be large and muscular? Smokey thought it unlikely, though Jenny herself was quite tall.

"Here, Smokey," Jenny cut into her thoughts. "Have another piece of cake."

Smokey accepted, and Jenny watched her. Smokey had no idea what to do with her cake plate as she already had a cup of tea in her hand. Jenny wanted very much to show her, but was acutely afraid of hurting her feelings. Jenny also realized that she was under Smokey's close scrutiny and was careful not to give notice.

Smokey was just about to ask Jenny another question about her family when they were interrupted. Polly announced that cook needed something in the kitchen. Smokey, already seeing that Jenny was very kind to her staff, watched as she rose immediately and went to lend assistance.

After she had gone, Smokey put her cup and plate down with a sigh of relief. Jenny made it look so easy as she balanced her plate on her lap, leaving her hands free to handle her cup and saucer. But Smokey's plate always tipped, no matter how hard she worked to keep her legs even.

And then there was the different way they held their cups. Smokey gripped her small china cup just as she held her large mug aboard the *Aramis*. Not so Jenny—why, her pinky finger even stuck out! Her pinky finger was always held at a most feminine angle as she drank. She made it all look as natural as breathing.

With a nervous glance at the door, Smokey reached for her cup and saucer. She held it just as Jenny had, one hand on the saucer, and thumb and forefinger of the other hand on the handle. Pinky finger pointing straight out, she tried to drink.

Before it even reached her mouth, the cup tipped and she burned her hand. Her hand smarting from the burn, a frustrated Smokey quickly placed her cup back in the saucer and positioned it back on the table. She had drenched her hand and dripped tea down the front of her dress. It wouldn't have mattered if she had been wearing the brown or navy blue dress, but this had to be the dark tan. It showed every spot.

Her napkin took care of her hand, but there was no hiding the spots on her dress. As she scrubbed, Smokey felt more than saw that she wasn't alone. She glanced up quickly to see Buck standing nearby, smiling kindly at her. Seeing her wet dress and tea-filled saucer, he had grasped the situation instantly.

"Hello, Smokey," he spoke gently as he sat and poured his own tea.

"Hi, Buck," Smokey spoke in return, not quite meeting his eyes as she tried to use her napkin to hide her wet lap.

"What have you and Jen been up to?"

Buck had a way of making Smokey relax, and she calmed at just the sound of his voice.

"We went to church this morning. This afternoon has been pretty quiet."

"Did you enjoy the sermon?"

"Oh, very much," she told him sincerely.

"We've been working our way through the book of James for some time."

"Were you at church, Buck? I didn't see you."

Buck grinned. "You didn't see me because the pipe organ nearly hides my frame."

"Oh, Buck," Smokey exclaimed in delight. "*You* were the one playing. It was just beautiful."

Buck inclined his head in true modesty. Jenny had joined them again, and she talked about Buck's musical ability, which was considerable. He'd been playing for years and had mastered the piano, organ, and violin. Smokey was impressed, but not at all surprised. She had believed Buck to be a very special person from the moment she met him. They chatted on for some time until Tate walked in the door. He had not been home all afternoon.

"I'm sorry I'm so late," he spoke as he moved to kiss his wife, "but the situation was more complicated than I originally believed. And I think you'll forgive me," he hesitated, and a sparkle lit his eyes, "since I found this character wandering around on the docks and decided to bring him home."

Smokey turned with the room and watched as a tall man, the best-looking she'd ever seen, stepped across the threshold.

"Dolly!" Jenny exclaimed and ran to kiss her brother.

Smokey's mouth closed with a snap, just before she was introduced.

Five

IF SMOKEY HAD THOUGHT HERSELF CLUMSY before Dolly arrived, she didn't know what to think now. She dropped her napkin, nearly upset the plate of sandwiches when it was passed to her, and when she did get a bite of sandwich into her mouth, swallowed wrong and nearly choked. Her cup would simply not sit quietly on the saucer, so she put it down and gave up altogether.

Jenny had introduced her brother, and he couldn't have been kinder, but his tall, good-looking presence seemed to rattle the normal good sense right out of Smokey.

Dolly, she learned in a hurry, was a nickname for Dallas, *Captain* Dallas Knight, to be exact. It had been Jenny's baby name for Dallas, and the name had remained in the family through the years. Smokey thought about how tender Jenny's voice became whenever she spoke of Buck or Dallas. They were obviously a very close family.

Smokey put her cup down and simply tried to be a part of the conversation, but she found that didn't work either. Time and again her eyes strayed to Dallas, and she found that she could have cheerfully done little else but stare at him for the remainder of the evening.

At the moment, his head was turned as he spoke with Jenny. Smokey's eyes nearly caressed his dark, wavy brown hair and crystal-blue eyes. His lashes seemed impossibly long.

A small gold hoop winked at her from one ear, and along with his snow-white shirt and black pants and boots, Smokey could easily imagine him at the wheel of a ship.

She sat up a little straighter and pulled her eyes away from his captivating looks when she realized she had been picturing him at the helm of the *Aramis*. Her thoughts so disturbed her that for a moment she lost track of the conversation. She came back with a jolt, but no one seemed to notice.

"Have you seen Greg Banning lately?" Tate inquired about another young sea captain.

"Indeed, I have. I asked him if he was trying to rival Clancy," Dallas said with a grin.

"Why was that?" Jenny asked.

"He told me he'd been racing in the coral reefs."

"Why, that's a treacherous stretch of water!" Buck put in.

"I know, but he doesn't seem to have a lick of sense."

The urge to come to Clancy's defense was so strong for Smokey that she had to bite her tongue. She sat very still and reminded herself that on many occasions her father had told her that in his younger days he hadn't had a lick of sense either.

"You're rather quiet, Smokey," Buck commented when there was a lengthy pause in the conversation.

"Oh, don't mind me," she spoke softly. "The name Clancy always brings a flood of memories."

"Indeed, it does." Tate's voice was reminiscent. "My father would gather us around his chair while he read to us about his exploits."

Smokey stiffened, waiting for Tate to make some outrageous claim concerning Clancy, one that she would instantly want to deny, but he only fell silent.

Smokey was just as quiet as she grappled with whether or not it was a lie to stay silent about her relationship to the famous Clancy. She had still not decided when Dallas rose.

"I was hoping you would stay for dinner," Jenny told him.

"Thanks, Jen, but Kathleen is expecting me. I'll be by tomorrow or the next day. It was nice meeting you, Smokey," he spoke kindly before kissing Jenny's cheek, shaking Tate's hand, and putting his arm around Buck so he would walk him to the door.

The evening passed in great fun for Smokey and everyone else, with a delicious dinner and then another card game, but something was missing for Smokey. It didn't take long for her to realize that the void she felt started when Dallas walked out the door.

Smokey would have been very surprised and at the same time dismayed to learn that Buck had noticed Smokey's reaction to meeting Dallas, as well as her reaction to his departure. The thought saddened Buck. Not because he hoped that Smokey would fall for him, for he was in love with Greer Rittenhouse, but because Dallas was so sought after by the local females that he had his pick.

Buck knew well that Dallas did not take advantage of his looks, but he also realized that his brother probably wouldn't give a girl like Smokey a second glance. It was unfortunate to Buck's way of thinking, because he saw something very special in Smokey Simmons, something he was quite sure the rest of the family had overlooked.

"What time is Buck expecting us?" Smokey wanted to know.

"Anytime," Jenny told her. "He doesn't work on Mondays, and he said we should plan to stay for lunch."

As soon as Jenny fell silent, Smokey's mind wandered back to Dallas. She had been doing that since he left the night before, and she knew she was going to have to order her thoughts back into control. She had never felt this way before.

Her father had said that when he'd seen her mother, it had been love at first sight for both of them. But Smokey knew she couldn't be feeling love. She was miserable, and wasn't love supposed to make you sing and dance? At least she wouldn't have to see him today, but then didn't she want to see him? Suddenly she was more confused than ever.

Stop it, Smokey, she thought sternly, trying to take herself in hand. *Get your mind off of Dallas Knight.*

"Jenny," she said out loud, her voice just a tad desperate. "Where does Buck work?"

"He owns and operates a small publishing company— Bridgeman Publishing. It was started by my maternal grandfather, Charles Bridgeman. Buck has worked there since he was a boy. My mother has no siblings, and my father already had a business of his own, so when Grandfather Bridgeman passed away he left everything to Buck. The company specializes in poetry and music."

Smokey was surprised and fascinated with Buck's occupation, and she also thought it rather fitting. She couldn't stop her mind from straying to Dallas and wondering at the fact that he and Buck could be so different. Brothers, with seemingly nothing in common. Smokey pondered the matter until Buck's house came into view.

Buck's house was as much a surprise as the man himself. He did not live on the ocean, but in a wooded area that would rival any ocean view for beauty. His house was a rustic one-story that at first glance did not seem to fit what Smokey knew of Buck.

Buck, who seemed to be watching for them, led them immediately into a large, pleasant room that was lined with bookshelves. Ever the gentleman, Buck helped the ladies with their sweaters, but Smokey took little notice. Her eyes were taking in the room with near astonishment; it was so unlike the outside's rough wood exterior.

The room was lovely. There were bookshelves everywhere; they literally lined the walls in tasteful elegance. The furniture was very ornate and colorful, and although many pieces didn't match, it was all artfully arranged. The effect was sophisticated, yet warm. The windows, nearly reaching the ceiling and gleaming with clean glass, were positioned in such a way that everyone had a beautiful view of the woods.

"Do you like books?" Buck broke into her inspection.

"I do, although I've never taken much time for reading."

"Well," Buck seemed delighted, "read anything you like. Pick some out and take them home."

Smokey, not used to such generosity, hesitated, but Buck's look of genuine warmth soon put her at ease.

"Thank you, Buck," Smokey finally said graciously as she moved toward the shelves. She immediately pulled a large volume on American history, then she spotted a slim blue-bound book that made her heart thunder. The title was *Kohls' Book of Etiquette*. Still holding the history book, she took it down and turned to the first chapter.

"What every young lady should know concerning afternoon tea."

"What was that, Smokey?" Jenny asked from across the room. Smokey realized she had spoken aloud.

"I was just looking at this book." She nearly stuttered at being discovered, but Buck rescued her.

"Take it with you. Here," he approached and without seeming to notice the titles, swept both books from her hands.

"I'll put them here under your sweater where you won't forget them. And here," Buck stopped and selected one more book. "This is a classic, lots of adventure on the high seas. I know you'll love it."

Something in Buck's voice made Smokey's eyes fly to his face, but she saw nothing to hint at his knowing about her sailing. The urge to tell Jenny and Buck all about herself pressed in strongly upon her at that point, but she didn't know how to begin, and it wouldn't have mattered anyway. Buck no more set the books with her sweater than one of his servants announced that lunch was waiting.

Smokey asked herself how many times she was going to make a fool of herself in front of this family. The meal had been a disaster. Buck had bowed his head to thank God for their meal, but before he could pray, Dallas walked in. Suddenly Smokey's mouth went completely dry as he sat opposite her and bowed his head for the prayer. Smokey didn't hear a word of it. She stared at the top of Dallas' head like a woman who'd taken leave of her senses. And that was only the beginning.

She spilled her water twice, once into her lap and once across the table. She poked herself in the cheek with her fork when Dallas was talking because she was giving more attention to his wonderful smile than to what she was doing.

Questions were directed to her throughout the meal as the family attempted to include her, but beyond monosyllabic replies, accompanied by a rather bewildered expression, she was mute. The meal seemed to last forever.

Over dessert Smokey berated herself without mercy. *Why in the world did it never occur to you that Dallas would be here today? He probably lives here when he's in port. He also probably thinks you belong in an asylum.*

"Well, I've got to be off," Dallas suddenly spoke into Smokey's riotous thoughts. "Thanks for lunch, Buck. I'll see you tonight." Dallas bid everyone goodbye, but beyond a strange little smile, Smokey didn't seem to notice.

Dallas made his way out of the house and shut the door, but paused on the front step and looked back at the closed portal.

Jenny's new friend is certainly an odd little thing, he thought in confusion. His mind moved backward over lunch, checking to see if he had said or done anything that might have explained her nervousness. He couldn't think of a thing.

As he walked up the street, his mind lingered on Smokey for just an instant more. She wasn't like any of Jenny's other friends, but Dallas mistakenly thought he understood the attraction. Smokey Simmons was a rather pathetic woman, and his entire family had always had a soft spot for abandoned pets.

"Do you really have to leave?"

"It's been wonderful, Jenny, but I need to get home. I can't thank you enough for the lovely time I've had, and please thank Buck too."

It was the afternoon of the next day and Smokey knew she had been rather abrupt.

"You'll come again, won't you, Smokey?" Tate put in when he saw his wife's crestfallen look. Smokey had announced at lunch that she would be leaving that day, and even though Tate was very busy, he knew that Jenny would need his support.

"Of course I will," Smokey said with a chuckle. "I'll be back so often that you'll be sick of the sight of me."

Jenny's hands came to Smokey's upper arms in a gesture that was almost fierce. "That's not going to happen, Smokey," she told her seriously. "I wish you could stay for the rest of the summer."

"Oh, Jenny, thank you." Smokey spoke with her heart in her eyes. "That means so much to me. I don't make friends easily, and I know there's a lot about me that I haven't shared, but—"

"None of that matters," Jenny cut in. "We'll be here, and you'll be welcome at any time."

The women hugged for a long moment before Smokey boarded the stage. Tate had offered to take her home that evening, but Smokey had wanted to leave that afternoon. They all parted on the best of terms, but Smokey felt something like an ache around her heart as the stage pulled away.

She didn't say much once she was back at Willa's, and neither Willa nor Darsey pressed her. In fact, she was quiet for the next two days. Not until she was aboard her ship and out to sea did she face all the hurts she was experiencing. Her men left her alone while she had a long, hard cry in her cabin, and when she finally emerged she felt a little more like herself, the captain of the *Aramis*.

Six

THE LONDON PORT WAS ABUZZ with activity, but Dallas took little notice from his place on the *Zephyr*. He had an appointment with a friend, and for the moment all he cared about was getting his ship unloaded so he could be on his way.

Dallas stood on the deck as his men, all stripped to the waist, carried crates to the docks. For the most part the operation was going smoothly, but a sudden crowd of sailors sauntering their way through his men and toward another ship suddenly made Dallas feel as if he should be on the dock himself; fights could break out so swiftly.

He'd no more gained his footing on the quay than a small sailor walking past him with the others and wearing a knit hat caught his eye. The sailor didn't look at him, but Dallas studied the smaller man's profile as he passed and pondered as to where he might know him.

He did a double take when he realized how closely the sailor resembled his sister's friend. Dallas figured she must have a brother. A huge fellow was with the small man, and just steps down the quay he had stepped between them so that the smaller man was lost to view. Dallas shrugged at his own imagination. He saw so many people in his work that after a while they all looked the same. He put the entire incident from his mind in order to finish the task at hand.

Two hours later, clean and pressed, a carriage was dropping him at the door of White's Club. He was resplendent in all black, save for a snow-white shirt and cravat, for his luncheon engagement with Brandon Hawkesbury, Duke of Briscoe.

"Well, Hawk, I understand that congratulations are in order."

"Indeed," Brandon inclined his dark, handsome head, his eyes sparkling with pleasure. "My son, Sterling, is three weeks old today, and Sunny is doing fine."

"Please give her my best and this," Dallas paused and brought a small box from his pocket. "It's for your son."

Brandon opened the box and laughed. A small gold loop, much like the one Dallas usually wore in his ear, winked at him from a bed of satin.

"I'm not sure his mother will appreciate the gesture, but I thank you."

Dallas grinned in reply, but Brandon's next words to him brought the conversation to a serious note.

"How is business?"

Dallas grimaced. "It could be better."

"You haven't been hit by Haamich Wynn, have you?"

"The pirate? No. In fact, I'm not sure I believe he exists."

"I felt the same way," Brandon admitted, "until a month ago when he hit one of my own ships. No one was killed, but I lost valuable cargo. Rumor has it that he's a peer of the realm."

Dallas whistled low. "I'll keep my eyes open in the future."

"I'd appreciate that for your sake, as well as my own. Now, you haven't really answered my question."

Dallas sighed and sat quietly before admitting, "In truth, I'm a bit discouraged. My long-range plan should have had me back in Maine right now, building my first ship."

Brandon took in his friend's grief and then spoke softly, "Dallas, if you'd only let me help you, I'd—"

Dallas forestalled him with a raised hand. "Thank you, Hawk, but I want to keep trying on my own. If things don't turn around by the first of next year, March at the latest, I may be in touch."

Brandon agreed with a nod and then said, "You're a fine captain, Dallas. What exactly is going on?"

"Smoke," he stated simply. "He's into port like a thief in the night, moving like mist on the water. I never get word of goods before he does, and he's come and gone before I can get the *Zephyr* moving." Dallas stopped talking when an odd look passed over Brandon's face.

"You haven't heard the latest rumor, have you, Dallas?"

"I guess not," he said quietly and waited.

"Smoke is a woman."

Dallas waited for his friend to thump him on the chest and laugh at his own joke—he did neither.

"You can't be serious," Dallas finally said.

"I'm very serious. She's been sailing for a few years now, but until quite recently she's kept her identity very low key. She sails the *Aramis*, and the talk I've heard is that there's no finer or swifter craft on the Atlantic."

Dallas' heart began to thunder in his chest. Images of Jenny's small friend Smokey, the sailor he had seen just hours ago on the dock, and the ship they had been moving toward all rushed through his mind.

"Hawk, what does the *Aramis* look like?" Dallas' voice was just over a whisper.

"I haven't seen her, but I can tell you what I've heard. She looks as new as the day she set sail. Clean lines. Ebony with a single gold stripe. No figurehead, but she flies a large American flag at the top of the mainmast, and another smaller one from the mizzenmast."

Dallas' eyes slid shut when Brandon was through. Upon Brandon's question, he shared the entire story, starting with his sister's friend and ending with the sailor and ship he'd seen at the dock.

"If the rumor mill can be trusted, she's an American and lives in Maine, so what you've said makes perfect sense. Look, Dallas," Brandon went on. "I can see that you're ready to hop your ship and follow the *Aramis* as quickly as you can.

"You haven't seen Sunny in ages or met Sterling," he added. "Why not come out to Bracken for a few days? It wouldn't be your original intent, but if you go chasing after the *Aramis*, you're only going to antagonize her captain."

Dallas nodded slowly in agreement and then shook his head in disbelief. It was all too ridiculous for words. The woman he had met at Tate and Jenny's and then again at Buck's couldn't possibly be one of the finest sailors to grace Atlantic waters.

Brandon was right, he did need to stop and think about his next move. Especially since this was almost certainly a case of mistaken identity. In just moments Dallas convinced himself that there was really no need to hurry.

"There's someone here to see you, Mr. Pemberton," Tate's secretary told him as he stepped into the private office of Pemberton Shipping. Tate looked up from his desk to thank the man, but could see that he was distressed.

"What is it, Scott? Something James can't handle?"

"Well, sir, they want to see you, and I—"

"If someone is upset," Tate cut him off, "just send him in. I'm sure we can work it out."

"It's the captain of the *Aramis*," Scott said. Although he still looked upset, Tate's face cleared.

"Smoke," he said with relief. "I've never worked with him before, but his reputation is flawless. Whatever the trouble is, we'll work it out. Send him in."

The secretary hesitated, but Tate ignored him and went back to his paperwork. A moment later the door opened and two people entered, closing the door behind them. Tate finished the entry in his ledger before looking up. He rose with a congenial smile on his face. When he spied Smokey standing just inside his office door, however, the smile became rather fixed, and his look turned to one of confusion. Beside her was a bear of a man. Both of them looked quite serious.

"I've been asking myself for weeks," she began softly, "if I was lying by not telling you what I do for a living. I'm afraid I never came to a solid conclusion one way or the other. I never dreamed that my shipment from London on this trip would be coming to one Tate Pemberton. I assure you, Tate, it was never my intention to be deceitful to you or Jenny."

Tate was so stunned he didn't know what to say, but not for the reason Smokey imagined. She would have been shocked to learn that his surprise was due almost solely to her manner, and not to what she did for a living. The Smokey he knew was endearing, but she was also quite shy and rather clumsy. This Smokey, the owner and captain of the *Aramis*, was in complete control of herself *and* the situation.

"Sit down, Smokey," Tate said, finally recalling his manners.

Smokey took the chair in front of the desk while Darsey sat in a chair under the window. Without further word, Smokey placed some papers on Tate's desk.

He reached for them and studied them carefully, taking a little longer than usual in an attempt to gather his wits.

"This is your price, the one written here at the bottom?"

"Yes."

"It's a bit steep," he said without hesitation.

"I believe it's more than fair," Smokey interjected with confident ease.

Tate's eyes came to hers then, and again he was struck by the change in her. Unsmiling, Smokey held his eyes without blinking. A slow smile began to spread across Tate's mouth.

Smokey then smiled in return, and Tate finally had to laugh with relief.

"I'm just so surprised," he admitted. "I mean, you obviously know what you're doing and I—" He seemed to run out of words so Smokey rescued him.

"What you're trying to say is that when I'm in your home, I'm a woman with a speech impediment and two left feet, and now you find I really do know how to walk and talk." She shrugged ruefully, her grin still in place. "I'm sure Jenny would feel as I have if ever she were to board my ship."

"I'm sure you're right," he agreed, his smile even larger at the thought of his wife doing Smokey's job.

"Now, Mr. Pemberton," Smokey brought him back to earth in a no-nonsense way. "Are you interested in my cargo, or do I travel farther up the coast?"

"You mean at this price?"

"Indeed, I do." There was a note of steel in Smokey's voice that Tate didn't miss.

"Sold," he said softly and shook the hand Smokey offered to him.

"When are you coming for another visit?" Tate asked without relinquishing his hold of her hand. His question so surprised Smokey that she didn't immediately answer.

"I wasn't sure I'd still be wanted," she finally admitted.

"Then you weren't listening very well when we said goodbye. Now, when can we expect you?"

Smokey was so moved by the sincerity of his eyes and voice that she felt warmly overwhelmed.

"Two weeks?"

"Make it ten days."

Smokey's laugh filled the room. She reclaimed her hand and stood. After introducing Darsey, who would handle the rest of the transaction, she made ready to leave.

"I'll tell Jen she can expect you," Tate called to her retreating back.

Smokey tossed a grin in his direction as she exited the office. She'd been buying and selling since before her father died, trading with shipping magnates and amassing a small fortune for herself in the last few years. But she didn't know when the sale of her cargo had ever felt so fine.

Seven

"I HAVE SOMETHING TO TELL YOU, SMOKEY." Jenny's voice was hushed as the two women sat close together on the large sofa in the Pembertons' parlor.

"What is it?"

"We haven't told anyone, and I need you to keep it a secret."

"All right," Smokey agreed and watched as Jenny's eyes glowed with excitement.

"I'm going to have a baby."

"Oh, Jen," Smokey whispered. The two women embraced for long moments, and when they broke apart their eyes were suspiciously moist.

"When will the baby come?" Smokey's voice was now as hushed as Jenny's.

"Next summer."

"That long?" Smokey's voice became quite loud, her brow wrinkling in disappointment.

"It does take time, you know." Jenny was laughing so hard over Smokey's reaction that she could barely talk.

"I know, but next summer! Why, that feels like years away!"

Again Jenny went off into gales of laughter. It was contagious, and Smokey laughed too. They talked of babies for the next hour, and then Jenny asked Smokey about her plans for Christmas.

"I'll be with Darsey at Willa's. Her children live in the area, and they'll all come on Christmas Eve."

"What about Christmas Day?"

"It's pretty quiet. By the time the family goes home on Christmas Eve, Willa is pretty worn out."

"Would they be terribly upset if you spent Christmas Eve and Christmas Day with us?"

Smokey blinked. "I don't know, Jen."

"Now what does that hesitant look mean?" Jenny couldn't have asked that question several weeks ago, but having Tate and Jenny learn of Smokey's occupation seemed to bring down the wall that separated them.

However, Smokey had not told anyone about the way she felt when she even *thought* about Dallas Knight. She didn't think she was ready to share, not even with Jenny.

"I'll think about your offer, okay, Jen? Maybe I'll discuss it with Darsey."

"Darsey means a lot to you, doesn't he?"

"Oh, yes," Smokey told her with a smile. "He was my father's first mate before he was mine, and he's been beside me since I was a baby. Willa told me that Darsey sees me as the daughter he never had."

"Do you miss your father?"

"I do, but the anguish is gone. That first year, the pain was so intense I didn't think I'd make it." Smokey suddenly grew very quiet.

"I'm sorry if the subject brings back all the pain."

"It's not that," Smokey told her. "You and Tate have been wonderful, but there's something more about me that I want to explain."

"All right," Jenny's voice was expectant, but something in Smokey's look made her heart thump with trepidation. Her mind ran with every crazy thing Smokey could possibly say, from being a pirate to having a husband and child of her own somewhere.

"Not now," Smokey said, much to Jenny's disappointment. "I want to talk to you when Tate is here too."

After two beats of her heart, Jenny agreed, knowing she would have to put her curiosity on hold. It would be hard, but she knew Tate deserved to hear the news firsthand. This was obviously something very important to Smokey. Jenny wanted to do all she could so Smokey would feel free to tell them in her time, secure in the knowledge that Jenny's love was unfailing, no matter what she shared.

"I'm not ashamed of what I do for a living," Smokey told Jenny and Tate that evening. They were alone in the library, and dinner was over. "But I find that I'm something of a curiosity."

"And you would rather we didn't tell everyone we know that you are the captain of the *Aramis*?" Tate interjected with an understanding smile.

"Well, that would help, but I need to explain why." Smokey stopped and took a breath. "You loved me and befriended me when we were strangers, and I was a bit hesitant with you because that's never happened before. I'm at sea so much, and when I am home and people learn what I do, they become quite curious. One question usually leads to another and I—"

Smokey stopped again, took a deep breath and went on. "My father was the most wonderful father a girl could ever hope to have. He was warm and caring, and he loved me to distraction. My parents were not married until later in life, and I wasn't born until he was 50 years old.

"I grew up at sea and loved it. I've never known any other life. My father loved God, and he instilled in me a deep faith in Jesus Christ. There was a lot he didn't know, and in turn, I have much to learn, but he tried very hard to teach me from his small store of knowledge." Smokey paused again, but Tate and Jenny, feeling a bit confused, were absolutely quiet. Smokey found she could no longer stay in her chair; she stood and paced as she continued.

"My father told me once that he never wanted to be a hero to me. He only wanted to be my father, teaching me God's way and making sure I knew he loved me.

"Nearly everything I know, I learned from him. My knowledge of God, sailing, and life in general was learned at his knee. He was my teacher, just as his father had been for him. Many have heard of my father, but most know him only by his first name. No one, not even when my last name is spoken, thinks to tie him to me, unless they find out that I sail.

"And as proud as I am to call him my papa," Smokey's voice dropped as she finished her speech and finally stood still before her host and hostess, "most of the time it's easier if people don't know that the legendary Clancy was my father."

The room was utterly still for the space of many heartbeats, and then Jenny was coming toward her, her eyes wet with tears.

There were no speeches about how blessed Smokey was or how honored the Pembertons felt to have her in their home, just a long, loving hug between friends. The hug ended with a bit of relieved laughter when Jenny shared that she thought Smokey *might* share about being a runaway wife or pirate.

"I have admired your father since I was a little boy," Tate told her when they were once again seated and Jenny had poured tea.

"So have I," Smokey told him with a smile.

"You know," Tate went on, "I always thought Clancy had been born over a hundred years ago."

"You're not alone in that belief." Smokey's voice was dry. "His father's name was Clancy also, so the name Clancy has been on the sea for many years. He told me once that to have done everything that's been credited to him, he would have to have been 200 years old."

"No wonder you're so good at what you do," Jenny complimented Smokey.

"Isn't that the truth! If our son wants to go to sea," Tate's face filled with excitement at the thought, "he could sail with you and learn from the best."

"Oh, no," Smokey said with a laugh. "I'd be an old woman by then, and I really hope I won't be sailing that long."

"Do you have to put some money aside before you can stop?" Jenny's voice was filled with tender compassion, but Tate and Smokey burst out laughing.

Smokey had just collected a small fortune from Pemberton Shipping, which, even though some of it would pay for business expenses, held a large chunk of profit. Jenny was clearly naive as to the success of Smokey's business.

"It's not that, Jen," Smokey took pity on the confused look on her friend's face. "It's just that until I met you, I thought I would be at sea until the day of my death, just as my father had been."

"What happened when you met Jen?"

"I wanted what she has. Not you personally, Tate," Smokey told him with a cheeky grin. "But a husband of my own, a home for us to share, and children, if God wills. There was a man who was in love with me a few years ago. He asked me to marry him for over three years, and even though I cared for him, and still do, I could never say yes."

"What happened to him?" Jenny wanted to know.

Smokey shrugged. "He gave up on me and eventually married someone else. I never see him anymore."

"Do you have regrets?"

"No, but I think I know why I could never say yes. I mean, he was romantic, and I love romance. I also enjoyed listening when he painted a lovely picture of us sailing the world together. But just recently I realized that if ever I marry, I want to have a home—a real home. And I don't want my husband to be a sailor who's gone for months at a time!"

Smokey's last sentence was uttered with great passion, and she was suddenly embarrassed at her own actions. She forced herself to sit back in her chair, her face heating as she looked down at her folded hands in her lap.

"We'll be praying that if God has a special man for you, you'll know it."

"Thank you, Tate." His words relieved some of her embarrassment. "That means a lot to me. I've thought about what Jen suggested when I was here before, and I've decided that I will make your church my own."

"Oh, Smokey, that's wonderful!"

"I'll still be gone at times; I do have a business to run."

"Of course," Jenny agreed. "But whenever you're home, we'll expect you."

It was growing rather late, so all in the room were surprised when Polly knocked on the door a moment later with a note from Buck. It was brief, just wanting to inform them that Dallas was in port and planned to visit on the next day.

Eight

STANDING BEFORE THE MIRROR in her room, Smokey frowned at her reflection. She had tried to do a little something different with her hair, but it had been no use; she felt all thumbs. With only enough pins for her usual hairstyle, nothing she had tried looked quite right.

With a resigned sigh, she whipped it into its usual bun and then stared at herself in disappointment. She knew very well that none of this had made a bit of difference to her before she had seen Jenny's hair and wardrobe, or met her handsome brother.

Why did Dallas have to come now? I had really hoped we would miss each other this visit.

Smokey's mind went back to the day she had seen him on the dock in London. It had been torture to walk by and not speak to him. She'd gained her ship and watched him from the deck until he was out of sight.

I don't know myself anymore. For so long my life was well ordered. I had my work and performed it well. Now, I feel discontent and confused.

Smokey took time to pray about her feelings and surrender them to God. Her heart calmed, and she realized that Dallas' visit didn't necessarily mean they would see each other. After all, she was going on a walk this morning and then meeting Buck for lunch. Tomorrow she planned to leave.

By the time she walked downstairs to breakfast, Smokey had convinced herself that she had no reason whatsoever to worry.

"Well, Buck," Dallas spoke in surprise when the older man came to the breakfast table. "You must have a date for lunch to be out of bed this early." Dallas' question stemmed from the fact that Buck was a night person. He loved to stay up late and sleep late. Dallas tended to be just the opposite.

"Indeed, I do." Buck answered his brother as he sugared the coffee just served to him.

"The lovely widow Rittenhouse?" Dallas asked expectantly.

"No," Buck's voice became quiet. Dallas carefully watched his face. "She thinks we should see other people. She also thinks she's still in love with her first husband and wants to be loyal to his memory."

"When did this happen?"

"Three days ago."

"I'm sorry, Buck." Dallas' compassion was real. "I know you really care for her."

"You're right, I do, and for that reason I'm not going to give up. I'm going to give her some time and then see if she's missed me as much as I already miss her."

"But in the meantime, you're going to see other women?"

Buck frowned at him in confusion, but then shook his head. "No, my lunch date is just a friend. What are your plans for the day?"

"I need to see Jenny this morning. It was too late to go last night," Dallas told him. "After that I've some work to do on the *Zephyr*. In fact, I'd best be on my way. I'll see you later, Buck."

"All right, Dolly. Take care."

Smokey walked along at an easy pace, her long coat slapping at her legs. The sea was a cloudy gray today, the sky overcast. It felt like it could snow at any time. Not headed anyplace in particular, Smokey felt she could walk for hours.

She kept a steady pace until she spotted a beautiful home, painted a bright white, sitting on a small point of land. Smokey stopped to drink in the scene.

Much like Jenny and Tate's, huge windows looked out over the Atlantic on both the first and second floor. On either side of this large home, however, were rounded rooms whose walls were nothing but glass. Smokey's inspection ended with the dormer windows in the roof, which gave the house a three-story look.

"Hello."

She jumped at the sound of a female voice but looked up to see that the woman was smiling.

"I'm sorry if I disturbed you," Smokey told her, "but I was admiring your lovely home."

The woman, having just been on a walk herself, turned with Smokey and stared up at the great house. "It is a beautiful home," she spoke quietly. "But it hasn't been the same since my husband died."

The woman turned to stare at Smokey then, as though surprised she had admitted such a thing to a complete stranger. Her face cleared when she recalled her manners.

"I'm Greer Rittenhouse," she voiced with a smile. "Are you walking anywhere in particular?"

"No. I'm staying with Tate and Jennifer Pemberton. My name is Victoria Simmons."

Greer's eyes now held recognition. "Of course, Buck mentioned you."

"Oh, you must be the woman Buck is seeing."

"Well," the lovely widow looked rather uncomfortable. "We're not dating right now, just friends."

"I'm sorry. That was rude of me."

"It's all right. You couldn't have known."

The women looked to the house again, and Smokey was very pleased when Mrs. Rittenhouse asked if she would like to see the inside.

It was more lovely than Smokey could have imagined. The huge windows to the east that Smokey had seen outside gave a view of the sea to rival that on her ship. The round rooms at the corners of the house were the most lovely sitting rooms Smokey had ever seen.

"It's a wonderful home," Smokey said with a touch of awe in her voice.

"Yes, it holds many happy memories, but I'm not sure I want to keep it."

"You would actually sell?"

"I might."

Smokey took a breath in an attempt to calm the frantic beating of her heart. "Would it be presumptuous to ask if you'd contact me if you're ever really serious about selling?"

"Not at all. I would want the house to go to someone who would cherish it as I do."

"Thank you. Jennifer Pemberton knows how to reach me, if ever you should try."

Smokey thanked her hostess, and Greer showed her out. The wind had picked up, so Smokey tugged her hood into place and continued on her walk. She hadn't gone ten yards, head down against the wind, when she walked straight into Dallas.

"I'm sorry," his deep voice sounded above her, and Smokey looked up for just an instant.

"It's my fault," she spoke quickly, but in that instant Dallas realized who she was.

"Smokey?" His voice sounded so pleased that Smokey looked up in confusion, knowing he had no idea what having his hands on her upper arms was doing to her heart.

"Hello, Dallas," Smokey said inanely.

"I was hoping I'd see you again."

"You were?" Smokey knew she sounded like an idiot, but her heart had done a flip-flop on those words and she felt mesmerized by the sight of his beautiful blue eyes smiling down at her.

"Yes, are you free for lunch?"

Smokey had little experience with men, but something in his eyes and voice made her come back to earth with a thud. He was interested in her, but not romantically.

"I'm not free for lunch." Smokey kept her voice as level as possible. "I'm meeting Buck at the hotel, and I really must be on my way."

Dallas opened his mouth to say something, but changed his mind. Knowing Buck was not interested in Smokey beyond being a friend, he'd been about to invite himself to lunch. But something in Smokey's huge gray eyes stopped him.

"How long will you be in Kennebunkport?"

"Not long," she said evasively.

"Are you leaving today?" Dallas was not to be put off.

"No."

"Well, I hope I'll see you before you go."

Smokey nodded and moved on without speaking. Dallas stood still and watched her go. He realized that he didn't just *hope* to see her before she left, he was banking on it. He hadn't had time to see Jenny that morning, but he would be at her house tonight for supper. If that didn't work, he'd camp on her doorstep in order to put his mind to rest about the true identity of Smoke.

The dining room of the hotel was warm and comfortably furnished. It was run by one of Kennebunkport's oldest families, and they prided themselves on good food and service. Smokey was hungry and very pleased that she was eating just five minutes after they had been shown to a table.

"How is your meal?"

"It's wonderful, Buck. Thank you."

"You seemed upset when you first came in, Smokey. Did something happen?"

Smokey took another bite of food and didn't immediately answer. "I saw your brother on my way here," she finally admitted. "I got the impression he wanted to talk with me, and I'm not sure I'm comfortable with what he might have in mind."

"It'll be easier for you when the whole family knows what you do for a living, won't it?" Buck said the words gently, but Smokey was still shocked. With a precise movement she laid her fork aside and stared across the table.

"How did you know, Buck?" Smokey asked, not wanting to believe that Tate or Jenny would have told.

"I'm a very observant man," Buck replied, carefully picking up her hand. "The look of your hands doesn't give you away, but the touch does. I noticed it the night we met. Your hands have worked hard for you for years. Your clothes are the next thing I observed. They're not frilly, but the cloth is of the finest quality.

"Added to these deductions is my insatiable reading habit. I receive newspapers from all over the world. I believe it was just a few months ago that rumors began to circulate through England and all of Europe that Smoke was a woman." When Buck fell silent, Smokey nodded ruefully.

"I didn't know how to tell anyone. It was never my intent to be deceitful. I had business with Pemberton Shipping just two weeks ago, so Tate and Jenny just found out; they were wonderful about the whole thing. And now Dallas wants to talk with me, and I don't know what he might be thinking."

"And you do care about his opinion, don't you?"

"I would love to tell you that I don't, but I just can't lie about it. I don't even know him really, but he's—" Smokey couldn't find the words.

"It's painful for you, and I shouldn't have pressed you."

"It's all right." Smokey hesitated and then went on. "I understand you have some pain of your own."

Buck's brow was knit with confusion, so Smokey continued softly.

"I met Greer Rittenhouse on my walk this morning. We talked, and she showed me her home. Your name came up, and she said you were just friends."

"It's the way she wants it," Buck admitted, pain now furrowing his brow.

"She talked to me about her house, said she was thinking of selling."

This was obviously new to Buck, so Smokey went on carefully. "She gave me a tour of the interior, and I fell quite in love with the place and its view. I asked her to let me know should she ever decide to sell."

"You and Dallas," Buck's smile was wry. "He's loved that house for years."

Smokey, not knowing how to answer, followed Buck's example and continued to eat. Buck didn't say anything for some minutes, and Smokey's mind began to wander. In a perfect daydream, she saw the widow Rittenhouse happily married to Buck, both of them settled comfortably in his home. To make the dream complete, she and Dallas were settled as husband and wife in the Rittenhouse mansion, with its lovely view of the sea.

Nine

ALL DALLAS' DOUBTS HAD BEEN PUT TO REST by the end of dinner at the Pembertons' that very evening. There was no conceivable way that this woman, who was so shy she could barely look at him, could be the renowned Smoke.

She hadn't spilled her water this time, but her knife clattered loudly against the edge of her plate whenever she set it down, and her hands shook slightly for most of the meal. Since she never once contributed to the conversation, Dallas was honestly beginning to wonder if there was something seriously wrong with her.

After they had retired to the parlor for tea, the horrible thought that she might have a drinking problem struck him so strongly that he retreated into a stunned silence for long moments.

Of course, he thought to himself. *That might explain why Jenny is so interested in her, but is that safe? Does Tate realize this?*

"Are you still with us, Dolly?" Buck wanted to know when Tate addressed a question to him and he didn't answer.

"I'm sorry," he said smoothly, pulling himself together mentally. "What were you saying, Tate?"

"I just asked how this voyage went. I think you mentioned seeing Lord Hawkesbury?"

"Yes. I even spent some time with him and his wife. It was a good trip overall, especially since I had some time with Hawk. Something funny happened when I was in London, however."

"Tell us about it," Jenny urged when Dallas paused. To everyone's surprise he turned to Smokey.

"Do you have a brother, Smokey?"

"No." Smokey answered after a surprised moment, knowing she sounded as breathless as she felt.

Dallas chuckled and shook his head. "I thought you might because I saw a sailor on the dock in London who looked very much like you. I mean, he had a knit cap on his head and baggy clothes, but it was his face I really noticed. He really looked enough like you to be your twin brother."

The room had grown so silent after this little story that Dallas' doubts returned in a flood. When he spoke again, there was no laughter in his voice. After sweeping the room, his eyes pinned Smokey to her chair.

"While Hawk and I were visiting, he mentioned the latest rumor to me. He said Smoke is a woman. Can you imagine? You might find it amusing," Dallas went on, even though he obviously didn't think it funny at all, "but when I saw that sailor who looked like you, and remembered your name was Smokey, my mind ran in some pretty ridiculous directions. I've actually been thinking that *you* might be Smoke." The soft emphasis he put on the word "you" caused shivers to run up Smokey's spine, but she forced herself to reply.

"I wear baggy clothes when I'm working," she softly stuttered. "And a knit cap over my hair." Smokey barely got the words out, thinking she might be sick.

"Dallas must have seen you just before you headed here with that shipment for me," Tate put in carefully, not at all pleased with the way his brother-in-law had handled this.

Tate's words caused Dallas to look slowly around the room. They all knew! Buck, Tate, and Jenny all knew she was Smoke. For some odd reason, he felt betrayed. He was also furious with himself for not taking the time to see Jenny that morning to gain some answers.

Though Dallas was unaware of just how angry he appeared at the moment, Smokey caught it all and blamed herself. She stood awkwardly, once again stuttering when she spoke.

"I'm going to turn in now. I have a big day tomorrow. Thank you for a lovely supper." Before anyone could gainsay her, she made her way from the room on legs that could barely support her. She was just out of earshot when Jenny let Dallas have the full blast of her fury.

"How dare you!" she spat at him in rage, coming to her feet in one magnificent move. "How dare you treat a guest that way in my home. You embarrassed the life out of her! You could have come to me, but no, you waited until you had an audience and then humiliated the life out of my friend."

Jenny would have gone on, but she was turned suddenly with Tate's hands on her arms. His voice was strict, but his touch was tender. "Calm down, Jennifer. I'll talk with Dallas. I don't want you this upset right now."

"He had no right—"

"I know," he gently cut her off. "But if you don't calm down, I'll call the doctor." He pulled her into his arms then and held her until she relaxed against him. He gave her a loving hug and kiss, and then held her in front of him, his eyes locked with hers.

"Go upstairs and check on Smokey. I'll be up in a moment." He released her when she gave a small nod and saw her to the door. Dallas spoke as soon as the door was shut.

"I'm sorry, Tate. I didn't mean to upset anyone."

"I realize that, but Jen is very protective of Smokey, and you did handle that poorly."

"Poorly?" Buck put in, censure filling his voice. "You were livid, and I can't understand why."

Dallas shook his head in disbelief. "I feel like such a fool. Do you really mean to tell me she's Smoke?"

"One and the same," Tate told him. "I know it's hard to believe, but Smokey's not at her best in social settings. I assure you, she's quite different when dealing with business matters."

"I'll apologize to her," Dallas said immediately. "Tonight, if you'd like." Dallas stood, willing to seek her out on the spot.

"No, I think tomorrow will be soon enough. Jen's with her now, and I suspect we all should sleep on it." Tate rose to leave, but Buck stopped him.

"There's more, isn't there, Tate? You looked almost frightened when Jen was upset. Can you tell us why?"

Tate hesitated for only an instant, hating to tell their wonderful news on such a sober note. "She's expecting, and although I've no reason to think she'll have problems, I'm not going to court disaster."

"When?" was all Dallas could say.

"Next summer," Tate answered and this time he did leave the room.

Jenny knocked on Smokey's door, but there was no immediate answer.

"Smokey," she called softly after a second knock. "May I please come in?"

"I'm going to bed, Jen." Smokey's voice was barely audible, and Jenny knew she would never sleep unless she talked with her. She eased the door open carefully and closed it with a soft click.

Smokey, still fully dressed, was on the window seat, the light from the full moon illuminating the tracks of tears on her face. Jenny came and sat across from her, not touching her or talking, but waiting and praying.

"He made me feel ashamed," she finally said, her voice quivering with emotion. "I saw him on that dock in London, but I never do anything to bring attention to myself while in port. We'd met so briefly that I thought it was best to walk on by. I never dreamed that he had noticed me. Now I feel like a liar and a cheat. I'm also angry because he's made me feel ashamed of the way I make my living."

Jenny's arms came around Smokey then, and the small woman, though older, sobbed in her friend's arms.

"Dolly is a wonderful man, Smokey," Jenny began. "And he's probably sorry right now for the way he acted. I was furious with him, but now that I've taken a few minutes to calm down, I can see that he reacted out of shock. That doesn't excuse him, but it might help you to see that it was nothing personal."

"I guess you're right."

"In fact, he probably greatly admires you. Buck was telling me before you came down for supper that your reputation is incredible."

Smokey shrugged and used her handkerchief on her face. "Like my father used to say, there's no magic in it, just a lot of hard work."

"It also must help to have the fastest ship on the ocean." Jenny's voice was very droll, and they both giggled.

Tate came for Jenny then, urging her to bed and sleep. Jenny made sure Smokey was all right before she left. She also refused to budge until Smokey promised to stay one day longer than she had planned. Smokey agreed, albeit reluctantly.

As Smokey fell asleep, she knew she would have to see Dallas again before leaving. It was not a comforting thought, but she told herself she would survive it. Of their own volition, tears started up again before she slept, this time because she wanted to talk with Darsey.

Ten

"You're an awfully hard lady to track down."

Dallas' deep voice so frightened Smokey that she started violently, and Dallas found himself apologizing over that before he could voice what he had come to say.

"I didn't mean to sneak up on you."

"It's all right."

They fell silent for a few minutes, each with his or her own thoughts, eyes out to sea.

Dallas had found Smokey in a craggy spot right above the beach. He had gone bright and early that morning to apologize, but Jenny had told him Smokey was on a walk. Dallas had other things he could do, many in fact, but until he had made things right between Smokey and him, he would not go to work.

"About last night, Smokey," Dallas finally began, and Smokey turned to look at him where he stood a short distance from her. "In my surprise I handled the situation very badly. I'm sorry."

"Thank you," Smokey said simply, and let her eyes rest on him for a moment more. His presence made her so aware of her rather plain looks and dowdy clothes that she couldn't get comfortable around him. After just a few seconds, Smokey transferred her gaze out to sea. She was surprised when Dallas did not bid her goodbye and leave.

She was even more surprised when he sat down on the rock beside her. There was nothing improper in the gesture, in fact he was two feet away, but she felt his closeness like an embrace.

"When do you sail again?"

Smokey answered without looking at him; it was easier that way. "We're scheduled to leave tomorrow."

"Will you be gone long?"

"We'll be back a few days before Christmas."

"May I sail with you?"

Even though the question surprised her, she answered immediately. "I don't take passengers."

"I meant as a crewman."

Smokey chuckled; she couldn't help herself. "Captains do *not* make good crewmen."

"I would." Dallas' deep, solemn tone forced Smokey to look at him. He was staring at her intently.

He's serious! she thought incredulously.

"Why?" she managed out loud.

"Because I want to study the *Aramis*."

"Why?" Smokey asked again, beginning to think this conversation absurd.

Dallas sighed. It was a reasonable question, but so hard to answer.

"I don't want to sail all my life." Dallas' eyes were now back to sea, his voice wistful. "When my parents moved south, a man they'd known for years took over my father's company. Buck had his own business to run, and I was too inexperienced to understand we were being swindled until it was too late. We were nearly broke in six months. Now I want to build the business up again, and my sailing is simply a means to that end. When I have enough capital, I want to build ships, and studying the *Aramis* would be invaluable to that trade."

"Knight Crafts," Smokey said when the realization dawned. "They're fine ships."

"I think so. I realize we were one of the smaller lines, but it's my dream to see the company in full production again."

"What happens to your ship in the next few weeks?"

"It needs repairs, and because it's been a busy year, my crew is ready for a break. I would work hard for you," Dallas added, "and take orders with the rest of the men."

Smokey wondered that she was actually considering it. Nate had impaled his hand on their last voyage, and as of a week ago, it was still infected. They could sail without him; it wouldn't be the first time they were shorthanded, or Dallas could take his place. Of course he probably wouldn't want the job when he learned it was the most insignificant position on the ship.

"I have an opening, but there's nothing very glamorous about it."

"I would take any job in order to be on the *Aramis* when you sail."

"You'd be a cabin boy of sorts, taking everyone's grief and seeing to every dirty job on ship, including the care of my clothes, my cabin, and the officers' quarters, and without a word of complaint."

"I was cabin boy to my uncle for two years. I can do the job." Dallas' eyes were alive with excitement.

"All right," Smokey agreed before she could change her mind.

"Great!"

Without even looking at him, Smokey knew his smile was a mile wide.

"Do your officers call you Smokey or Captain Simmons?" Dallas asked, his voice respectful.

"Captain Simmons," Smokey said with an unladylike snort. "I should be so lucky!"

It was a cryptic remark, but Dallas was given no chance to question her. Smokey pushed to her feet, jumped down to the beach without help, and took a few steps away. She turned back to him, as though suddenly remembering he was there.

"Be at the docks here at six bells tomorrow evening. Be on time, or we'll sail without you." She gave him no chance to reply.

Dallas watched her walk on down the beach, his heart and mind aswarm with questions. None of them mattered for the moment, however. He was going to *sail* on the *Aramis*. He still had his doubts as to whether Smokey could sail her way out of the harbor, but that wasn't important—studying her ship was.

"Did Dolly find you?" Jenny inquired of Smokey when she came back to the house.

"He did," she told her with a decisive nod.

"And did he apologize?" Jenny prompted.

"Yes, we actually talked awhile."

"Why, Smokey, that's wonderful! What did you talk about?"

"My sailing. I actually was able to converse with him this time without stuttering or staring at him like I was demented."

"So the wall has come down between you?"

"I wouldn't say that," Smokey shook her head. "He asked if he could sail with me when I leave tomorrow, and I actually agreed."

Jenny's mouth swung open. As funny as she looked, Smokey did not feel like laughing. She gave Jenny a short rendition of the conversation, and when she finished, the younger woman was still speechless.

"What are you thinking?" Smokey needed to know.

"That you're wonderful," Jenny told her lovingly.

"What do you mean?"

"Smokey, I know Dolly hurt you last night, and here you are helping him out. It's been his dream to build ships for years, and I think your assisting him is wonderful." Jenny paused and bit her lip. "Do you feel a little used?"

"A little," Smokey admitted. "Your brother is kind, but he really couldn't have given me the time of day before he found out who I was."

Jenny nodded with understanding. "I'll be praying that

you two will get to know each other and be friends. Knowing you both, I think you would get along very well."

"Thanks, Jen, but first I need you to pray about my having to tell Darsey. I don't even want to think about what he's going to say."

As it was, Darsey said nothing. He simply stared at Smokey for one full minute. When he spoke, his voice was even.

"What about your plans for China Island?"

"We can still do it, if we don't forget the book this time."

Darsey fell silent again.

"I can send word that it won't work out," she finally said, looking so young and vulnerable that Darsey sighed deeply. She was so naive of other ships and crews. Didn't she realize how unusual their life on the *Aramis* was?

"It's not me I'm thinking of, lass, it's you. The boys know how to give you your privacy, and you give us ours. We don't know this man. It certainly wouldn't be the end of the world if he didn't work out, but it would be an awful bother getting rid of him."

"I don't think he'll be any trouble. Like I said, he's been a captain for years, and he just wants to study the *Aramis.*"

"In other words, we won't be getting much work out of him."

Smokey shrugged. "I hope that's not the case, but I can't make any promises. I don't want to talk you into this, Darsey." Smokey's voice changed suddenly, and Darsey knew his captain was speaking.

"Because if I do talk you into this, you'll say 'I told you so' if it doesn't work out. So speak up now or keep still."

"I'll abide by your decision, lass, but hear me well. I'll not brook a moment of improper conduct out of him where you're concerned."

Now it was Smokey's turn to sigh, heartfelt and deep. "I'm sure that won't be a problem, Darsey." Her voice was resigned. "No problem at all."

She turned and went upstairs before he could question her, but in truth he had heard enough. He sat in Willa's parlor for a long time, wondering how many years he had prayed for this, and then asking himself, now that it had finally happened, why it scared him witless.

Eleven

THE NEXT DAY DARSEY GATHERED the officers of the *Aramis* as they set sail from their home port in Kennebunk. He explained that Nate would not be sailing with them this trip, and that they would be picking up a man Smokey had hired to take his place in Kennebunkport.

"Does Nate know he's being replaced?"

"He's not being replaced, Mic," Darsey patiently told him. "It's just for this one voyage."

"He wants to study the *Aramis*," Smokey interjected when she came across the group gathered on the deck. "Since he won't be sailing with us again, I'd like you to be of help to him if you can. Answer any questions he may have. Outside of that, it's business as usual."

The men nodded, and Smokey's eyes lingered on their faces. There wasn't a man under 40, and most were nearer to 50. Darsey was that and then some. Each of them—Darsey, Mic, Robby, Pete, and Scully, who was the ship's cook—had sailed with her father for years before he died. She knew them to be capable, reliable, and loyal to a fault. What would they think of Dallas Knight? Indeed! What would Dallas think of them?

Hers was not a normal group of sailors. Most men enjoyed full-time work, but Smokey had a tendency to stay closer to

home than her father had, so she could be in port more often.
The older these men became, the more that seemed to suit
them. She was a generous captain, and they always shared in
the fruits of her labor, which included time off for weeks at a
stretch.

The men dispersed while Smokey was still deep in thought.
She walked to the bow, her body moving to the rocking of the
ship with the ease of a willow tree in the wind.

Once at the front of the ship, the sight of the waves and the
speed with which the *Aramis* moved did not thrill her as it
usually did. She barely noticed either. Her mind was already
in Kennebunkport and on the man who would be waiting in
port to meet them.

"I've never seen you like this, Dallas," Tate commented to
his nearly delirious brother-in-law. Buck was quick to agree.
The three men were standing on the dock Sunday evening,
awaiting Smokey's ship.

"It's hard to explain," Dallas told them, his eyes still alight
with pleasure even as he tried to calm down. "It will mean so
much to the business, and I think this is a once-in-a-lifetime
opportunity."

"I hate to be a prophet of doom," Buck interjected, not
unkindly. "But have you thought about what will happen if you
don't get along with Smokey or her men?"

"What's not to get along with?" Dallas asked in genuine
confusion. "I'll do my job, observe the workings of the ship,
and come home rich with knowledge." Dallas' voice was so
matter-of-fact that neither man commented.

Dallas himself was still thinking on his brother's words,
but the more he thought about Smokey Simmons' personality,
the more assured he felt that they would get along fine. After
all, she was very shy and quiet, keeping mostly to herself, and
that would suit him fine.

He reminded himself that she had talked more on the beach than he had ever heard her, but that was obviously credited to the fact that she was more comfortable talking about ships than any other subject.

Dallas hoped that if she were really knowledgeable, he would learn some things from her, but he had no illusions. She was young and timid, and Dallas believed he would learn more from her ship and her men than he would from her.

He wouldn't have admitted it to his family because they all liked her so well, but in the brief time that he had known he would be sailing with the *Aramis*, Dallas had convinced himself that Smokey must be little more than a mascot.

The big man he had seen with her in London was her first mate, a man named Darsey. Dallas knew he was almost as well known as Smoke. As soon as Dallas remembered who the man was, he realized that he must be the driving force behind Smoke. It was like this with many ship's captains—Smokey owned the ship, Darsey did all the work, but as owner and captain, Smokey took the credit.

An hour later, as Darsey introduced himself to Dallas and showed him to the crew's quarters, Dallas was more convinced than ever about Smokey's uselessness aboard ship. In his thrill of being on the *Aramis*, he forgot just how much his own first mate did for him on the *Zephyr*. His mind even went so far as to feel a bit of disgust that Smokey couldn't stay home where she belonged.

She hadn't really struck him as that kind, but she was clearly the type of female who had to have attention. He figured she must have inherited the ship from her father and then gotten it into her foolish, female head to be a captain. He tried to adjust his attitude as he stowed his gear for the voyage.

Dallas would have been amazed to learn that Smokey and Darsey had run into sentiment like this before. He would have been surprised beyond speech if he had known that Darsey had interpreted most of his thoughts on their first meeting.

As the first mate made his way topside, he hid a smile. Young Mr. Knight would have to find out the hard way that Smoke Simmons was no figurehead.

Their first morning at sea, Smokey sat at the desk in her cabin and pored over her maps. She had to be in Savannah by tomorrow morning and then into Florida the morning after. That would mean their trip to China Island would have to wait until the end of next week. A knock on her cabin door interrupted her thoughts.

"Come in," she called. Darsey entered and shut the door behind him. The chair he took creaked under his weight as he made himself comfortable in the small space.

"Did Dallas get settled?" Smokey wanted to know.

"I believe he did."

"What did you think of him?"

Darsey grinned. "I think we've got another one who's giving me more credit than I deserve."

"Oh, no." Smokey's look was one of exasperation. "I really thought better of him than that. Oh, well, we won't be out that long."

"Long enough for him to learn he's wrong," Darsey said, a mischievous glint appearing in his eye.

"You don't really think we're going to tangle, do you? I mean, he will take orders, won't he?"

"That's up to him, now, isn't it, lass?" Darsey spoke honestly.

Smokey agreed with a nod. "I guess it is, but you know, since I'm not out to prove anything, you could simply handle all problems on this trip."

"That's true, but it's unlikely that such a plan would last for more than a day."

Smokey laughed. He was right. It was just as she'd said to

Dallas, captains did not make good crewmen, and she was no exception.

By the time the *Aramis* pulled into the port of Savannah, Dallas had all but forgotten Smokey's presence on board, which only confirmed his earlier belief that she was quite useless as a captain. With this in mind, he was surprised to hear her greet him as she came onto the deck. He had begun to think she preferred to spend all her time in her cabin.

"Good morning, Dallas," Smokey said congenially as she moved past him and approached Scully. He noticed that she was dressed as she had been in London—baggy clothes, black boots, knit cap, and all. She stopped next to Scully and waited for him to face her. Dallas, without effort, overheard their conversation.

"You've got a few hours, Scully, to make sure you're ready." Her voice was a bit stern. "If you don't have proper food on this trip, I won't be at all happy."

"Aye, missy," Scully said with a frown, and Smokey turned away.

Dallas had to duck his head in order to hide his expression. *So, she's a prima donna to boot!* He didn't know when he had been more repulsed. He watched as she went below. A minute later Darsey appeared. Darsey handled the load and later the casting off, and although Dallas did his job silently and efficiently, he was beginning to feel a strong aversion to his captain.

Their next stop was Barbados. Dallas' duties were minimal once they were out at sea, and he found himself feeling a little bit of heaven on earth. In just a few days' time, he had become adept at ignoring Smokey and at the same time studying her clipper.

Dallas had never been on a ship that could move with such speed. The *Aramis* was a yare vessel, and he had never seen her equal. She cut through the water with the ease of a sharp blade against tender beef. If he hadn't understood before, it became increasingly clear now why this boat was in and out of port before the *Zephyr* could even get moving. The cut of her bow, the placement of the sail—in fact everything Dallas could see—contributed to her grace and speed.

He smiled to himself on more than one occasion as he worked. *There may be aspects of this job I don't enjoy, but studying this craft more than makes up for every one of them.*

The afternoon of the sixth day saw Smokey on the deck more than any other day previous. Quiet as they sailed, she allowed Darsey to handle most everything, but her eyes were watchful. Everyone on deck knew that the ship would be in the midst of a storm before the night was through. What remained a mystery was how hard it would hit, and for how long.

The afternoon was swiftly disappearing when they moved into heavy cloud cover. The north wind seemed to pick up as if by magic, but still no rain fell. The wind had begun to whip the craft as though the magnificent clipper were but a toy. Hoping to beat the rain that was sure to come, the crew was lowering the sails as fast as they could.

They worked fast and hard, but the wind was stronger and trouble came. Smokey had never left the helm, so no one had to summon her when the rigging of the mainsail would not come loose. The sail had to come down or be ripped to shreds.

Dallas, who had been working with Mic and Robby securing the other sails, turned to offer his services to Darsey. He had climbed the mainmast dozens of times in his day and would be only too glad to make repairs on this one if needed. What he saw when he turned, however, stopped the words in his throat.

Darsey and Smokey had come down on the deck, and Dallas watched in horror as Smokey clamped a knife between her teeth, jumped up onto the mainmast, and began to climb. Dallas swiftly tied off the line he'd been holding and ran toward the mast. With one foot on the base he reached to haul himself upward, but Darsey's huge hand stopped him.

"Don't do it, lad," he shouted over the wind.

"You can't be serious," Dallas shouted back, knowing he would never get past Darsey if he prevented him.

"You've misjudged her, Dallas," Darsey returned, speaking his name for the first time. "She *is* the captain of this ship, and she's been climbing the rigging since she was three years old. If you interfere, I can promise that she'll land you in the next port and leave you to make your own way home."

Dallas could do nothing but step back and look up, just as the rest of the crew had done.

Smokey had removed her tunic, and the wind now plastered her white blouse to her slim form. She had tangled her small-booted feet in the ropes and balanced herself, much like a circus performer, in order to free up both hands for the work.

Dallas didn't think he could breathe as he watched her swaying dozens of feet above the deck, but her face, although determined, was almost tranquil. Her hands, he also noticed, moved with skill and dexterity until the job was done.

She came down as swiftly as she had gone up, and Darsey, catching her around the waist, swung her onto the deck where she joined her own hands to the men's as they brought the sail under control.

There was no pomp or ceremony. To the rest of the crew it was routine. For Dallas, however, it was like a blow. All his notions concerning her abilities as a captain were falling into a heap about him. As he worked, he stole glances at her.

Some of her crew had been sailing for more years than she had been alive, but she made them seem almost clumsy. There were no hesitations or mistakes in her movements, no shirking of any job. Her eyes missed nothing, and with a minimum of effort, all was put right for the storm.

Not ten minutes later, as the clouds broke loose above them and the rain began to pour, Dallas realized that his bias had colored his every thought. Smokey had behaved no differently since they left Maine than he had on dozens of voyages. The crew was extremely capable in their performance, leaving Smokey free to comport herself as she should—as the captain of the *Aramis*. Dallas knew he had a lot of soul-searching to do.

Twelve

TWO DAYS LATER, DALLAS STOOD at the stern of the ship, swabbing the deck, checking lines, and coiling rope with Pete. Save the cleanup, all signs of the storm were over. Although it had not been the worst storm he'd ever seen, neither had it been the mildest. The wind and waves had actually moved them ahead of schedule, so the *Aramis* was not in a hurry but moving along at a steady clip.

In the time that had passed Dallas had prayed during his every waking moment. He had come to the conclusion that while he did not need to verbally apologize to Smokey, he must by his actions show her his respect. She certainly deserved it.

Contrary to what he had thought, there was nothing or no one aboard the ship over which she was not in complete command. Dallas found that the *Aramis* was only an extension of the woman herself. There was nothing showy or bossy about her, but with a gesture or softly spoken word, her every wish was obeyed. Dallas found that he wanted to laugh when he thought about how full circle his thoughts had come. He had moved from nearly despising her to being slightly in awe.

He realized now that he had experienced a taste of her authority when they'd talked on the beach. She had said more to him than ever before, and there had been no hesitation or shyness. It was almost impossible to relate the woman he saw at the helm of the *Aramis* to the woman who had spilled her water glass twice during lunch at home.

"Dallas," Darsey called to him from the helm. "Run to the captain's cabin and bring the large glass."

Dallas trotted down the stairs to do as Darsey bid. When he returned to the helm, Smokey put her hand out for the instrument.

"Thank you," she spoke almost absently. Dallas followed her eyes and spotted the ship in the distance. He watched as Smokey placed the glass to her eye, and then again as a huge smile broke across her face.

"It's the *Clausen*," she told Darsey, who was right beside her. She handed him the glass.

Dallas felt more than saw that the other men had become almost tense. All had stopped their duties and were watching the captain and her first mate intently.

Smokey took the telescope from Darsey and had one more look. When she lowered it again, she sported a look that Dallas had never seen before but would come to love.

"Let's catch him." The words were almost whispered, but the crew went into action as though on strings. Dallas felt the blood pump in his veins as Darsey tacked off and headed due south and he and Mic ran down to man the lines.

The sails whipped and cracked as they let loose, and the entire vessel seemed to lift out of the water for the chase. Dallas looked up at one point to see Smokey behind the wheel. For a moment he was distracted in his duties, thinking how well the position suited her.

They were some three miles away when the crew of the *Clausen* realized their ship was under pursuit. The crew of the *Aramis* watched with glee as *Clausen's* canvas blew to full sail and the other ship tried to outrun them. The *Clausen* stood no chance.

Dallas was amazed at how quickly they pulled alongside of the other ship. Smokey stood on top of the wheelhouse, the glass again to her eye as they sailed past. The crew heard her shout of laughter when the captain of the *Clausen* stood high and waved his handkerchief as a white flag.

Smokey waved to him in obvious friendship as they pulled easily ahead. Dallas could not wipe the grin from his face; he didn't know when he'd had such fun. Like a diamond in the rough, there seemed to be more to Smokey Simmons than he ever considered possible. In fact, that very evening he was to see yet one more facet.

"Dallas," Darsey approached him on the deck where he was repairing some line, "Smokey wants to see you in her cabin."

"Right." Dallas put his work aside and went directly below. He knocked on her door and waited for her to acknowledge him before going inside.

Smokey was at her desk when he stepped in. She motioned him to a chair.

"How is everything?" she wanted to know as soon as he was seated.

"Fine."

"Good," Smokey said, taking him at his word. "The rest of the crew has known me for some time, and they would never hesitate to voice a complaint or concern. I wanted to be certain you felt the same."

Smokey paused long enough to pick up a sheaf of rolled papers from her desk.

"I found these in my files, and I thought you might like to study them. You can't have them, but as long as you're on board you can look at them. They're the plans for the *Aramis*."

Dallas took the pages she offered to him and slowly unrolled them. His eyes drank in the lines and measurements with the ease of an experienced builder.

"These are excellent," Dallas spoke, almost to himself.

"It's a fine vessel," Smokey agreed, causing Dallas to look up. He studied her across the small space for a long moment.

She was as relaxed and confident as she could be behind the desk. She smiled easily, transforming her entire face whenever she did, and there was nothing forced about her voice or movements.

"I hope I'm not out of line to say that you're different on your ship than when you're at Jenny's."

"Or at Buck's, when I'm dumping water on myself?" Smokey said dryly and laughed, freeing Dallas to join her.

"How long have you been sailing?" Dallas was suddenly overcome with curiosity about this unique woman.

"My father was a sailor, so I've been at sea all my life, but as an actual captain, just a few years."

"How old are you—19, 20?"

Smokey laughed again, and Dallas found he liked the sound. "I'm 25, and I've been the captain of the *Aramis* since I was 23."

"Twenty-five?" Dallas face showed his shock. "You look younger," he admitted softly, and even though he knew he was a crewman under her authority, he allowed his gaze to become rather warm.

Smokey, still so attracted to him she had to work at keeping her composure, wanted very much to ask him what he was thinking, but Darsey knocked and entered. His stern gaze pinned Dallas to the seat for a moment, making him feel closer to 15 than 28.

"Here's your supper, lass—and yours is waiting in the galley, lad." Darsey stood expectantly on these words until Dallas stood and moved toward the door.

"Thank you, Smokey," he told her before exiting.

He stowed the papers in his bunk and then made his way topside, wishing for the first time that he was in command of this vessel, a position that would allow him to sit and talk with the fascinating Smokey Simmons for hours if he so desired.

Scully, Darsey, Mic, Dallas, and Robby were crowded into the galley having supper and swapping stories when Smokey entered. Dallas watched in amazement as she slammed her plate on the table, slopping some of its contents onto the wood surface.

"This has spinach in it, Scully," Smokey spoke between clenched teeth, her face bright pink with anger. "I told you in *Florida* to get some decent food."

"Now, missy," he tried to placate her. "You need spinach. Remember what your father used to say, he—"

"You have got exactly 15 minutes to get a decent supper to my cabin," she cut him off ruthlessly. "Or I'll have you keel-hauled." She slammed out in a fury to match the storm they had just been through, and Dallas spoke.

"*What* was that all about?"

"She hates green vegetables, always has. And Scully always tries to get her to eat them. You shouldn't have tried it, Scully," Darsey now said to the old cook. "She can always tell."

"She doesn't eat right," he insisted. "I don't know how she tasted them. If only she would—"

"Oh, stow it, Scully," Mic told him. "Just make her something and take it down."

After a fierce glare at Mic, Scully went to work, grumbling the entire time. After just ten minutes, he set a fresh plate on the table and turned to Robby.

"Take that to her, Rob."

"No way, Scully; you made her mad, you take it down."

Scully tried Mic, pushing the plate in his direction. "Take this down."

Mic didn't even acknowledge him, so Scully looked to Darsey.

"Don't look at me. I won't go near her when she's been kept from her dinner."

Dallas suddenly found the entire table staring at him. "Now wait a minute," he protested but was cut off.

"Go on, lad," Darsey said with a huge grin. "You're low man this voyage, so get moving."

Dallas rolled his eyes, scooped up the plate, and walked below. He thought the lot of them were overreacting. *Just like a bunch of old women. She's probably forgotten all about it by now.* Nevertheless, he knocked very softly on her door.

"Come in." Smokey's curt reply brought Dallas through the door.

He set the food down, and she examined the contents as though looking for clues to a crime. When she stayed silent, Dallas took that to mean she was satisfied; he couldn't have been more wrong. As soon as he started toward the door, he found himself getting the sharp side of her tongue.

"Dallas, this cabin may be your idea of clean, but it's *not* mine. See to it first thing in the morning."

Dallas turned back and stared at her for the space of several heartbeats. Her eyes were still flashing with fire, turning them from gray to black. The top of her head didn't even reach his shoulder, and yet she rose to give him orders like a giant. He wanted to laugh so badly that it hurt to hold it in.

"Yes, Captain," he finally said. "Will there be anything else?"

"No." Her reply was short, and her eyes narrowed, daring him to make one move out of line. "You're dismissed."

Dallas obeyed, letting himself slowly out of the room. After shutting the door softly, he paused in the passageway and grinned, his mind's eye still seeing the darkness in her eyes and the flush on her face. Dallas slowly shook his head, his grin still in place. He could honestly say he'd never met another woman quite like her.

Thirteen

ABOUT A WEEK AFTER the spinach incident, Dallas woke one morning and realized something was amiss. It was early, and without taking time to pull on anything more than his pants, he went topside.

He found the *Aramis* docked near a small island. This voyage had been something of a pleasure trip for Dallas, and he'd had no need to keep track of their location. Now he wished he had paid a little more attention.

Robby was the only one about, and he was standing calmly on the deck watching Dallas approach. The ship felt so deserted it was eerie.

"Where are we?"

"China Island," Robby answered.

"I've never heard of it."

"Not many have. Smokey's pa used to bring her here; it's where she learned to swim."

"Is she over there now?"

"Um hmm. Along with most of the crew."

Dallas' gaze turned to the small island and lingered on the rowboats that were pulled up on the beach. He knew the ship boasted several rowboats, but it was an easy swim and the thought of walking on terra firma strongly appealed to him at the moment.

"Is Darsey about?"

"On the island. Along with Mic and Pete."

"I think I'll swim over."

"All right," Robby agreed easily enough, figuring that the island was large enough to guarantee the captain's privacy.

Since Dallas was dressed only in pants, there was no need to go below for anything. He stepped to the railing, and Robby's brows rose with appreciation when a perfect dive was executed, one that caused little more than a ripple on the surface of the water. Impressed, Robby watched as Dallas surfaced and struck out with long, clean stokes. In no time at all, he was walking ashore. Robby only hoped that Smokey was in a secluded place.

"What does it say next?" Smokey wanted to know as she watched her first mate from across the table.

Darsey turned another page. "A lady must keep her knees pressed together at all times; her legs should be gracefully crossed at the ankles. Ah, lass, do we have to go on with this?" Darsey put the book down and frowned at her.

"Yes. Now keep reading."

"Why didn't you do this at home with Willa?" Darsey asked, ignoring her order.

Seeing that she was going to have to explain, Smokey sighed. "She would have asked what kind of people my new friends were, that they expected me to put on airs in their company. She just wouldn't have understood."

"I'm not sure I do," Darsey admitted. There was no censure in his tone, only tenderness, and Smokey tried to make herself understood.

"I'm not ashamed of who I am or where I've been, Dars, but I don't fit into the world outside of a ship. I don't know how to hold my fork or cup, and I'm so nervous and uncomfortable that I end up dropping things and spilling water in my lap."

"You're exaggerating, Smokey; those things aren't going to happen."

"They already have," Smokey told him with tears in her eyes. Darsey's heart melted. She didn't cry easily, and those tears made him see how much she hurt over this.

When she had explained why she wanted to stop at China Island, Darsey had looked at her as though she'd taken leave of her senses. Even that morning as he had loaded a small table, two chairs, and a china tea set aboard the rowboat, he'd thought it was too fantastic to be real.

Then they had gone ashore and found a secluded area, set things up according to Smokey's wishes, and she'd handed him a book on etiquette. That was two hours ago, and until he saw those tears pooling in her eyes, Darsey had begun to think it was all rather silly.

Without so much as a sigh of resignation, Darsey opened the book and began to read again. He would have loved to hand this job over to someone who was better qualified, but he was all Smokey had. If they had to sit there for a week, he would see her through this.

Once on the island, Dallas found a shallow pool and took a quick dip to wash the salt from his pants and hair. The water was cool and refreshing, and he started on a tour of the island after he'd bathed.

There appeared to be more birds than other wildlife, but he did spot a few snakes and lizards amid the fronds and leaves of bushes and trees. He was making his way through a rather dense section of bushes when he came across Darsey and Smokey.

Thinking he was imagining the sight of his captain and her first mate having tea on the island, Dallas inspected them for the space of several heartbeats. They were all too real. He watched as Darsey read, lowered the book, and then read some more. He continued to watch as Smokey picked up a teacup, working to balance it carefully with just two fingers. Realization of what she was doing dawned just before he was spotted.

Smokey knew the moment she saw Dallas that he had been watching for some time. Her face flamed in humiliation, but her embarrassment did nothing to temper the sternness of her tone.

"Get back to the ship, Dallas." Smokey's voice was like a lash, and Dallas immediately moved to do as he was bid.

He'd only taken two steps, however, when an overwhelming feeling of tenderness for his captain overrode his good sense. He stopped and turned back.

"I gave you an order, sailor." Smokey was livid, and her voice told Dallas as much. Still he did not obey.

"I know you did, Captain." Dallas' voice was quiet and respectful as he took careful steps toward the table. "However, I'd like to show my appreciation for your helping me by returning the favor. With no offense intended, I think I can be of more assistance than Darsey."

Darsey came out of his chair so fast that he tipped it over backward. He righted it quickly, and even though Smokey was glaring at him with fire in her eyes, he turned to Dallas.

"Take my seat, Dallas." The older man's voice was filled with relief. In truth, insult was the farthest thing from his mind. "I'm ready for a break, so go ahead and sit here and read for Smokey."

As Dallas collapsed his tall frame into the chair Darsey had vacated, shame washed over Smokey so quickly that she had trouble breathing. *Never* had she been so mortified. She turned frantic eyes to Darsey, but he was headed through the trees without a backward glance.

"Now," Dallas' voice was as calm and collected as if this were an everyday occurrence for him. "I believe you were working on tea service."

Dallas began to read. Smokey kept her eyes on the table, her face still aflame. She would have given anything at that moment to be able to walk away, but something detained her. For some moments she only half-listened to the book. Then Dallas spoke her name, his voice tender and compassionate.

"Okay, Smokey, pick up the teapot with your right hand." Smokey moved to obey him without ever looking in his direction.

"Put the fingers of your left hand over the lid and pour us some tea. Oh, now, that won't do at all!" Dallas suddenly said, and Smokey looked up in surprise, wondering what she'd done wrong.

"Darsey didn't even take time to put water in this. Here," he handed her the book, "you read that first page yourself while I fill this."

Smokey watched him walk away and then glanced at the trees overhead. The sun was headed high into the sky, and the day was growing warm. Smokey looked at the book in her hand and for a moment forgot about the heat. On the opposite page was a lovely ink sketch. The picture showed a beautiful parlor where three ladies were seated, one of whom was pouring tea. Smokey scrutinized the picture, studying it with intense longing.

So consumed by the picture and the words of the chapter, Smokey reached without thought to remove her knit cap. Dallas came through the trees from the pond and stopped dead at the sight of Smokey with her hair down her back.

It fell to her waist in black waves, and he continued to gawk as she unconsciously ran her fingers through the mass and gently rubbed her head. Dallas got ahold of himself just before she glanced up to see him.

"All right," Dallas said as he worked at not staring at Smokey. He placed the teapot back on the table and resumed his seat. "Now, try it again."

In the last moments, Smokey had become completely relaxed. All humiliation over Dallas' presence deserted her, as with studied concentration she lifted the teapot and filled their glasses to the three-quarter mark, just as the book instructed. Her hand never wavered, and when she put the pot down, she gave Dallas a huge smile. Dallas couldn't stop himself from laughing. Smokey joined him before asking him to read on.

In the next hour Dallas read while Smokey set the table, served from a standing position and drank her "tea" without spilling a drop. Dallas thought she might go on forever, but his stomach suddenly growled very loudly.

"I didn't take time for breakfast," he said with a sheepish grin.

Smokey frowned. "I didn't either, now that you mention it. I guess we had better head back."

They were gathering the tea set to return it to the box when Smokey realized she couldn't find her cap. She searched around a bit, but stopped on Dallas' words.

"Why do you need it?"

"Because I don't want to cut my hair."

"Why would you have to do either; I mean cut it or cover it?"

"The wind, Dallas," Smokey explained patiently. "I can't let it hang down while on the *Aramis*. It blinds me."

"Here," Dallas stepped toward her, "turn around a minute."

Smokey did as he directed without question, but she stiffened when she felt his hands on her hair. When they were both working on her ship, it was easy to remember their positions; she was the captain and he was part of her crew. But in Maine or here on the island, she was a woman and he was a man, and Smokey found herself unable to remember anything.

Dallas was feeling the same way at the moment and was tremendously relieved that Smokey's back was to him, allowing him to hide his expression. He efficiently braided the length of her hair, amazed at how soft and thick it was, and tied the end with a thin leather strip he wore about his wrist.

"There," he said proudly when the work was done. Smokey's hand went to her nape as she turned to face him.

Until that moment, she had given no thought to his bare chest or the dark stubble on his cheeks, but he suddenly became more male than she had ever noticed. The breadth of his shoulders and the muscles in his arms, along with the way his gold ring hung sparkling from his ear, were so distracting that Smokey could only gaze hopelessly into his crystal-blue eyes.

"Your hair is beautiful." Smokey heard Dallas' voice, although he sounded a long way off. "It seems a shame to cover it." Smokey made no reply, but continued to look at Dallas, her heart in her eyes.

"Smokey," Dallas' voice had turned hoarse. "If you don't stop staring at me like that, I'm going to kiss you."

Smokey unconsciously raised her face, and Dallas lowered his. Darsey had come upon them, but had discreetly moved away this time in order to give them privacy. Dallas' lips were just a breath away from Smokey's when a bird suddenly flew from the trees and startled them both. The interruption broke the spell.

Smokey, her heart still madly pounding in her chest, spoke to Dallas, but her eyes never left the ground.

"It's time to get back to the ship. I'm sure Darsey is nearby. He can help you take the table and chairs back to the boat. I'll see you on board."

Dallas watched her walk away, knowing he had no choice but to obey. Within moments she had gone from a very warm, embraceable woman to the businesslike captain of the *Aramis*. Dallas understood, but it didn't change the way he felt inside— like a man who had been offered a lovely gift, only to have it snatched away a moment before he could grasp it.

Smokey had been right about Darsey; he appeared just moments later. Dallas was thankful for his help as well as his silence. He needed that time to pray. He was still praying when the *Aramis* set sail less than an hour later.

That evening when all was quiet on the ship, Darsey found Smokey alone at the railing. The moon was a crescent in the sky, but there was still enough light for the first mate to see his captain's face.

"Are you all right?" Darsey asked without preamble. Smokey nodded, turning to look at her friend and confidant.

"I think so," she told him. "I was afraid for a few moments on the island."

"Of Dallas?" Darsey's voice held legitimate concern.

"No," Smokey reassured him. "I think my fear stems from the intensity of my feelings. By the time I gained my cabin, frustration had set in. There's nothing I can do about the way I feel."

Darsey had no argument for that. They were both professionals and rightfully believed this was not the time or place to pursue a romance. Smokey reassured Darsey that she was going to be fine and talked of other things before going down to bed. Upon her departure, Darsey went on watch.

When the older man was finally alone, he let his mind drift to the youngest crewman. As quiet as Dallas had been when they had left the island earlier, Darsey was quite certain that he understood the situation as well. Darsey found his respect growing for Dallas every day.

Fourteen

WITH THE SHIP HEADED toward London, the next days passed in an uneventful fashion, and neither Dallas nor Smokey could have said exactly why. Maybe it was because they forced their minds away from the incident on the island, or maybe it was the amount of praying they both did when apart from the rest of the crew.

Only when Smokey was alone in her cabin and Dallas lay in his bunk did they allow their minds to drift back to the near kiss and the way they felt. On the heels of their thoughts, they turned to God.

Smokey begged God to help her forget Dallas, sure that he could never be serious about her. Dallas, on the other hand, prayed for patience where Smokey was concerned, knowing she did not recognize his feelings for her as yet. He also prayed for a gentle way of telling Kathleen that he was falling for another woman.

Women like Smokey were a complete mystery to women like Kathleen. Kathleen never read a newspaper or cared to talk about anything beyond the latest dress pattern she had seen or who was getting married next and how pretty the bride's dress would be. It wasn't that Kathleen was slow, it was just that her world was so small.

Dallas clearly remembered the first time he'd tried to talk

to her about the ships he dreamed of building. "Oh, Dallas," she had laughingly said. "I'm just a woman, and a woman can't understand those kinds of things."

Dallas had had to bite his tongue to keep from telling Kathleen that Jenny knew all about ships, or to ask her what being a woman had to do with anything. Kathleen changed the subject soon after that, however, and Dallas still regretted that he hadn't questioned her when he'd had the chance.

Worrying about his relationship with Kathleen when they were miles from home was not going to change a thing. Dallas determined to speak with her as soon as he returned. He had no guarantees that he and Smokey had a future, but he couldn't go on seeing a woman whose company paled so dramatically in the light of his captain's.

When they docked in London, Dallas listened while Darsey put some men on watch. The older man then turned to Dallas and invited him to clean up and go with them ashore.

They'd come in and delivered a load of coffee and taken on half a holdful of wool. He hadn't seen much of Smokey since they'd docked, but she now appeared, hair brushed smooth and in a fresh braid that hung down her back, and wearing a different, brighter-colored overtunic than she usually wore.

Smokey and Darsey stood on the deck and talked while the officers readied themselves, all turning up freshly shaved and clothed just 15 minutes later. Darsey led the procession off the ship, Smokey following behind him. Consumed with great curiosity, Dallas brought up the rear. That this was routine for each of them was more than clear, until he saw where they were headed.

Darsey walked calmly into one of the roughest parts of the

docks, to a waterfront tavern that was so hidden, Dallas would have missed it had he been alone.

Clancy's Place was painted on the door in faded, chipped letters. Dallas watched as Darsey opened the door and held it for Smokey to enter. If Dallas hadn't already been captivated with this woman, he would have been stunned at the events of the next moments. As it was, he was more than a little surprised at the spaciousness of the tavern *and* his captain's welcome once she stepped in.

As if someone had blown a whistle, the place grew very still. Heads turned, and drinks and cards were placed on the table with an almost reverent quiet. Smokey began to make her way through the crowd. As she passed each table, the occupants stood. Dallas listened in fascination to the words exchanged.

"Hello, Timmy," Smokey spoke to a man who looked well over 100.

"Hello, Cap'n. How's business?"

"Smooth. How's Betsy?"

"Fine, she asks about you."

"Give her my love."

And on it went. She had a word for nearly everyone in the room. As they neared the bar, she spoke to one man who hadn't stood.

"Hello, Hector."

Hector only grunted.

"Well," she spoke wryly, "you grunt as well as you always have, so I guess that means you're doing well."

That said, she used two fingers and flicked the cap from his head. Dallas listened as the room erupted with laugher, and watched a grudging smile cross Hector's face even though he never stood or even looked at her.

Finally they were at the bar. A man who was nearly as wide as the wall behind him stood opposite them, his grin as toothless as that of a baby's.

"Is the back room open tonight, Bart?" Smokey asked with an innocent smile.

"Well-l-l," the heavy man said with a twinkle in his eye. "I'll tell you, Smoke, there was a great group of nuns just in here and wantin' my back room. I didn't know if you was coming, you see," he shrugged at this point, and Smokey hid a smile. "So I had to turn them away. I'm sure I lost a great deal of money."

Another nonchalant shrug accompanied these words, and suddenly a coin left Darsey's fingers and spiraled through the air. With speed and dexterity that belied his size, the big man snatched it out of the air, his face alight with triumph. With a flourish of his hand, he spoke.

"It's all yours, Captain."

"Thanks, Bart. Tell Meg we're starving, and I want my tea strong."

The men resumed their chatter as the group disappeared to a private room at the rear of the building. Nearly every man in the place had a story about Smoke, some stretching the truth only slightly. The only table that remained silent sat in the darkest corner of the room. Two men occupied this secluded table, and they were as different in size and appearance as two men could be.

"Who is she?" the taller man wanted to know, his eyes never leaving the door that Smokey and her men had disappeared through. His complexion was fair and his hair light, but all was hid under a cap and the shadows of the room.

"Have you not heard of the Smoke?"

"Yes, but I'd forgotten the rumors that Smoke was a woman. I'd like to know her. See what you can do."

"I'd never get past the first mate. Guards her like mother bear, he does."

"Then it might be worth my having a try." The big man's smile was surprisingly boyish at the thought.

"You're willing to give up the sea already?"

"Who is to say I'll need to?"

The smaller man fell silent then. There had been a note in his master's tone that he did not like; one that he knew better than to argue with. After a moment of staring at the larger man, his eyes followed his captain's to the door of the back room. He couldn't help but wonder what was going on inside.

"Why can't Scully cook like this?"

"He'd pout for days if he heard that, Robby."

"Oh, I don't know. Maybe he'd just learn to cook."

Smokey shook her head at their antics and poured herself another cup of tea. They had been telling stories and carrying on for the last two hours.

When Dallas saw Smokey pouring out, he pushed his mug toward her and she filled his also. The move was so relaxed and feminine that for a moment Dallas could only stare at her. Smokey stared back, thinking of their time on the island and wishing she had Dallas to herself. Dallas' thoughts nearly mirrored Smokey's, but he knew that now was not the time or place to pursue the matter.

Indeed, had they been alone they might have leaned close and begun to talk in quiet tones, but Mic began a story just then and Dallas forced himself to turn and listen. What he heard caught his full attention at once, and romantic thoughts were momentarily swept aside.

"I swear we'd be out forever with Smokey's pa. My wife gave birth to my twin boys while I was out roaming the world. Not Smokey, though. She likes to stay close to home, much to the pain and frustration of every captain sailing the North Atlantic." All the men laughed, and he went on.

"Do you remember the time when we beat the *Katie Lynn* out of Halifax? You could have hung a shark hook on the captain's mouth, it was so wide open. Dallas here is too much of a pup to appreciate all I'm speaking of, but believe me, the captain here has been the victor for more than her share of spoils."

"On the contrary," Dallas put in smoothly, his voice dry, but not bitter. "I'm well aware of Smokey's effect on the trade."

"Meaning?" Darsey wanted to know.

Dallas shrugged, growing a bit uncomfortable. "Like Mic said, most captains have experienced the aftermath of her expertise."

A brief silence fell over the group.

"And in your case," Smokey spoke softly, "it keeps you that much further from realizing your dream to build ships." These words were said thoughtfully as Smokey stared intently at Dallas.

Dallas didn't answer, but returned her look for just a moment and then lifted his mug to drain the contents. As soon as he set it back down, Smokey stood.

"It's growing late. Walk me back, will you, Darsey?" Again her voice was soft. They left then, and the men followed soon after.

No one mentioned Smokey's proficiency or the speed of the *Aramis* again that night. In fact, it was not spoken of for many days, not until they were headed home and about a day's sail from Kennebunkport.

Fifteen

SMOKEY WONDERED IF THERE COULD BE a sight more breathtaking than the view of the sun rising over the Atlantic horizon. The sky was a bit cloudy on this morning, which only added to the glow as she stood at the stern of her ship and gazed in awe. As she did every time she witnessed this spectacle, she prayed. This morning's prayers concerned the future.

I want to give him something, Lord; I want to give Dallas a chance to realize his dreams. I haven't been in the east for a long time, and I feel like my time behind a ship's wheel is drawing to a close. Smokey hesitated when she realized the thought did not upset her. It must be time for a change.

Close the door if I'm headed astray, Father, and give me wisdom in the days to come. One more long voyage to let Dallas have a chance, and then I'll think about selling the Aramis.

Smokey prayed until she heard footsteps behind her. It wasn't like any of her men to disturb her at this hour, but she assumed Darsey had a question.

"If you'd rather be alone, just say the word."

The sound of Dallas' voice washed over Smokey like a warm spring shower. For just a moment her eyes slid shut. She was not some giddy, wide-eyed girl who lived her days in dreams and fantasies, but the thought of starting each morning with the sound of that voice made her want to jump and

112

dance on the polished wood beneath her boots. Instead, she opened her eyes, uttered one more silent prayer, this time for strength, and turned to face him.

"I don't mind if you join me. It might be nice to have company."

Dallas stood beside her, taking no care to keep his distance. He desperately wanted to thank her again for letting him join her crew, but even after he had prayed about what he wanted to say, no words would come. A good five minutes passed in silence, each enjoying the glorious morning sun, before Dallas felt he had found the right words. But Smokey spoke before he had a chance to share them.

"I've given a lot of thought to what you told us at Clancy's Place, Dallas, and I've made a decision that I hope will be a help to you." Having spoken to the waves, Smokey shifted then to see his face.

"I've decided to trade in eastern waters for a time. I usually stay close to home, but the men won't mind the change and I haven't been to Pakistan in years."

"How long will you be away?" Dallas asked, amazed that he sounded so calm.

Smokey shrugged. "We'll leave in late January and be gone six months, maybe a year. We'll see how it goes. I've a few leads coming up in February, so I can pass those along to you if you're interested."

It was all so selfless and matter-of-fact that for a moment Dallas could find nothing to say. When he did speak, only one word would come.

"Why?"

"Why what?" Smokey frowned in genuine confusion.

"Why are you doing this?"

The real answer to that question was the last thing Smokey wanted Dallas to know, but rather than admit this, she shrugged and answered as best she could.

"Jenny is my friend, and you're her brother. I think you're my friend too."

"Is that what we are, Smokey, friends?" Dallas' voice dropped in intensity, and for a moment Smokey misunderstood him.

"I realize that on this ship I'm your captain, but we're almost home, so..." Smokey hesitated when a horrid thought occurred to her. "If you think I'm going to be a nuisance when we get to Maine, you needn't worry. I'm done with spilling my water and staring like a fool."

"That's not what I meant," Dallas cut her off before she could go on, his voice filled with pain. How in the world did he tell this woman what he was feeling, when he could barely identify the emotions himself? Was he in love? He didn't know. Was he captivated? Extremely.

"It's a long time for you to be gone," Dallas finally managed, but Smokey's stance was still guarded. "I'll miss you," he finished quietly. For a moment Smokey could only stare at him.

"Did you mean that?" She had to know.

"Yes."

Again Smokey stared. "I'll miss you too."

Smokey truly believed it would happen this time. Dallas' gaze was locked on Smokey's mouth, and his head was lowering. The small brunette's face tipped in anticipation. Smokey's crew had other ideas, however. Scully came topside before seeing about breakfast, and Robby came to check on Darsey, who had been at the wheel since 3:00 A.M. Again the spell was broken, only this time Smokey did not immediately turn into Dallas' skipper. Taking a step away from him, she spoke for his ears alone, her eyes mirroring the pain inside.

"I honestly wonder what it would be like to kiss you, Dallas. But now that I'm thinking a little clearer, I've remembered that you have a girl at home. It's probably best we forget this."

Dallas had no clue what to say to this kind of honesty. For the moment he had forgotten all about Kathleen. In all fairness to both her and Smokey, he knew he owed Kathleen an explanation before pursuing someone else. He determined once again to take care of that soon after he returned. It wouldn't change the fact that Smokey was going away, but at least he could bid her farewell with a clear heart.

"Thank you for reminding me, Smokey. I hope we'll know each other much better in the future, but you're right, for now I am somewhat committed."

As hard as it was to thank Dallas and walk away, Smokey managed to gather her wits and do so. She had never felt for anyone the way she felt for Dallas, but he was not free to return her feelings and might never be. Smokey knew that the sooner she realized this the quicker the ache in her tender, young heart would heal.

"I feel as if you've been gone forever. Did you have a good Christmas?"

"I did," Smokey told her friend. "I thought about your offer, Jen, but I missed Willa and hadn't seen some of her family for a while, so—"

"I understand," Jenny told her with a smile. "We did miss your being here, though. To make up for it we're throwing you a party."

"A party? What for?"

"A going-away party. Dolly told me what you're doing for him, and I thought of the party last night when I was supposed to be sleeping. The only person I've told is Buck...oh, and Tate too. It will be a dinner party, a week from this Saturday, and we'll invite all your friends."

"I don't have many," Smokey told her good-naturedly.

"You have more than you think," Jenny told her cryptically. "What do you mean?"

"You remember Greer Rittenhouse?" Jenny went on at Smokey's nod. "I saw her while you were gone. She was very impressed with you, and extremely pleased with how well you liked her home. Buck is going to ask her to come with him."

"Are they seeing each other again?" Smokey asked eagerly.

Jenny shook her head sadly. "I'm still praying. Buck is trying to give her the time she wants, but he's truly a man in love."

        ❧ ❧ ❧

"Why, Buck," Greer spoke with genuine pleasure at the sight of him.

"Hello, Greer. May I come in?"

"Of course." The lovely widow stepped back, and Buck moved across the threshold. As always, her home was immaculate, but Buck had eyes for Greer alone.

"How have you been?" he asked softly.

"Lonely and confused," she admitted, her voice just as muted as Buck's. "And yourself?"

"Lonely, but not confused."

Greer knew exactly to what he referred. He was still as much in love with her as ever. She looked into his eyes and desperately wished she could return the words, but she just wasn't sure.

When she had first met Hank Rittenhouse, many years before, the situation had been reversed. She had fallen for him immediately, and he'd been unsure of her. At one point, he had confessed his love for her, only to come two days later and say he'd spoken in haste. He had been in love with another woman, and he confessed that he had begun seeing Greer to put the other woman from his mind.

Greer's young heart had felt so used, she thought she would die. The year that followed was a long, painful one, but in the end Hank had in fact come to love her. Once married, their time had been joyous. Greer felt as if something had been wrenched from her when he died.

And then Buck had come into her world. He was as different from Hank as any man could be, but he made her laugh and forget some of her loneliness. At first she'd been sure that he was God's gift for her, but then thoughts of Hank would crowd in upon her in the night. By morning, she would convince herself that she was acting unfaithfully whenever she saw Buck. The only time she had been more confused was when she and Hank had been courting.

"Are you all right, Greer?" Buck interrupted her thoughts.

"I think so," she admitted. "As usual, my thoughts are running wild and working to make me anxious."

They moved into one of the spacious sitting rooms where huge windows opened out toward the sea. Each took a comfortable chair by the fire.

"If you'd like to share, you know I'll listen, but I'm actually here to ask you out to dinner." Buck ignored the way she stiffened and continued in an easy tone.

"Jenny is giving a dinner party next Saturday night. It's for Smokey Simmons, and she told me to feel free to invite you."

"I liked Smokey when I met her, Buck. She's very sweet. Is it her birthday or some special occasion?"

"She's going away for a time, and the party is something of a sendoff."

Greer hesitated and then spoke with a measured tone. "I would like to go with you—"

"But you want to be certain that I understand it's just as friends?" Buck finished for her. Greer's eyes filled with tears over his understanding.

"It's all right, Greer." Buck's voice was soothing; he'd prepared himself for just that. "We'll go as friends because that's what we are—friends."

"Thank you, Buck," she whispered.

He leaned close then and took her hand. Greer was so thankful for his tender touch that she began to tremble. Buck desperately wanted to hold this small woman who fit into his arms so well, but he kept his seat and prayed that in time she would know that his love was a safe thing and nothing to be feared.

"Are we friends, Smokey?"

"Why, Jen," Smokey said with a laugh. "What are you talking about?"

Jenny's frown was in reality a good-natured scowl. "Your party is just a week away, and I've made some decisions."

"About?" Smokey prompted her and tried not to laugh at the determined look on her friend's face.

Jenny hesitated, and Smokey was more confused than ever. She was telling herself that being pregnant must change a person. Jenny had been acting strangely for two days.

"I want to dress you and do your hair for the party," Jenny suddenly blurted and then held her breath.

It was on Smokey's tongue to laugh and tell her friend that she'd been dressing herself for years when she suddenly understood her meaning. She stood and came to sit close to Jenny on the settee.

"Do you mean that, Jen?" Smokey's eyes had turned eager. Jenny smiled.

When the younger woman answered, her tone was dry. "You're one of the finest captains on the Atlantic, Smokey Simmons, but you have wretched taste in clothing."

Smokey laughed until her side hurt. In control once again, she confided, "I've been wanting to ask for your help with my hair and wardrobe, but I didn't know how you would feel about it."

They both laughed over the misunderstanding, and then the plans began. There wasn't much time, but Jenny had thought it all out while Smokey had been away. Jenny would introduce the *new* Smokey Simmons at her going-away party.

Sixteen

"JENNY WAS HOPING YOU WOULD COME for lunch, Dallas," Tate told his brother-in-law as he led the way into the dining room.

A place had been set for him, but Dallas immediately noted that his was the only extra setting and that Smokey was not in attendance. He had looked for her at church but seen only Jenny and Tate. All the way over he had hoped he'd only missed her.

"I saw Kathleen this morning just as she was leaving," Jenny chatted as the entrée was served. "She's very excited about the party, but said you had forgotten to tell her. She said you had been awfully busy since you returned and it must have slipped your mind." Jenny prattled on without immediately looking at her brother's face.

At that moment, Dallas was calling himself every kind of fool. He had put off talking with Kathleen because he'd been so busy working on the *Zephyr*. He had barely taken time to sleep, let alone see Kathleen.

"Dolly," Jenny finally took a moment to look across the table at her silent sibling, "have I been out of line?"

"It's all right, Jen," Dallas quickly reassured her when he saw a look of panic on her face. "It's my fault for not telling you. I *have* been busy, but I should have made time to see

119

Kathleen. My feelings have changed, and I have realized it's not fair to her to let it go on."

"Oh, Dolly," Jenny murmured.

"Will you tell her now or after the party?" Tate wanted to know.

"I'd like us to be friends, so maybe I can talk to her and we can still attend together." Dallas doubted the idea the moment it was out of his mouth, but he stayed silent. His sister was just as skeptical, but she felt as if she'd already opened her mouth one time too many.

"I thought Smokey was here," Dallas tried to comment casually a few minutes later, but couldn't quite hold the tone. Jenny and Tate had to force themselves not to look at one another.

So that's the way the wind blows, Tate thought. However, he said only, "She decided to go home for a few days. She'll come back Thursday or Friday."

"And the party is Saturday?" Dallas double-checked.

"Right."

The table fell silent then and remained so until dessert was served. They discussed ships over cake and coffee. Nothing more was said about Smokey, Kathleen, or Dallas' relationship to either woman.

"Now tell me again who you invited?"

"Buck and Greer, Pastor and Mrs. Chase..." Jenny went on to name a few more people and then watched her friend's face carefully as she finished the list. "And Dolly will be coming and bringing Kathleen."

Smokey nodded but said nothing. She watched Jenny watching her and knew what she was thinking.

"Did you expect me to react?"

Jenny had the good grace to blush. "I'm sorry, Smokey. I

really wasn't trying to set you up, but I guess I do wonder if you and Dolly are any closer to each other now than before you left. But then that's none of my business."

"It's all right," Smokey told her contrite friend. "You could have asked me; I wouldn't have minded. If the question bothered me, I'd have just told you."

"You're so honest with me about your feelings, Smokey. You can't believe how much I admire that. I'll remember not to ever drop hints or attempt subtlety. Either I'll come right out and ask you or keep my mouth shut."

"Thanks, Jen," Smokey told her sincerely and then went on. "I thought a few times while we were gone that something might be starting up between Dallas and me, and believe me, it would have been welcome on my part. But to tell you the truth, I'm going to be away for a long time, and it's probably best to leave things alone."

"How does that make you feel?"

"A little sad, but then I'm trying to be somewhat pragmatic about the whole thing. I don't believe anything would have ever come of it."

"Why do you say that?"

"Because to have Dallas fall for me as I have for him would be a dream come true, and I've never put much faith in fairy tales."

"But we have a God who loves to give us the desires of our heart."

Smokey had never thought of it that way. She said nothing for a moment. Jenny watched her.

"I haven't been fully trusting the Lord where Dallas is concerned, so your point is well taken, but what about the desires of Kathleen's heart?"

This time it was Jenny's turn to be silent. She let out a small sigh and spoke quietly.

"I don't have an answer for that, Smokey, but even though I have nothing against Kathleen, I'm not going to stop praying that God blesses you with every dream of your heart." Jenny punctuated her words with a warm hug. The subject was dropped then, and the women went on with their plans for the party the following night.

"Well, now," Tate said softly and for his wife's ears alone, as the new Smokey Simmons joined them in the parlor on Saturday evening. He clearly remembered that first evening when Smokey had dined with them and how she had been embarrassed about not changing her dress. Tate had regretted her discomfort then and smiled at the fact that she had no such worries tonight. In fact, Jenny had told him that Smokey had *five* new dresses.

The one she had chosen for tonight was a pale gray silk with a rounded neckline and long, tapered sleeves. The fitted bodice revealed her small rounded bosom and trim waist. The skirt flared into yards of folds and tucks that dropped in layer after layer all the way to the floor.

In truth Smokey looked like a princess. Jenny had brushed her hair straight down her back and then carefully swept the sides back with matching dark gray combs, letting the back hang free. She put her own hair atop her head, but she had never seen Smokey's hair down before, and after she did, she refused to put it back up.

"Well, Tate," Jenny turned to him and spoke so that Smokey could hear. "What do you think of our guest of honor?"

Tate bowed low and spoke with a twinkle in his eye. "You are enchanting, Miss Simmons."

Smokey didn't smile in return; she wrung her hands in despair. "Do I really look all right?"

"Yes, Smokey," Jenny told her patiently. "You look lovely."

"What if I spill something down the front of me? This pale fabric will show the smallest drop."

"You're not going to do that," Jenny told her, and Tate's

heart turned over a little. She was so unsure of herself. For a moment he wondered if Smokey might think this was more trouble than it was worth. He found himself wishing he had gone himself and tried to convince Darsey and his sister to come. Tate was certain that Smokey would be more at ease if they were present.

"I'm acting silly," Tate heard her say at last. "I know all the people who are coming—well, almost all—and I've no reason to be nervous."

"Right!" Jenny agreed with a decisive nod. Then both women went into gales of laugher because Smokey hadn't convinced herself in the least. A moment later, however, they quickly tried to school their faces as the first guests started to arrive.

"Kathleen!" her mother barked as she came into her daughter's bedroom and found her sitting in front of the mirror at her dressing table, the hairbrush forgotten at her side. "Put that book down and finish with your hair this instant! He's going to be here any moment."

"But Mother, this book is all about the pyramids in Egypt. There are even some drawings."

Mrs. Wagner snatched the book from her daughter's hand and tossed it onto the bed. "How many times do I have to tell you, you're never going to find a husband like that. Dallas is the finest catch this town has to offer, and if you don't play your cards right, you'll never land him!"

"He's not a fish, Mother," Kathleen said tiredly.

"You watch your mouth, young lady! Now I want your word that you'll say nothing this evening of the latest mathematics or history book you've read."

Kathleen continued to work on her hair without answering. She knew that now was *not* the time to tell her mother that Dallas had told her he just wanted to be friends, and that she had agreed; in fact, she had been relieved. It had nothing to do with Dallas, but more to do with herself and lingering feelings over a man she hadn't seen for months. She stayed quiet a little too long, and a glance in the mirror told her that her mother was furious.

"All right," she agreed to avoid a scene.

"Good." Mrs. Wagner's demeanor changed as if by magic. She was always easy to live with when she got her way, and Kathleen hated confrontation. It was a relief when her father called up the stairs to say that Dallas had arrived.

"I'll go down and talk with him. You stay here awhile."

"But I'm ready to go," Kathleen told her as she adjusted the last hairpin. "It's already a little late."

"Do as I tell you," Mrs. Wagner hissed at her. "A man hates to be kept waiting, but it adds mystery to the romance." On that note the older woman sailed out the door, and Kathleen was left looking at herself in the mirror.

How awful to live your whole life as a lie, Kathleen thought, not for the first time. It had started when Kathleen had been ten and a neighborhood boy had called her a bookworm. Her mother had overheard and given her a long talk that evening on how she must never appear to be smarter than a man. Kathleen remembered her words very well.

"I always got better marks than your father did, but I was a poor girl from a poor family and I knew if I didn't play it right, I would never better myself. A man wants his wife to be slightly dull in a cute sort of way, and helplessly dependent on him."

Kathleen could never get her mother to explain why a man wanted this, but that had been the way she was raised. Looking in the mirror again, Kathleen wondered if it was time to go down.

She knew she would never get the hang of this deceitfulness. She also knew that her mother had never fooled her father, not with herself or her daughter. Every time she left for an evening out, as she was now doing with Dallas, he would hug her and whisper for her ears alone.

"Be yourself, honey; just be yourself."

The ride from Kathleen's home to the Pembertons' would take nearly 30 minutes. The first part of that half hour was spent in silence. Kathleen was dying to ask Dallas about his ship's repairs, but she knew her mother would be furious.

Of course, Kathleen told herself, *you're just friends now. Maybe it would be all right to be yourself.* But old habits die hard, and when Dallas asked her how she'd been, she once again fell into the helpless female routine.

"Mother and I are doing some decorating on the house. We're starting in the kitchen. I love to sew, and of course Mother will hire someone to do the painting. Father is too busy, and mother and I don't know how."

Dallas nodded, not sure what to say. He'd have been surprised to know that Kathleen was biting her tongue to keep from telling Dallas the truth—that she could paint an entire houseful of rooms if she put her mind to it, and for that matter, probably learn to make her own paint to boot. Kathleen found herself wishing she had refused Dallas' invitation; it was certain to be a long evening.

Seventeen

KATHLEEN WAS RIGHT. The evening did prove to be long, but despite the fact that she was learning some hard lessons, she had a good time. Since Dallas clearly had eyes for another woman, she was thankful that she'd never fallen head-over-heels in love with him.

Smokey Simmons, the guest of honor, was the object of Dallas' attention, and Kathleen couldn't blame him. She was the most fascinating woman she had ever encountered, and clearly Dallas shared that belief. At first Smokey seemed a bit nervous, but as the evening progressed she laughed and shared in all of the conversations.

Some of the couples left early, so by 11:00, Smokey, the Pembertons, Buck, Greer, Dallas, Kathleen, and the Chases were all who remained. It had just come out that Smokey was a ship's captain, and Pastor Chase was truly intrigued.

"Where do you usually sail?"

"Wherever I need to in order to receive or deliver goods."

"England?" Mrs. Chase wanted to know.

"Yes, all over Europe actually."

"How about the east?" Kathleen put in.

"It's been some time since I've sailed in those waters, but I'll be headed in that direction when we set sail next week."

"Do you ever see Dallas and the *Zephyr*?" Greer asked.

"Not often, but I have seen him."

126

"I never see anything but the wake of her rudder as she sails *back out* of port with a holdful of treasures." Dallas' tone was so wounded that eveyone in the room laughed. Smokey, who was as relaxed as she'd ever been, teased him, her eyes wide with innocence.

"You could always remain a crewman, Dallas."

"Ohhhh," both Buck and Tate interjected when they saw the mischievous light in Dallas' eyes.

"And run the risk of being stuck with another Captain Bly?"

Now Smokey's eyes took on a glint, but Dallas, who was warm to his subject, ignored the signs.

"Do you know that she's cruel to her cook?" he said to the room at large, but never took his eyes from her face. "Her cook brings perfectly good food to her cabin, and she refuses to eat it. She forces him to put his own meal aside and make her something else."

The occupants of the room were on the edge of their chairs with fascination. Dallas and Smokey sparred back and forth as though they were alone in the room.

"This is insubordination, sailor," Smokey told him, trying to look stern.

"We're not on ship, Captain," Dallas reminded her smugly.

"Lucky for you."

This last comment caused everyone to roar. When the laughter died down, Buck had a very serious question that only led to more hilarity.

"Smokey, how do you handle disobedience?"

Smokey and Dallas chuckled.

"I don't," she admitted, and Dallas went on to explain.

"Smokey has the most unusual crew I've ever met. No man is under 40, and they all have appointed themselves guardians of their captain. I was watched like a hawk."

"Why?" Buck asked.

"They do tend to be rather protective," Smokey answered, "because they've known me from the time I was a child. On the other hand, they don't know Dallas, and trust for a new man comes hard in a crew as close as my own."

"So you really never discipline anyone?"

"It wouldn't do a bit of good," Smokey said with a wry shake of her head.

Dallas jumped in at that point and told the story about the spinach. Jenny and Pastor Chase had tears rolling down their faces as he recounted the tale. Smokey laughed at Dallas' version of the event and added when he was done that it happens nearly every voyage.

Pastor and Mrs. Chase said their goodbyes soon after that, and everyone stood to stretch their legs. The room was very warm to Smokey, so when Jenny and Tate saw them to the door, she headed out the French doors of the parlor for a bit of air. Dallas watched her exit and without a word to anyone, followed.

Kathleen took all of this in without distress. Turning away so Dallas would feel free to follow his heart, she began to visit with Buck and Greer.

It was cold outside, but the cool air felt wonderful as Smokey stood above the beach and listened to the pounding of the waves against the shore. The nearly full moon sent a ray of light across the surface of the Atlantic that was mesmerizing, shimmering and winking at her like a thousand tiny jewels.

She felt more than heard Dallas' presence behind her on the grass and turned to find him approaching. He stopped beside her and stared at her for a long moment.

"Did I tell you that you look lovely this evening?"

"Thank you, Dallas. I was thinking you look wonderful too."

Again Dallas stared at her. "I've never before waltzed with a woman, but right now I wish there was music."

Smokey smiled at the very thought and then at herself. "I'd probably step on your foot."

Dallas smiled in return. "With your little feet, I wouldn't even notice."

Smokey chuckled softly, a sound that sent a shiver down Dallas' spine.

"Now how would you be knowing about the size of my feet?" she wished to know.

Dallas' vast hands came up, and he held his fingers about seven inches apart. "You forget I've sailed with you. Your boots are only this big."

Suddenly Smokey didn't feel like laughing. It seemed such an intimate, tender thing to have Dallas know the size of her feet. The thought of leaving him, perhaps for the better part of the year, felt like a knife in her side.

Smokey watched as those hands came forward now to frame her face. He made no move to kiss her, but she felt his thumbs stroke gently over her cheekbones. His eyes in the moonlight were warm and intimate like a man in love. Smokey was afraid to hope.

"Dallas," Kathleen's voice came faintly from the direction of the house.

"Yes, Kathleen?" Dallas turned but did not take his hands from where they'd dropped on Smokey's shoulders.

"Buck and Greer are leaving now. Would you like me to ride home with them?"

"No, Kathleen, I'll be there in a few minutes."

They both watched as she moved back to the house, and Smokey was pleased at how calm Kathleen had sounded. It didn't change the inevitable, however—she was still sailing next week.

"I have so much I want to say to you," Dallas spoke. Smokey tipped her head to see him.

"Dallas—" Smokey began.

"Kathleen and I are just friends."

"I think I figured that out already, but it doesn't change the fact that I'm leaving."

"And you'd rather that I leave things unsaid right now?"

"I might regret it someday very soon, but yes, I do. I don't want you here, not able to get in touch with me if you change your mind."

"You don't understand if you think that's going to happen." Dallas wanted to say more, but Smokey was adamantly shaking her head.

"You need to go, Dallas. Next time we see each other, we'll talk. We'll both have had time to think, and then we can share where we are."

Her logic and ability to keep calm in an intense situation was one of the things he admired most about her, but at this particular moment, he wanted desperately to kiss her. He'd have loved for her to put her logic aside for just a few minutes. Instead he did as she asked. His hands slid tenderly down her upper arms before he reluctantly broke contact.

"Go with God, Smokey. You'll be in my prayers."

The words were barely audible. Then Smokey stood alone and watched him walk away.

"I think I owe you an apology, Kathleen."

"No, Dallas, you don't." Kathleen's voice was tight with anger, and Dallas sighed.

"Yes, I do. You're furious and I—"

"You're right," she cut him off in rage. "I am angry, but not with you."

Dallas pulled the buggy to a halt and shifted in the seat to see her. It was getting colder by the moment, but he had to learn the truth.

"What's going on, Kathleen?"

"You wouldn't believe me if I told you." Her voice was self-mocking, and Dallas persisted.

"Try me."

"My mother," Kathleen began but did not go on.

"I get the impression that she desperately wants you to marry."

"She does, Dallas, and I would love to be married, but not her way, not through pretense and deceit."

"Pretense?" Dallas was adrift. "I'm not sure I understand."

"Ask me anything about ships, Dallas," Kathleen blurted in anger. "Go on...ask me...ask anything you wish. I've done extensive reading on the subject. Or maybe you'd rather know about the pyramids. I was reading a book about them before you picked me up this evening." Kathleen blurted the words out, forgetting her promise to her mother.

Dallas could only stare at her as she came to a stop and tears flooded her eyes.

"My mother," she whispered tearfully, "believes that all men want a wife who's a little bit stupid and very clingy. She's been teaching me since I was a child that if I want a man, I can't let anyone know I am intelligent."

The tears were flowing freely now, and after Dallas produced a large white handkerchief, he slipped his arm around her. She sobbed into his shoulder, and Dallas said nothing, only listened as she told the truth for the first time in years.

"I don't know if you remember Harvey Blanchard, but we were seeing each other last year." Kathleen was developing a hard case of hiccups, but continued to unburden her heart. "I admire Harvey more than any other man I've ever known. He's brilliant and sensitive and I fell for him our first time out. At first I thought he might be feeling for me as I did for him, but Mother insisted that I play dumb, and quite frankly he was bored out of his head with my wide-eyed looks and inane chatter."

The memory was so painful for Kathleen that she sobbed anew, her frame shuddering with harsh weeping. Dallas still kept one arm around her shoulders and let her cry. He didn't know when he'd heard anything so foolish as to pretend ignorance to attract a man. What rot!

"I made a decision tonight," Kathleen lifted her head and attempted to repair her face. Her voice shuddered some, but Dallas could tell that her mind was resolute.

"My father is always telling me to be myself, and now I'm going to be. He's always up when I get home. I'm going to tell him that I'm done pretending and that I'm going to stand up to Mother. I'm sure he will side with me, but if worse comes to worst, I'll contact my aunt about moving in with her. She lives in Biddeford and is always asking me to come. I won't live a lie for one more day."

"I'm glad you told me, Kathleen. I hope your parents see your side. I'll be praying for all of you."

Kathleen's eyes were filled with peace as she answered, "Thanks for everything, Dallas. By the way," Kathleen went on, unable to remember when her heart felt so light, "does Smokey know what a wonderful husband you're going to make?"

"I don't know," he said with a grin for the compliment. "I can't ever get that girl to stand still long enough to listen to me."

"That's part of the problem isn't it, Dallas? She's not a girl, but a woman who knows who she is and what needs to be done. Unless I miss my guess, the very thing that frustrates you is also what you admire the most."

Amazed at her insight, Dallas stared at her. "Did Harvey stick around long enough to learn that you read minds?"

Kathleen laughed, her first heartfelt laugh in a long time. "Take me home, Dallas, and on the way I'll tell you all about the pyramids."

Eighteen

SMOKEY DROPPED INTO HER DESK CHAIR and with a huge sigh, leaned back and closed her eyes. She had begun to wonder if they were ever going to get away. With plans to be gone longer, it seemed every crewman had some problem with getting there on time. Any other captain would have found himself another crew, but not Smokey. She smiled at the thought.

The smile also had to do with the comfort she experienced to finally feel the gentle rocking of the ship beneath her. She opened her eyes to look around the familiar cabin and then spotted Jenny's letter. It had come two days ago, and she hadn't even had time to open it. She'd have missed it altogether had they not been delayed. Even fearing that it might make her sad, Smokey decided to read it now.

> Dear Smokey,
>
> I miss you already and have to force myself not to think about how long you might be gone. Did Willa cry harder than usual? I hope not, but I know how she felt.
>
> The baby is really moving these days, and I get so excited every time I feel it. I'm glad you liked the wallpaper and fabric I picked. I hope the baby will.

Tate has had a busy week—I feel like I've hardly seen him. It's been the same for Dallas, but his efforts have paid off. The *Zephyr* is well on her way to readiness, and he plans to sail next week.

Jenny had more to say, but Smokey put the letter down and stared into space. Dallas' face swam into her mind, and her whole frame shuddered with yearning. What if he met someone and married before she returned? What if he simply didn't mean what she thought, or he had been carried away by the moonlight and late hour? Smokey hated the questions she asked herself, but she wanted to be prepared for the worst.

She stood and wandered to the wardrobe, where three of her five new dresses hung, not sure even now why she had brought them. Smokey fingered the sleeve of the gray dress, still able to feel the pressure of Dallas' hands on her arms as they had stood above the beach.

With a careful movement Smokey shut the wardrobe door and began to pray. "Thank You, Father, that You've promised never to leave me or forsake me. Help me to leave Dallas in Your hands. I love him and I want to be with him, but I can't let that rob me of my peace and joy in You."

Smokey prayed for herself for a long time before she began to lift Dallas to the Lord. Peace settled over her as she surrendered all to God, and as she finished, she wondered just where Dallas might be at the moment.

The skeletal beginnings of the ship they had been working on when Knight Crafts had gone out of business stood stark against the gray sky. The sight of it had a saddening effect on Dallas that he felt determined to fight. He asked the Lord to help him persevere and be more resolved than ever before to raise the capital to start the business again.

He thought of the orders and leads Smokey had left with him and praised God for her generosity. If he could make the most of his time and effort, this would be one of the most successful voyages he'd ever sailed. He knew Smokey had one stop to make in England and then she was headed south. Dallas found himself wishing that they might meet there, and then he knew that wouldn't be possible; she'd be well on her way before he arrived.

"Hello, Dallas," a voice cut into his thoughts. He turned to find Harvey Blanchard approaching. Dallas took the space of a heartbeat to cover his surprise and extend his hand.

"Hello, Harvey. What brings you out this cold day?"

"I take a walk along here most days. Sometimes I stop to take time to think." Harvey stopped speaking, and both men stared at the ship in silence.

"Will you ever be in operation again?" Harvey voiced the question he had often pondered in the past.

"I hope to be," Dallas answered and turned slightly to study the younger man without appearing to do so. He remembered him of course, but seeing him brought back a clearer picture. He was tall and slim, with keen brown eyes and a serious brow. He and Kathleen had been several years behind him in school, but Dallas did recall that Harvey had been more than a little precocious.

"In fact," Dallas continued, "I sail next week, and when I return I hope I'll be in better shape to assess that possibility."

"Great," Harvey told him sincerely. "If you've a need for investors, my uncle is always looking for opportunities."

"Thanks, Harvey, but I'd like to continue on my own for as long as I'm able."

"I can understand that. I'm the same way."

The men fell silent, and Dallas prayed. How could he bring Kathleen up without looking obvious? He quickly concluded that uncomfortable or not, he had to give it a try.

"It's a bit ironic that you came by today, Harvey. I mean, Kathleen mentioned you when I saw her a few weeks ago."

"Are you still seeing Kathleen?" Harvey asked, and Dallas wondered if he detected a note of sadness in his tone.

"Actually, we're just friends. But she mentioned you with fondness, and I thought it was funny that after she said something, you came by."

"It's unfortunate."

"What is?"

"I don't know exactly. I cared for Kathleen, but there were some things I couldn't get comfortable with."

"Sometimes things are not exactly as they appear," Dallas told him softly. Harvey stared at him. "I know she misses you."

"Are you saying she might welcome a visit from me?"

"She talked about going to see her aunt, but if she's home, I know she'd like to see you."

Again Harvey stared. "And you're sure I'm not stepping between the two of you?"

Dallas smiled. "I'm sure. There's someone else, and Kathleen knows all about that."

A small smile lifted the corners of Harvey's mouth as his hand came out. The men shook. "Best of luck to you when you sail, Dallas, and with your someone else. Thanks for telling me about Kathleen."

Dallas nodded and shifted his eyes back over the water when Harvey moved away. He answered even though Harvey was already out of earshot many yards away.

"You're welcome, Harvey. I hope you and Kathleen work things out." He fell silent then as his thoughts turned to his own "someone else."

LONDON

"We're loaded, Captain," Robby reported to Smokey and waited for her orders.

"Thanks, Rob. Tell Pete and Nate they're on watch and tell Darsey I want to go to Clancy's Place."

"Will do," Robby replied and shut her door. She threw the bolt and began to change. She was feeling rather tired, but it would be some time before she was back here, and even though they were running behind schedule, she wanted to see Bart and Meg.

An hour later the group left the ship. The men knew very well they were welcome to go elsewhere, but they loved Clancy's, so following Darsey and Smokey was more than just habit.

The usual exchange of conversation and coin took place inside, and before long, Smokey and her crew were seated around the back table with plates of food and mugs of tea or ale.

Halfway through the evening, Meg reappeared. She dropped her considerable bulk down at the far end of the table and beckoned to Smokey with one finger.

"A've told Bart he can 'andle things for a spell. I want to talk with me girl."

Smokey smiled at her friend, who wasn't really old enough to be a mother to her but had always treated her with maternal care.

"Where's that good-looking sailor ya had with ya last time?"

"Dallas," Smokey supplied. "He was just with us for the one voyage."

"More's the pity. I thought there might be something a cookin' there."

"Oh, Meg," Smokey laughed. "You're a hopeless romantic."

"*I'm* romantic! 'ear her talk!" the older woman exclaimed. "*I* wasn't the one a gawkin' at ya with calf's eyes the whole evenin'."

"He was not," Smokey told her and laughed at Meg's round-eyed expression.

"Ya spend too much time in the salty air, love. He could barely keeps 'is eyes from ya. In truth, he didn't even try."

"Do you mean that, Meg?" Smokey had grown as serious as her hostess.

"I've been working in this tavern for many a year, love, and I know a smitten man when I sees 'im. He was gone, I tells ya." Meg reached and tugged the braid that fell down Smokey's back. "And you've never worn your 'air down afore this bloke sailed with ya. I says ya feels the same for 'im."

A huge smile broke across Smokey's face, and Meg cackled with glee. They talked on, fun talk, girl talk, until Bart shouted for Meg from the main room.

"'is lordship bellows," Meg said and rolled her eyes, but she rose without further ado and went to him. Smokey had just stood to move back to her place with the men when she realized her tea was visiting her and she would need to excuse herself for a moment.

"Are you ready to go?" Darsey asked.

"No. I hope Meg will come back in, but right now I need to step out."

"Watch yourself," Darsey called to her, but Smokey's head was in the clouds. The mate watched her go before turning back to listen to Scully. When five minutes passed and she had not returned, he began to study his pocket watch. When two more minutes passed and there was still no sign of her, Darsey came to his feet in a flash. He checked Meg's private rooms and found them empty. He and the crew hit the main tavern at a full run, and on his shout the room quieted.

"Smokey!"

A murmur went around the room before a man cried out.

"That table in the corner is empty, and there were two men sitting there not five minutes back."

Darsey didn't answer. He ran for the door and out onto the docks, many men behind him. Frustration rose within him over the moonless night, but still he ran, telling himself he'd find her if he had to tear those docks apart.

Nineteen

THE SACK THAT HAD BEEN THROWN over Smokey's head, as well as the sweet-smelling cloth that had been held over her mouth, were suffocating. Only moments passed before she lost consciousness, making her unaware for the remainder of the night that she had been carried and deposited onto a strange bed in a strange cabin on a ship she'd never seen before.

When she did awaken, it was getting light—that much she knew without having to look. Her head was pounding, and she didn't want to open her eyes, but she told herself she must try. Something wasn't right.

Trying to sort out what felt so wrong, she realized she must have dozed off before telling Darsey that she wanted to go to Clancy's. Smokey's eyes flew open with a start. She'd already been to Clancy's and talked with Meg. On her way back from the "necessary," someone had grabbed her!

From her place on the bed, Smokey let her eyes roam. She was in a huge cabin; it was at least four of her own and garishly decorated in red and black. She'd never seen anything like it.

Her eyes widened in surprise when she caught sight of a nearly life-size statue in the corner. It was a naked woman, her arms raised seductively over her head.

Realizing the entire room was full of such "art," Smokey sat up slowly. On the wall opposite her was a painting of a man and a woman in an intimate scene. Smokey's face flamed as she looked at it, and her heart fought down the panic rising within her.

She tossed off the quilt someone had lain over her and swung her feet off the side of the bed. A glance out the window told her they were docked, but before she could think to call for help, her head began to hurt so badly that she was forced to close her eyes again.

Questions as to where they might be, and who had taken her and why, swarmed her befuddled mind. Her head pounded on until she knew she would have to lie back down or be sick. Even after her head hit the pillow, questions surfaced, but no answers followed. Fight as she might, sleep was crowding in once again.

"Well, now," a smooth male voice spoke to Smokey as she stirred again many hours later. "I had begun to despair of ever seeing your eyes; they are as lovely as I imagined."

Smokey had come fully awake at the sound of that voice and moved herself backward on the bed until she was pressed stiffly against the headboard.

A huge man with sandy brown hair and a boyish smile sat in the chair nearest the statue. He seemed as composed and pleased as if he were entertaining a close friend and not a woman he had abducted.

"Who are you?" Smokey managed.

The big man's eyes twinkled, and he stood. Bowing from the waist, he spoke.

"Haamich Wynn at your service, my dear. I'm sorry our first encounter had to be so rough, but I promise to make it up to you." This said, he again took a seat.

"Haamich Wynn?" Smokey asked. "The pirate?"

Inordinately pleased that she had evidently heard of him, his grin widened.

"One and the same. Now, my dear, you have me at a disadvantage. I know your nickname is Smokey, but I wish to know your real and full name."

"Why?"

"Well, my dear," he spoke as if it were obvious. "We're going to become intimately acquainted, and I want to know what I should call you."

Smokey was silent.

"Oh, my dear," the pirate spoke, his voice tender, almost hurt, "you're not going to talk with me? How can we ever be... *friends*—" he said the word with a malicious grin—"if you don't talk to me?"

"Friends?" Smokey questioned flatly, not at all impressed with his smooth tone.

"Oh, yes, my dear," the pirate chuckled, "we'll be very *good* friends."

It was all said with such smooth confidence that Smokey's fear escalated until she thought it would choke her. He was serious, dead serious.

"Now," he went on in that same easy tone. "Most women do not like surprises, so I'm going to tell you about the remainder of the evening. You're going to tell me what I want to know, and then I'm going to leave and give you some time to get used to the idea of our *friendship.*"

"Speak plainly." Smokey's eyes smoldered with disgust. "It is not for friendship that you keep me here."

An amused smile turned up the corners of the pirate's lips. "As you can see," he nodded his head toward a tray of food, ignoring her words, "I've ordered some food for you, but I imagine you're too upset to eat. After I leave you, I'll want you to change. When I come back, we'll continue to talk, but at that time we won't be separated by the space of this room; in fact there won't be anything separating us at all.

"And one last thing," Haamich's voice dropped, and his eyes lost their sparkle. "I want you to keep in mind that I *can* force you to do anything I wish... but I'd rather not."

The pirate fell silent to allow his guest to digest this and was satisfied with the fear he saw in Smokey's eyes.

"Now about those questions. Well, first I wish you to stand up. Come now," his voice grew persuasive. "I'll not touch you yet. Just get off the bed and let me see you."

Smokey, still shaking so badly she thought she might be sick, came stiffly off the bed. She watched his eyes move slowly over her and when she would have folded her arms over her chest, forced them back to her sides at the slow negative shaking of his head.

"Take the tie off your braid," he instructed her. Smokey looked down to see that the braid had fallen over her shoulder to lay across her breast. With trembling fingers, she complied.

"That's it," he encouraged. "Now shake your head so your hair falls free. Oh, yes, I guessed that your hair would be one of your lovelier assets, although I'm sure you have many. Now, you may sit down again if you wish and tell me your name."

Smokey did sit, her hair now a riot about her shoulders and back, but she did not reveal her name.

"I don't suppose it would do any good to tell you I want to leave this ship."

"You're right, no good at all. Your name?"

"What if I were to offer you money?" Smokey tried.

Haamich Wynn laughed in true amusement. "I've found you, Smokey, and you're mine. Now for the last time, your name." His tone changed just slightly and the smile evaporated. Smokey saw no hope for it.

"Victoria Simmons."

"Victoria. I like it, but I also like the name Smokey, so while you're changing I'll decide what I'm going to call you. How old are you?"

"Twenty-five."

"Really," he seemed truly amazed. "I'd have guessed younger. And an innocent, no doubt?"

Smokey's breath caught in her chest, and she blushed to the roots of her hair. Her captor's smile became very tender as did his voice. "That more than answers my question."

Without giving her time to say the angry words that were caught in her throat, he stood. Smokey stiffened, but he did not approach. Going to one of two wardrobes, he opened the door and brought forth a dress. It was dark red and gold, and Smokey could see, even from a distance, that it was very near her size.

"Now," he spoke as he laid the dress across the chair he had vacated. "I'll leave you to change. When I return, I will collect the clothes you're wearing, so don't bother trying to hide them. I actually like you in trousers, but I prefer my women to look like women."

"How many of us are there?" Smokey finally spat in fury, which oddly enough seemed to please her companion.

"There have been many, I will admit to that. But after seeing you, my dear; well, I have quite frankly lost my heart."

"So I'm supposed to be flattered by this abduction?"

"Indeed," he told her sincerely. "Now, do change, my little love, because if you don't put the dress on, I'll put it on you myself, and I don't think you want that."

He gave her no further chance to reply, but exited. Smokey heard him lock the door from out in the passageway. She stared at the door before her eyes fell on the dress. Bile rose in her throat.

"I don't know what else to do," Smokey began to sob, even as she unbuttoned her tunic. "Please help me, Lord," she cried as she undressed and quickly slipped into the dress. She had left her trousers on, but the dress was so tight-fitting around the waist that she couldn't button it without removing them.

She felt utterly bare in only the dress, her underdrawers, and boots, but she feared what he might do should he come back and find she had disobeyed. As she buttoned the last button at the neckline, she stared in horror at her front. Tugging and pulling, she searched for more fabric that might be hidden, but it was no use. It was the most revealing gown she had ever seen. A full-standing mirror stood in one corner and Smokey moved toward it with dread.

"I look like a doxy," she whispered to her reflection. Her eyes slid shut to blot out the image, and she began to pray.

"I'm going to trust You, Lord. Please calm my fear so I can think clearly. Right now I don't see a way out of this, but You're a God of miracles, and I pray that You will show me what to do."

Smokey's prayers were cut short when she heard someone at the door. She continued to pray silently as the door opened and Haamich Wynn entered. He looked very pleased to see her in the dress, and Smokey felt an amazing calm come over her as she watched him move about the room lighting each lantern.

Until that moment she hadn't realized how dark it had become. When every lantern was aglow, Haamich turned to her and smiled. His eyes moved carefully over her.

"I can see by your eyes that you have either resigned yourself to your fate or decided to fight me."

"I have decided to fight you, but not the way you think." Smokey paused and nodded above her captor's head. "I'll fence with you. If I win, you set me free; if you win, I'll submit without a struggle."

Smokey wondered where that came from and why she had never before noticed the gold foils that sat high on the wall in a beautiful glass and wood case. If she had seen them, she would have met Haamich Wynn armed and ready when he came through the door.

It shouldn't have surprised him, but it took a moment for Haamich to see that she was serious. It was incredible to him that she actually knew how to fence. The more he thought on it, the more he liked the idea. The pirate's eyes glowed with excitement and lust as he spoke.

"I have never in my life met a woman like you, Victoria, and I have no plans to let you go."

"Then there is no point in the wager. I thought you might be a man of honor," she told him coldly.

"Ah, but I am a man of honor. I'm only warning you that I *will* win the match and you will be mine."

"*I'm* ready to take that risk. Are you?"

"Yes, more than willing."

Smokey watched as Haamich removed his coat and laid it across a chair. He then flipped a catch at the top of the case, the back of his hand nearly touching the ceiling. Lifting the foils out with care, he placed them both on the bed. He selected one, backed off, and waited for Smokey to take her own. He was quite confident that she didn't stand a chance, but he would not be so foolish as to give her an opportunity to strike out when he was unprepared.

Smokey grasped the handle and took up her position. The face of her opponent told her that he found this all to be little more than an amusing game. Smokey, on the other hand, knowing this man to be big but not clumsy, realized fully that she might be fighting for her life.

"En garde," Haamich said, and Smokey took the offense. In a move that was nothing short of lightening fast, she sidestepped and cut nearly to the skin across his stomach. Haamich deflected her next move and held her blade in midair. His smile no longer in evidence, he was now completely alert, cursing himself for agreeing to fight her. He was going to have to cut her to disarm her, and the thought infuriated him.

While he hesitated, Smokey moved again. For the next several minutes all was quiet as they fought with equal skill and dexterity. Haamich's strength far outweighed hers, but Smokey was so fast and agile that she more than made up for her lack of muscle. She could see that her opponent was flagging.

In a move of desperation, Smokey did something she had never done before—something for which her father would have thrashed her. She went for his face. Slightly horrified at the dark red line that appeared and immediately began to bleed, Smokey stepped back and stared. The pirate seemed to freeze in his tracks.

Smokey watched as he lifted his free hand to his face. He touched the cut that was deeper than it first appeared, and brought bloody fingers out to examine. Smokey's eyes were huge at his reaction. His head began to roll, his eyes went back in their sockets, and a moment later he fell full-length on the floor between them. Smokey scampered back, ready to fight if it were a trick, but he seemed to be completely out. Her breath coming in quick gasps, she approached and poked him with her weapon. He didn't budge.

She fell on the bedsheets and began to tear them like a woman possessed. In less time than she would have dreamed possible, she had tied his feet and hands. She stuffed a great wad of sheeting into his mouth and then tied a gag so tight she knew he would be in agony when he woke.

All the time she worked, she thanked God—and Darsey for insisting she learn her knots. Her final two moves were to bend the pirate's knees so she could attach the ties that were on his feet and hands. Lastly, she secured him to the bed so he wouldn't be able to roll to the door.

A mad dash around the room did nothing toward finding her clothes. She hadn't even seen him take them. She had just started a more thorough search when he moaned. The sound panicked her, and she knew she had to flee while there was a chance. She rushed to the door and, with a final glance back, turned the key.

She moved silently out into the companionway, locked the door, pocketed the key, and stood still, trying to calm the frantic beating of her heart. She knew that to go on the docks dressed as she was could be just as dangerous as staying on the ship. A sound from within propelled her forward, however, and with silent steps she gained the upper deck.

No one seemed to be about. She spotted one man by the wheelhouse, but he was lifting a bottle to his mouth and seemed oblivious to everything about him. The ship was much larger than her own, but it made no difference as Smokey moved with quiet expertise among the familiar surroundings, staying in the shadows until she reached the gangplank. The pirate must have dismissed most of his crew for the night, believing he had everything in hand with his young captive.

In order to actually leave the ship, she would have to leave
the shadows, for there was no other way. She was halfway
down when a shout rang out from the drunken watchman and
the remaining crew began to gather. Smokey took off at a run,
thankful that she'd kept her boots on. A slight sound of panic
and pounding feet followed her, but Smokey knew that as long
as no one else got in her way, she would get away.

There was no other port in the world quite like London.
Although she knew generally where she was, this section was
somewhat unfamiliar to her. She knew she could never outrun
the men, so she took to hiding. She shot down an alley and
took a moment to catch her breath.

She stood between two buildings, and even though she
could hear people talking inside, she felt safe for the moment.
The moon was bright and the sky was clear, so she knew she
must keep to the shadows. Suddenly she heard men running.
They were still a ways off and beyond the corner of the
building, but she knew she would have to keep on.

She turned and ran up the alley as fast as she could. As the
narrow lane emptied out onto the other side, her mad dash for
freedom was halted instantly when she ran full tilt into a big
man's chest. He immediately lay hold of her, and Smokey,
knowing she had been caught, began to fight with all her
strength.

"Easy, easy," a deep voice spoke above her as the man tried
to calm the wild thing in his hands.

Hearing that voice, Smokey stilled, but not before she
threw her head back to see his face. Only one word escaped
her lips.

"Dallas!"

Twenty

"SMOKEY," DALLAS SAID with surprised pleasure, and the small black-haired woman felt tears burn her throat.

"Oh, Dallas," she cried softly as he drew her into his arms and held her tenderly against his chest. Smokey didn't know when anything had felt so wonderful. To be at the mercy of an unprincipled pirate and now to stand in the secure arms of the man she loved was almost more than she could take.

"Your hair isn't braided," Dallas whispered almost to himself, and Smokey was brought abruptly back to earth. Haamich Wynn was still looking for her.

"Dallas," Smokey pushed away from him slightly, although Dallas did not relinquish his hold. Images of the pirate in a fight with Dallas made Smokey shudder, and her voice was filled with fear as she spoke.

"I can't explain right now, but I have to go. I—"

Smokey's words were cut off when a door opened and flooded them with light. Smokey felt Dallas' frame tense and his eyes darken when he saw the way she was dressed. His eyes dipped down to her neckline and then back to her eyes. There was no warmth in his voice when he questioned her.

"What's going on, Smokey?"

"I don't have time to explain," she began and tried to move out of his hold.

"No," he told her abruptly. "You're not going anywhere until I have some answers."

Smokey's head whipped to the right at the sound of someone entering the opposite end of the alley. She began to struggle and whisper frantically.

"Let me go. I can't explain it right now. You've got to let me go," Smokey begged him, but it was no use; he held her with ease.

"What are you—" he began.

"Please, Dallas." Smokey was becoming frantic, and Dallas was on the verge of releasing her when she acted out of desperation. Her hand shot out and captured the back of his head, and at the same time she threw her entire body toward the building with all her might.

Before Dallas could form another thought, he found himself holding Smokey against the building and kissing her, or was she kissing him? For a moment he was too stunned to act. Then his senses swam, and taking action or even thinking was the farthest thing from his mind.

For long moments nothing else existed. He didn't hear the men that passed and took him for a man enjoying the pleasures of a dockside prostitute. He didn't realize that all around him men were looking for the very woman he held.

All he knew was that Smokey was kissing him in a way he hadn't thought possible. She was soft and warm, and her arms wrapped around him with a type of tender desperation. Her lips were sweet, and Dallas thought he would drown in her kiss.

As much as it pained her to do so, Smokey began to scoot away. Her hands went to Dallas' chest, where she felt the thunderous beating of his heart. She spoke with regret.

"Dallas, I've got to go."

"No." His voice was hoarse.

"Yes, Dallas, please listen—"

Smokey tried to explain, but Dallas' lips came back to claim hers again. Feeling as swept away as he, Smokey let him kiss her again, and then with a sob, broke free. With all of her strength, she pushed him away. She never completely escaped his hands, however, as he quickly caught her wrist.

This is the woman I love, his heart said to him. *I'll never let her go*. Unfortunately for Dallas, Smokey was desperate.

"Let me go," she tried one last time, knowing that the men would eventually come back.

"No, Smokey." Dallas sounded like a man in a dream, and Smokey lashed out, fearing for his safety. Her small-booted foot swung hard and connected with Dallas' shin. His own boot offered some protection, but the action served its purpose. Dallas released her as he bent nearly double to grab an aching leg.

Tears pouring down her face over what she'd been forced to do, Smokey ran like she had never run before. This time there was no stopping and hiding. She slowed to a walk at times, but pushed on until she thought she would collapse, and in fact, at one point did. Her side ached and she had a few close calls with various sailors, one of whom tore her dress.

Cold and disoriented, Smokey finally stopped. She stood in the shadows of the dock and gasped for breath. Recovering somewhat, she turned her head and looked out over the ships, their masts silhouetted against the sky.

For a moment she thought her eyes were playing tricks on her. Then she realized it was true—the *Aramis* was docked not 50 yards away. Smokey's heart pounded in her chest at the thought that she was so near to safety.

Don't give yourself away now, Smokey, not when you've come this far, was her heart's prayer as she made herself walk slowly toward the ship. At the foot of the gangplank stood Scully. Smokey approached and spoke with what she believed to be a normal tone.

"Scully," she began, not realizing that her voice was a high-pitched squeak. "Is Darsey on board?"

"No, Captain," he told her, feeling as if he were looking at a ghost. "He's out searching for you."

"Is it safe to come aboard?"

"Safe?" the old cook was nonplussed. "Aye, it's safe," Scully answered her finally and began to be afraid at the change in his captain.

"Very well. I'll be in my cabin. Please send Darsey to me when he arrives."

"I'm here," his voice sounded behind her. Smokey turned.

"Is the crew here? Is there any reason we can't set sail immediately?"

"No, Captain," Darsey told her. "I'll inform the men."

Smokey moved up the gangplank then, still not understanding that she had gone into a state of shock. Darsey silently followed her, his heart pounding as roughly as Scully's over Smokey's manner and appearance.

The trembling began when Smokey gained her cabin. Darsey followed and lit her lanterns.

Darsey felt his stomach heave when he finally saw her in better light. The hem of her dress was torn in many places, and the neckline had sagged even lower over her breasts. Her face and hands were filthy and tearstained, and he thought they might have to cut her hair to remove the tangles. Grabbing a blanket, he wrapped it around her shoulders as anger raged within him at whoever had done this to his girl.

"Robby and Mic are casting off. Scully will prepare a bath for you. Would you like that?"

Smokey didn't answer but continued to shake like a leaf in a storm. Darsey saw that she was in no shape to know anything. He left her for just a few moments to make sure all was well on deck and then came back to find her just where he had left her.

He had never invaded her privacy before, but when her bath was ready and she was still standing in a trancelike state, Darsey gave her a little shake.

"Smokey! Get cleaned up now."

She seemed to finally see him, and Darsey turned away as she began to unbutton her dress. As he let himself out, he prayed that she would be able to function. Questions swarmed through his mind as he went topside to take over.

He wasn't the only one to have questions. Dallas had come on the scene just after the *Aramis* pushed off. He prayed that Smokey was aboard and safe, but never had he been so hurt and confused. His hands balled into fists as he thought about her dress and the way she'd kissed him. He had no idea when he would see Smokey again, but when he did, he felt she owed him a long explanation.

Two hours later, Smokey was finally bathed, in her night-gown, and tucked under the covers of her bed. Darsey sat in a chair nearby and watched her. She hadn't wanted the light out, nor had she wanted to talk. It took some time, but after staring at the shadows on the ceiling for a while, her eyes finally slid shut. Darsey watched and listened as her breathing evened out and sleep claimed her. A single tear slid down his weather-roughened cheek as he prayed.

"Help me, Father," he whispered. "Help me as I help her. I don't know where she's been or what's been done to her, but I know she needs me. Help me to be there and help her to get over this awful night."

Darsey prayed until his own body grew limp with exhaustion. It never once occurred to him to leave Smokey's side to seek the comfort of his own bed. Slouched in his chair, sleep came to claim him also, leaving the night's pain and worries for the morrow.

Twenty-One

"HOW IS JENNY FEELING?" Greer asked Buck as they lunched at the hotel.

"Her only complaints are fatigue and feeling like she can't get anything done."

Greer smiled. "She needs to baby herself a little right now. She'll be busy enough in a few months."

"That's true, but she pushes herself too hard. Tate has told her she should rest, and in fact, when I saw him this morning, he said she'd taken a nap yesterday."

Their conversation was interrupted when their food arrived. Buck began his meal with a better appetite than he had enjoyed in weeks. Greer had made no promises, but this was the third time she had agreed to see him since Smokey's going-away party. They grew a little closer each time.

"You and Hank never had children, did you?"

"No, we didn't," Greer told him. She wasn't at all offended by the question, but a look of sadness crossed her face.

"Maybe I shouldn't have asked you that."

"It's all right, Buck. You see, all five of my children are in heaven. My body simply refused to carry a baby to full term."

"I'm sorry, Greer," Buck told her, his eyes filled with love. "I'm sure you would have made a wonderful mother."

"Thank you, Buck, but I'm not sorry anymore," Greer told

him. "I wouldn't have wanted to raise them on my own." Greer smiled at a sudden thought, and Buck questioned her.

"I'm just laughing at myself really," she admitted. "I nearly asked you if learning about my pregnancies will change the way you feel about me, but I think I already know that answer."

"As a matter of fact," Buck told her seriously, "I was just thinking that some of your reluctance to accept my proposal might stem from the fact that you think I would press you to have children." Buck stopped for a moment to hold the lovely widow's eyes with his own.

"It's you I want, Greer, no one else. I had no desire to marry until I met you, and it's you alone that I'm going to want for the rest of my life."

"Oh, Buck." Greer's eyes flooded with tears. "I'm trying, I really am."

"Shhh," Buck said softly. "I didn't tell you that to distress you or scare you away. I just want you to know that nothing is going to change my feelings."

Greer reached across the table and took Buck's hand. She gave it a light squeeze before releasing it. Both of them were ready for a change in subjects, and the topic turned to Smokey.

"I so enjoyed the party. I was utterly amazed to learn that Smokey is the captain of her own ship, however."

"She certainly didn't look the part that night, but Dallas tells me she's magnificent. He said if his heart wasn't set on building ships, he would gladly sail around the Atlantic for the better part of every year with Smokey."

"Do you suppose they'll see one another?"

"I doubt it, Greer. Smokey's plans were to be halfway to the Orient by now."

"So there's been a change in plans?" Robby asked Darsey the morning after they had left London.

"I don't know. She was still sleeping when I woke in that chair. Until she wakes up and gives orders or seems able to function," Darsey shrugged, "I just don't know."

"Did she say *anything*?" Scully wanted to know.

"Not yet. There were no bruises that I could see once the dirt was off of her, but I realize that doesn't mean a thing."

The men all exchanged looks. Faces darkened with anger. It was all too easy to imagine what could have happened in the hours she was gone. The fact that she found her way to the ship, however, was nothing short of a miracle, and that gave the men cause to hope she would really be all right.

"So what is our present course?" Mic pressed Darsey.

"Home," the older man told him simply. "I'm going to head below and see if she's stirred, but for now, set a course for Kennebunk."

Smokey had been awake for some time, but had not moved from her bed. Her entire body ached, especially her legs, but in a very real way she welcomed the pain. It meant she had fought hard and survived. Right now she was praying and thanking God for the strength He had given her.

She praised Him for His love and care and for sparing her from anything worse. She had been grabbed and frightened and forced to fight, but as upsetting as all of those things had been, Smokey was all too aware that the situation could have been much worse.

Praying and surrendering her hurt pride, her fear, and every known sin to her Lord, Smokey knew the peace that only He could give. By the time Darsey appeared with a mug of tea, she was ready to talk.

"How are you, lass?" he asked softly as he sat on the chair on which he had spent the night.

"I'm going to be all right. I hope I never have to repeat a night like the last, but I'm going to survive."

"Can you tell me about it?"

"Do you remember my going out?"

"Yes."

"When I came out of Meg's private rooms, I noticed a man standing there. I was thinking about what Meg and I had been discussing and never gave him any thought. He grabbed me from behind. I struggled, and because he was small, I nearly got away. But then he pressed a sweet-smelling cloth over my mouth. I woke up aboard a ship in a strange room."

"Who did this?"

"Haamich Wynn."

"The pirate?"

"Yes." Smokey's voice was soft.

"I've heard he's a huge man."

"He is. I don't know who it was that grabbed me; obviously someone who works for him."

At that point Smokey went on to give Darsey the entire story, from the moment she woke up, fought with the pirate, escaped, and saw Dallas to where she found the *Aramis*.

"You actually kicked Dallas?" Darsey asked her.

Smokey nodded regretfully. "I panicked when he wouldn't let me go. All I could think about was Haamich Wynn finding him with me and killing him. I don't know if he'll ever forgive me."

"I'm sure you just need to explain."

"I hope you're right."

The two fell silent for a moment, and then Smokey went on. "Darsey, how did the *Aramis* come to be docked in the south quarter?"

Still trying to deal with all she had shared, Darsey took a ragged breath and began to tell of his nightmare in the last 36 hours.

"I didn't give you much time to return to the back room. When you hadn't shown in five minutes, I got nervous. When two more went past, I hit the door running. There was no sign of you.

"Someone in the tavern said that the table in the corner had recently been occupied and was now empty. Hearing that, I ran for the docks. As you well know, there was no trace of you. I searched for a time—many of us did—but I didn't wait very long before going back into Clancy's and asking about the men who were missing.

"No one seemed to know a thing about them, and for Clancy's, that's not normal. Meg and Bart know everyone who walks through the door, or they do soon afterward. Evidently those two were not new, but neither were they regulars until some weeks ago. Any and all attempts to gain information from them were met with blank stares, and since they kept to themselves and always paid their bill, Bart let them alone.

"When Clancy's came up dry, I did a little more inquiring in the neighboring taverns. Bart went with me. Even though others had seen the men we spoke of, no one knew their names. I felt frantic at that point, and on the off chance that you'd returned, decided to head back to the ship. Docked some yards away from us was a huge frigate. I don't know why it caught my interest, but it was so heavily guarded that I couldn't get it out of my mind.

"When they pushed off, we followed them. I knew there was a chance that I could be leaving you high and dry on the docks, but I simply had to follow that ship. Strangely enough, they did not head for high seas. They docked again, this time in the—"

"South port area," Smokey finished for him, now understanding exactly where she had been. All this said, both Darsey and Smokey fell quiet. When Smokey spoke, she sounded weary.

"I want to go home, Darsey. I want to go home to Willa's cooking and scolding and loving."

"We've set a course for Kennebunk, lass," Darsey told her, watching as her eyes briefly slid shut with relief. She hadn't eaten anything yet, but for the moment there was no need. Darsey watched as she scooted low beneath the covers and closed her eyes, this time to sleep.

Twenty-Two

SMOKEY LAY IN HER BED at Willa's and stared at the white ceiling above her. She had been home for over two weeks and had done little but sleep, eat, and take long walks to the beach, where she would sit for hours and pray.

Her encounter with Haamich Wynn made her feel as if something precious had been wrenched away from her. She had escaped physical harm, but the emotional effects went deep. She knew such men existed, but she had never faced one personally.

Smokey also spent hours every day thinking about Dallas and wondering where he could be. She asked herself all the questions she wanted to ask him. Did he understand that she panicked on the docks that night? Was he angry over the way she was dressed, or was it concern? And always, her last question—why, if he was angry or upset with her, did he pull her back for another kiss?

All these questions and many more swam through her mind. She longed for answers, but when none came she repeatedly forced her mind back to God's sovereign will, asking for His peace in this troubling time.

She also prayed for Jenny. She hadn't been to see her since she returned, but it wasn't for lack of want. In truth, she wanted desperately to see her, but Jenny was not expecting

Smokey back for weeks. An appearance now would bring a myriad of questions.

Smokey had no idea how Jenny would respond to all she had been through. With Jenny's present condition in mind, and real concern for the baby, Smokey made herself stay away. It was one of the hardest things she had ever asked herself to do.

"Why, Dolly," Jenny exclaimed as her brother opened the door to her bed-sitter after a soft knock.

"May I come in?"

"Of course," Jenny assured him and stayed on the settee after he had waved her back down.

Dallas bent and kissed her cheek. "Motherhood agrees with you; I've never seen you look lovelier."

"Thank you," Jenny told him sincerely. As her hand moved to her distended stomach, she wished she could return the compliment. Dallas was smiling and looked genuinely glad to see her, but as she took a moment to study his face, Jenny saw something that disturbed her.

"Did I misunderstand you, Dolly, or are you back before you had originally planned?"

"I am early, yes, and I'm afraid I can't stay. I'm looking for Smokey."

"Smokey?" Jenny frowned in confusion and studied her brother's face once again. He was working hard to hide his anxiety, but it was there.

"She isn't here. Did you really expect her to be?"

He shook his head regretfully. "I only hoped. Has she been in touch?"

"No. Dallas, what's going on?" Jenny's use of his real name told him she was frightened.

He hesitated and then spoke with a measured tone. "I saw Smokey when I was in London, but she was in a terrific hurry and we didn't really get to talk. I was rather hoping she had come home, since I had an early shipment for Tate." Dallas did not tell Jenny that he altered his course in hopes of seeing Smokey. "I just wanted to make sure everything was all right with her."

Jenny looked instantly relieved. "I'm sure she's fine, probably running a little behind schedule. Knowing Smokey, she's made up for it by now and is halfway to the Orient."

Dallas worked to put a smile on his face. "Just in case she did come this way, I think I'll ride over and check with Darsey's sister. Where did you say she lived?"

Dallas had finally managed to use his normal voice, and Jenny gave him directions to Willa's without the slightest reservation.

Willa poured coffee for Darsey and Smokey before refilling her own cup and sitting down at the table again. They had just eaten a wonderful meal of baked fish, and everyone was full and content.

"That was wonderful, Willa," Smokey told her. The older woman smiled. Smokey had been off her food for the first week she was home, and it was nice to see her face filled out again.

"My mother's recipe," Willa said and smiled at Darsey. "Do you remember those Saturday clambakes, Dars?"

Darsey chuckled and explained to Smokey. "Mother hated clams, couldn't even stand the smell of them. So as a new bride, when the rest of the family was eating clams, Mother always baked fish for herself. Mother was so good at it that Father wasn't long in joining her and abandoning the clams.

"Before their first anniversary the whole family was eating fish on Saturday afternoons. They never stopped calling it a clambake, but they all ate fish."

Smokey listened with rapt attention to their reminiscences. She'd never had a family life like the type they had known, and it was all very fascinating and wonderful to her. She thought she could sit all evening and hear them go on, but there was a knock at the door.

Willa rose to answer it, saying that their neighbor, Mrs. Bright, had planned to bring some fabric over so Willa could help make some clothes for her baby granddaughter. Neither Darsey nor Smokey noticed when they did not hear the sound of Mrs. Bright's voice, but when the deep tones of a masculine voice floated from the front room, they both tensed.

Smokey's back was to the kitchen door, but she kept her eyes fixed on Darsey's face and knew the exact moment their guest entered.

"Hello, Dallas," Darsey spoke easily. To his credit, he did not look at Smokey. "Would you like to sit down and have some coffee?"

"Thank you, but I'll pass. I'd like to talk with Smokey if I may."

Smokey's heart was doing funny things just hearing his voice, but she forced herself to turn and, with a semblance of calm, look at Dallas.

"May I talk with you, Smokey?" he asked when her eyes locked with his.

"Certainly," Smokey said and rose slowly from the table. "We can go into the front room." Smokey mentally congratulated herself on how normal she sounded and hoped that he wouldn't notice how she was trembling as she led the way to the parlor.

Once seated across the room from each other on the old, comfortable furniture, an unwelcome silence fell. Smokey spent a few moments looking at the hands in her lap and then out the window, dark as it was. She glanced up to find Dallas' eyes riveted on her.

"Am I out of line to ask why you were so set on leaving me when we met in London?"

"No," Smokey began, "but it's a long story and I—"

"I have time," Dallas cut in.

Smokey nodded. "First of all, I'm sorry I kicked you. That was terrible, and I only hope you can forgive me."

"Were you afraid of me, Smokey? Did you think I was going to force you to do something against your wishes?" Dallas' face and voice were so pained that Smokey nearly cried.

"No, Dallas, no!" Smokey's hand went to her mouth in horror. "It wasn't that at all. I just panicked out of fear for you. I acted without thinking."

"Fear for me?" Dallas' face was now a mask of confusion.

Smokey took a deep, calming breath and began to share. "We were running behind schedule as you might have already guessed, or we would have been out of London before you arrived. We really should have rushed on, but I knew we wouldn't be back for some time and I wanted to see the folks at Clancy's.

"I left the back room long enough to take care of a personal need, and when I came out of Meg's private rooms, a man grabbed me. I fought, but he held a drug-soaked cloth over my mouth. Everything went black, and when I woke up I was on a ship."

The hair stood up on the back of Dallas' neck, and fear pounded in his chest. He shifted in his chair, his face intense as he waited for her to continue.

"There was no one with me, and I was lying on the bed. The room was rife with lewd art and paintings, but I wasn't given much time to look around. When the door opened, a man came in." Smokey wondered how detailed she should be. She would be horribly embarrassed to repeat all the pirate had said.

"The man was Haamich Wynn."

"The pirate?" Dallas broke his silence.

"Yes. He told me that my capture was deliberate and that he wanted to get to know me better. He insisted that I put on that red dress."

A flicker of skepticism lit Dallas' eyes, but Smokey, thinking she had imagined it, kept talking. She was babbling slightly, and some of her facts were getting muddled.

"I noticed some fencing swords on the wall, and I told him I would fight him. He agreed to set me free if I won. I've never done such a thing before but I cut his face. He actually fainted at the sight of his own blood. I tied him up and ran away.

"I ran from the ship, but my escape was immediately noticed, and his men came after me. That's when I ran into you. I was afraid of your being found with me, so when you wouldn't let me go, I panicked." Smokey ended with a small shrug and noticed that Dallas looked almost angry.

"I'd heard that Haamich Wynn was a huge man."

"He is. As big as Darsey, if not bigger."

"And you want me to believe that you had a duel with him and won?" Dallas could no longer hide his doubt.

Smokey's whole body stiffened at his tone. She stood, her entire being radiating anger.

"I apologized for kicking you, Dallas, but I did not owe you an explanation."

Dallas stood also. "No, I guess you didn't, but there are some things that bother me. I'd like to get the entire picture."

"No," she told him. She could see that she had surprised him. "I've told you all I'm going to, and if that isn't good enough, then that's too bad. As I said, I owe you nothing, and I might add that I don't deserve your judgment."

"I'm not judging you." Dallas fought to keep his voice even.

"So you believe me?"

Dallas hesitated, and it cost him.

"Get out, Dallas," Smokey told him, her voice low with fury. "Get out and do not come back, not until you're ready to apologize for believing me a liar."

"Smokey, if you would just tell me again how you came to be in the dress, I—"

"Get out." Smokey's voice was whisper soft, and Dallas knew he would have to give her some time.

It was on his tongue to apologize, but he felt so muddled at the moment. With regret he moved toward the door. Knowing that he'd handled the situation very badly, he looked back, but Smokey was already leaving the room. He noticed that she did not even turn as she strode back toward the kitchen.

Twenty-Three

TWENTY-FOUR HOURS LATER the *Aramis* set sail with a full crew. Darsey was at the helm when Smokey came topside to check on the men.

"I want answers, Darsey," she told him as she stood next to the older man. "I won't be home until I get some."

Darsey, having already read her motive for leaving Willa's, only nodded.

"You might be asking for trouble," he told her, his face and voice calm.

"Well, I've never been afraid of trouble," she said logically. "And since I can't go on as I am, wondering and upset, I think I'd best do what I can."

Darsey only nodded. The old sparkle was back in her eye. He knew that she had prayed constantly while they had been home, but he also recognized as Smokey just had, that she had been hiding. Now she was facing her fears and acting with the good sense she normally had.

If she had wanted to head out and trade in southern waters as she had originally planned, Darsey would have been all for it. But now she needed to fit together the pieces of this puzzle, and Darsey understood that just as well. He prayed for her and her responsibility as captain of their vessel. He also prayed for

Dallas, who was certain to come looking for Smokey again and find her gone.

"She's not here," Willa told Dallas the afternoon after Smokey left.

"When do you expect her back?" Dallas asked, never dreaming that she was on her ship.

Willa was as unflappable as ever when she answered. "It could be weeks, but I'm thinking it probably will be months."

"You mean she's left on the *Aramis*?" Dallas asked in astonishment.

"With Darsey and the whole crew. I'm not sure how much trading they'll do, but Smokey needed to find some answers."

Distracted, Dallas ran a hand through his hair and stood in frustration. He turned to leave, barely remembering to bid Willa goodbye.

Willa shut the door and then watched from the front room window. "That Darsey's got me to answer to when he returns! Why didn't he ever tell me that Dallas was in love with her?"

"He's good, Darsey; I'll give him that," Smokey told her first mate some seven weeks after they had set sail.

Darsey could only shake his head. Their search to know more about the pirate Haamich Wynn reminded him of the night that Smokey was taken. One dead-end lead after another.

They had been to London, France, the Netherlands, and even up into Norway and Sweden, and had still come up empty. They weren't discouraged, but more curious than ever.

Smokey was wondering if this wasn't God's way of telling her to let the matter rest. She was quite certain of this and praying about heading home or doing some trading when the weather stepped in and answered for her.

A storm hit hard and fast, and the *Aramis* and her crew found themselves stranded just off China Island making repairs. They had plenty of stores to survive, as well as to fix the ship, but it was going to take time. Time that Smokey would rather have spent doing something else.

❀ ❀ ❀

When Smokey did not turn up in the first two ports Dallas visited, he knew he would have to go back to work. He simply did not have the finances to keep searching for her. He was able to trade and deal with great profit in the days that followed, but he never stopped looking for Smokey or asking every merchant he met about her.

Never had he had so much to say to someone. How could he have treated her that way after all she had been through? The story seemed outrageous to him, but he had been around long enough to know that didn't make Smokey's words false. Had he stopped and thought about that rather than verbally attacking Smokey in her own home, he might have her with him now, rather than having to confess his anxiety to the Lord with nearly every breath he took.

"Ready for me to take her, Cap'n?" Dallas' first mate asked, effectively breaking into his thoughts.

"Sure, Cliff. I've set a course for China Island. We'll dock there tonight and head out in the morning. We're not due in Denmark for over a week."

"Aye, aye, Cap'n."

Dallas headed to his cabin to check the charts and work on his books. His heart and mind dwelt on Smokey again, and how much she meant to him. After just a few minutes though, he forced his mind back to the business at hand.

Smokey would ask herself for years to come how they got the drop on them. It might have been the stealthy way they approached, or the fact that the entire crew had been concentrating on the repairs, or possibly a combination of the two. Nonetheless, the facts remained.

Night was falling fast on the second day of repairs when Smokey heard a knock on her door. She called entrance and froze in her desk chair when Haamich Wynn walked in, looking and acting as calm as ever.

"Did you really think I would give up on you, my dear?" the pirate asked, seeming genuinely glad to see her.

"Come on, Smokey," he went on smoothly. "Come topside. I have a few things I want you to say to your men."

Standing on legs she was sure wouldn't hold her, Smokey moved out the door. She couldn't repress a shiver when she felt Haamich close behind her. Her heart pounded as she prayed. Her only fear at the moment was for the safety of her men.

"Cliff sent me down, Cap'n," the bos'n told Dallas some hours later. "He said you should come up right away."

Dallas left his cabin without question. He took the glass from Cliff's hand the moment he was up top and looked in the direction Cliff had been gazing. His heart plummeted over what he saw.

The light of the full moon clearly displayed the *Aramis*,

but anchored beyond her was another ship. There was nothing patently obvious to warn Dallas that the *Aramis* was in trouble, but the fact that neither of Smokey's flags were flying caused him to believe that something was amiss.

He handed the glass to his bos'n and spoke quietly to Cliff. Just minutes later the two men left the ship in a longboat, moving silently toward Smokey's ship and praying that they could be of help.

Smokey's eyes moved over the deck of her ship. She knew she had never been so helpless. Darsey and Robby, the biggest men of her crew, were already bound. The rest were scattered around under close watch of the pirate's men, who seemed to be everywhere.

They were a scurvy lot, Smokey concluded swiftly, without a trace of moral fiber to their names. *Of course*, she asked herself, *what should I have expected after meeting their captain?*

"Now," Haamich Wynn spoke expansively. "Let's get right down to business. I regret that we have been parted this long, my dear, but you've been moving around so much that I couldn't get ahold of you."

"You've been following us," Smokey stated with anger.

"My dear," the pirate spoke as though addressing a child. "I told you I want you, and I will have you."

"For a man who lost during our last encounter, you're awfully quick to claim your victory now!" Smokey spat the words, and Haamich Wynn laughed.

"That's one of the things I love about you, my dear—your honesty. But alas, I am honest too. I freely admit that I was foiled last time. So now attend to my words, Smokey, because I will *not* be thwarted again.

"Now," he said, becoming businesslike at once. "Line your

men up and tell them that I am their new commander. I've seen what this ship can do, and I want the *Aramis* as well as you."

Smokey was so thoroughly shocked that she could only stare at him. His back was to the wheelhouse and even though Smokey's peripheral vision caught some movement there, she was too stunned to move or speak.

"Tell them, Smokey." His voice was now deadly soft. "Unless you do as you're told, I'll give you to my men right on the spot. They like a woman who fights, only this time you won't have a blade."

Smokey began to tremble. She knew there would be no escape this time. With a heavy heart she turned her back to the pirate.

"Line up, men." She spoke softly, but all were able to hear. Even Robby and Darsey, hands bound behind them, moved into place.

Smokey's eyes roved over them and then paused and blinked when she saw that Dallas was lined up with her men. She forced her eyes away from his intense stare, a stare that seemed to be trying to tell her to trust him, and spoke.

"There has been a change in command." Smokey's voice remained soft. "Your new captain is Haamich Wynn."

"Very nicely done, my dear." The pirate's voice was delighted. "Now you just head down to your cabin, and I'll join you in a moment."

Smokey turned, her chin thrust forward, ready to fight. She was trembling from head to foot, but the thought of going to her cabin and submitting to this man made her furious.

"Ready to fight me, Smokey?" The pirate's voice had turned mocking. He turned to a man at his side. "The biggest man— Darsey, I believe it is... cut his throat."

"No!" Smokey shouted. No one moved. They all watched as she took a deep breath and moved toward the companionway.

The pirate's men went to work then, and the entire crew was tied. Darsey ended up next to Dallas and spoke in a low tone.

"Please tell me you didn't come aboard alone."

"I didn't" was all Dallas said, and the older man nearly slumped with relief.

Twenty~Four

ALL THE WEAPONS HAD BEEN REMOVED from Smokey's cabin. She had never thought to hide them before, so her foil, small knife, and pistol were all gone. Seeing this, Smokey began to know real fear. She tried to resign herself to the next few hours or days, but her insides were in turmoil.

Even though Smokey heard footsteps in the companionway, she jumped when her cabin door opened. Haamich Wynn stood there, but he was still speaking to one of his men outside. Smokey heard his man say the name "Lordlin" before he left. She had no time to wonder on the matter, however, since the pirate had finally come in and shut the door.

From where she stood by the desk, Smokey watched him lean against the jam. His smile was tender as he stared at her, and the young captain noted that very gently, almost affectionately, he ran a finger repeatedly down the scar on his face.

"I've missed you, Smokey. I was quite frantic when you left. I found myself terribly frustrated that I never found out where you make your home."

He pushed away from the door then and moved toward her; his presence seemed to fill the cabin. Smokey felt suffocated. Her braid was again lying on her breast, and this time Haamich picked it up and began to wrap it around his fist. Smokey panicked and moved away. Haamich shook his head.

"I promise you, Smokey, there is nothing to be afraid of. I'm going to take very good care of you."

Smokey licked her lips in fear as he started toward her. She didn't like standing close to the bunk and began to move away. This time Haamich anticipated her move and reached for her upper arms. With strong hands he drew her slowly but inescapably closer. He was so big, frighteningly big.

Please God, Smokey prayed, *show the men how to help me.*

"You're going to learn to love me, my dear." Haamich spoke then, and Smokey saw his head bend toward her. "You're going to learn that you can't live without me."

His words infuriated her, and she acted in desperation. As his head neared, she spit, hitting him full in the face. The pirate paused for the space of two heartbeats before balling up his fist and punching Smokey across the upper cheek and eye. She barely saw the blow coming, and then she saw nothing at all.

Smokey had no idea how much time had passed before she woke. Her head was spinning, and her wrists hurt. It took a moment for her to understand that her wrists were tied and secured to the bed frame on either side of her. She found herself praising God that she was still completely dressed.

Smokey heard her desk chair move and turned her aching head to see Haamich Wynn pushing himself up. She watched as he sat on the bunk beside her and leaned a hand over her to rest it on the bed.

"I'm sorry, my dear. I never meant to hurt you. You are very shook up over nothing."

"Nothing?" Smokey whispered, not believing her ears. "You call this nothing?"

"I am really the best thing that has ever happened to you," he spoke with conviction. "As soon as you get to know me, you'll see how right I am."

His hand lifted toward her blackened eye, and Smokey's chest rose and fell quickly in fear. The movement drew his eyes downward, and Smokey wanted to sob.

"Please don't do this," she said in a breathless voice. The pirate's eyes came back to hers.

"I must. I am consumed with you, and I won't stop until you are mine."

His hands went to either side of her then, and he bent to kiss her. Smokey closed her eyes to blot out the image of his face.

Before he could touch her, however, there was a knock. Smokey opened her eyes and watched with fear as rage contorted his features.

"I told you not to disturb me!"

"But Cap'n," the fearful voice of one of his men sounded through the door. "We need you."

"Don't bother me!" he shouted.

"But Cap'n," the voice began again, and Haamich Wynn came off the bed with a snarl. He wrenched the door open, and Smokey heard the sound of flesh meeting flesh. She craned her neck to see Haamich Wynn's head snap back, but he remained standing.

From her awkward position, Smokey caught a glimpse of Dallas. Then Darsey's frame came through the door. Haamich Wynn's punches were wild and without effect as he attempted to fight back. Darsey's blows, however, were perfectly aimed. Smokey's neck strained as she watched his fists pounding the man.

The fight seemed to go on forever as the men fought over nearly every inch of the cabin. When Smokey didn't think she would be able to take any more, Haamich Wynn, with much moaning and carrying on, fell hard to the floor.

Smokey suddenly found Dallas above her. A knife flashed, and the blood rushed back to her hands as they were released.

Smokey wanted to sit up, but not until that moment, as she stared at Dallas with one eye, did Smokey notice that her other eye was nearly swollen shut. She didn't think she could move at all.

Dallas placed a hand on either side of Smokey, much the way the pirate had done, and leaned over her. This time Smokey was not afraid. She watched Dallas lean close, his eyes giving proof of the pain within.

"I'm sorry." The words were whispered.

Smokey reached and placed a hand on his arm. "You won't let him get me again, will you, Dallas?"

"No," his voice was whisper soft. "We're going to take him back to England and turn him over to the authorities. He can't hurt you again."

"Are my men all right?"

"Yes, they're fine; just worried about you."

Smokey nodded, and a shadow fell across her. Darsey had come close to see her. On spotting him, a delayed reaction swiftly rushed in. She began to shake all over. Try as she might to hold them back, tears flooded her eyes.

Dallas, without waiting for permission, gathered her in his arms. She cried against him for a few minutes, tears of pain and tears of relief.

"Is it finally over, Dallas?" Smokey asked as she calmed.

"It's over," he assured her softly.

Tenderly cradling her with one arm, Dallas used a handkerchief to wipe her tears. He didn't try to comfort her with any more words or tell her to stop crying, but just held her until she slept.

He saw that it would not be a restful sleep as soon as he laid her back down on the pillow, but Darsey was near and Dallas knew she would be in good hands.

As much as he hated to leave her, he had no choice. There were arrangements to be made concerning the pirate, his ship, and his men, and Dallas had volunteered to see to them.

He didn't see Smokey again before all three ships set sail for England, but by the time they had arrived and turned Haamich Wynn over to the authorities, he had established a plan.

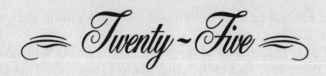

Twenty-Five

SMOKEY'S FACE WAS STILL SWOLLEN when the London authorities came to take Haamich Wynn away. She watched as they cut him loose before putting him in the huge, black coach. Something didn't seem right to Smokey. His look was almost smug as he spoke to one of the constables. Smokey knew there was little she could do about it, so she tried not to dwell on the possibilities.

Dallas and Darsey handled everything in the next two days, giving Smokey plenty of time to think. It occurred to her that the pirate might have friends in high places who would overlook his acts, or even listen when he claimed that it was her word against his own. She hadn't had a chance to ask Dallas about the pirate's ship, but Smokey knew that a holdful of stolen goods would add weight to her story.

For the moment, she had an important decision to make— did she head home, as she longed to do, or out to sea, as she had originally planned? If she went home now, she could be there when Jenny and Tate's baby was born. Smokey had nearly convinced herself to return to Maine when Dallas arrived and ruined all her plans.

"They'll need you to testify."

Smokey hadn't even thought of that. She glanced at Darsey, who had been with Dallas during this time, and then back at the man himself.

"When do they need me?" she wanted to know.

"In about two weeks. Without you they don't have a case."

Smokey hid her disappointment and spoke carefully. "We could do some trading down the southern coast in the next week and be back here in two weeks."

Darsey's mind was already obeying orders, but Dallas stepped in again.

"No."

"What do you mean, no?" Smokey asked him with raised brows. They'd had no time alone since their confrontation in Willa's living room, and even though the apology had been spoken, their relationship was not yet on solid footing.

"I mean that you need a rest, and I know just the place. I've contacted a friend. He and his wife would be glad to have us."

Smokey glared at Darsey when he covered a laugh with a cough. The older man was thinking that Dallas was digging himself in deep.

"You took it upon yourself to arrange leave for me?" Smokey's tone told Dallas he was in trouble, but his determination to get this girl to himself for a few days never wavered.

"Yes, I did," he told her calmly. "You look exhausted, your eye is still black and swollen, and you *are* going with me to Bracken. If I can't convince you, I'm sure Darsey can."

"Did you know about this, Darsey Brennan?" Smokey nailed him with a glance.

"Not a bit, lass, but if you ask me—"

"No one's asking you, Darsey," Smokey cut him off, and it was Dallas' turn to muffle his laughter.

He was truly desperate to get Smokey someplace safe and restful, but Dallas knew from the thundercloud on her face that he was going to have to change tactics. He stepped close and spoke low.

"You asked me not to let him get you again. I can't do that if we're not together."

In the light of his tender gaze and caring voice, the indignation drained out of Smokey. Running her tongue over her suddenly dry lips, a shiver of fear resurfaced.

"So you think they might not hold him?"

"I don't know. Something didn't feel right to me, but I can't put my finger on it."

Smokey nodded, knowing just what he meant. She glanced out over the Thames in indecision and then at Dallas' shirt-front. Dallas reached out two long fingers and placed them under Smokey's chin. With a gentle move, he tilted her face until her eyes met his.

"Please come with me to Bracken so I can take care of you. Darsey will be there as well, and I know you'll love Brandon and Sunny."

Smokey thought she could agree to anything when he spoke low and touched her so tenderly.

"All right," Smokey said and felt suddenly cold when Dallas immediately removed his hand and stepped away. He turned to leave then, calling absentmindedly over his shoulder to say that they would be leaving for the country in an hour.

Dallas completely missed the vulnerable look on Smokey's face. Darsey, on the other hand, saw it all. He walked down the gangplank with Dallas and stopped him with a few words when he would have walked away.

"Don't play games with her." The older man's voice was a growl.

"What are you talking about?"

"I'm talking about touching her and saying sweet things just to manipulate her."

Dallas stared at him in true surprise. "Does she feel that way?"

"You saw the look on her face. You know she does."

Dallas looked back to the deck, but Smokey was gone. He honestly hadn't noticed any distress on Smokey's part. In truth, he thought Darsey was being overly protective.

When Dallas looked at Smokey's first mate again, he was given one final, serious warning before Darsey boarded the *Aramis*.

"Don't play with my girl, Mr. Knight, because I won't stand for it."

Dallas stood for just a moment and recounted his scene with Smokey. She wasn't some child to be easily fooled, and Darsey knew that. Dallas was not a man who believed that the end justified the means. He didn't feel he'd been out of line. He hoped to have a chance very soon to tell Darsey that he was overreacting.

It took Dallas just ten minutes into the carriage ride to Bracken, Lord and Lady Hawkesbury's home, to see that Darsey had read the signs correctly. He had hurt Smokey. Her set face and the way she held herself spoke volumes.

Dallas had complimented Smokey on her dress, a lovely rose-colored day dress, as soon as he had seen her, but he realized now that her thanks had been rather stiff.

His desire to ask Darsey to ride with the driver so he could be alone with Smokey was nearly overwhelming. But he knew that both Smokey and Darsey would take that request as an insult. It would only make things worse.

If only they weren't so tired right now. Darsey looked ten years older, and Smokey's good eye sported a dusky circle, a sure sign of fatigue. Dallas' own eyes had a gritty feel when he blinked. He was glad that evening was approaching, knowing they could all get some rest soon after they arrived at Bracken.

He told himself he would make things right with Smokey in the morning. All that mattered right now was her rest and safety. Dallas found himself wishing he didn't have to sail to Denmark, but the shipment could not wait. At least he didn't have to leave until tomorrow afternoon and would only need to be gone three days.

He watched the small brunette nod off from his seat in the carriage across from Darsey and Smokey. Darsey himself looked like he would surrender to sleep at any moment, so Dallas let his own head fall back against the squabs where he dozed off and on for the next hour.

Twenty-Six

SMOKEY BLINKED AS SHE READ THE CLOCK on the mantel in her room, certain that it must be wrong. It said 2:00, and the sun was streaming through her window. Could she have slept that long?

They had arrived at Bracken, the most gorgeous home Smokey had ever seen, about 8:00 the evening before. She'd met the Duke and Duchess of Briscoe, a couple much younger than she had envisioned, and then been shown to a small dining room where she, Darsey, and Dallas had been given a light supper. She could not at the moment even remember what she ate.

Directly after the meal she had been shown to a bedroom the size of Willa's entire house. Smokey didn't believe she would ever fall asleep in such a cavernous space, but sleep she did *and* for nearly 17 hours.

Smokey was just thinking about rising when someone knocked. Tugging the covers up a bit higher, she called an entrance. Darsey walked in and softly shut the door.

"Good afternoon," Smokey said after he'd taken a chair by her nightstand.

His eyes twinkled when he spoke. "I'm glad to see you decided to join us. I've been checking on you all day, wondering if you were ever going to wake up."

"I was rather surprised to read the clock a few minutes ago."

"So you *just* woke up?"

Smokey gave a sheepish nod and then grinned at him. "Have you ever seen a house like this in all your life?"

"House?" Darsey questioned her. "I believe mansion or palace would be more fitting."

"I think you're right. Willa would spend all her time cleaning, certain that no one could do a better job. It would put her in an early grave."

Darsey agreed and then glanced around the room. He said his own bedroom was just as magnificent. "I was offered lunch," Darsey added, "but I wanted to wait for you."

Smokey nodded. "I'd be a little intimidated to be here without Dallas," Smokey admitted. "I hope he's around when I get downstairs."

"He won't be," Darsey said flatly, and Smokey wondered at his tone. "He had to leave for Denmark. He's got a shipment due in. Said he'd be back in three days, maybe four."

Smokey was so surprised that she did not immediately speak. Darsey watched her face and knew that he would have thrashed Dallas if he could have laid hands on him.

"I can't stay here without Dallas," Smokey finally said. "I mean, they're his friends and I just wouldn't feel right."

"I must admit that I was feeling the same way."

"All right." Smokey made a swift decision. "Give me a few minutes. I'll get dressed and come downstairs and explain."

Darsey left then, but with a heavy heart. If Dallas really cared for Smokey, why would he go off and leave her? It seemed to Darsey that he'd had plenty of opportunity to explain his plans. Smokey was just starting to look rested, and the last thing she needed was to travel all the way back to London today.

Darsey went to his own room to pack up, completely unaware of the way Dallas had paced the floor of the library like a caged animal that morning, waiting for Smokey to come down.

Less than an hour later, captain and mate appeared downstairs at Bracken. Darsey was holding the handle of his own ragged case, as well as Smokey's satchel. They stood in the quiet entryway gripped with indecision.

Smokey was on the verge of knocking on one of the numerous doors off the foyer, hoping to find someone to whom she could explain their sudden departure, when a voice spoke behind them.

"Mr. Brennan."

Startled, both Smokey and Darsey turned to find a tall, nearly cadaverous individual with a very proper air addressing Darsey.

"I am Parks, head of housekeeping here at Bracken. Lady Hawkesbury is expecting you in the salon. If you and Miss Simmons would please follow me."

Smokey and Darsey exchanged a puzzled glance but followed nonetheless, Darsey still holding the bags. Parks went to one of the numerous doors and opened it. Darsey stood back and let Smokey precede him. Their hostess was inside.

"Oh, here you are!" Sunny Hawkesbury exclaimed with pleasure. She was a picture of grace and beauty as she rose from her place on the sofa. "I hope you both slept well. I know you must be hungry, so I've ordered tea to be served and—" Sunny, a warm and sensitive hostess, suddenly noticed her guests' bags.

"Is something wrong?" she asked Darsey kindly, making Smokey hesitant to speak. Did they all misunderstand and think Darsey was her father? She didn't know, and when her mate stayed quiet, she knew she had no choice but to speak.

"We appreciate your kindness, but we need to get back to London."

"Oh," Sunny's eyes swung to Smokey for an instant, and although her mind was racing, her look was calm.

"Is there something we can do?" Sunny finally asked, automatically addressing herself to Darsey.

"You've been more than kind," Smokey put in again, "and I thank you for the good night's sleep, but we really must be on our way."

Panic began to spiral through Sunny. She knew that Dallas expected them to be here when he returned, and why in the world was Mr. Brennan so silent?

"Well," Sunny smiled a smile she didn't feel and again spoke to Darsey. "Since you haven't eaten, will you at least stay for tea?"

"Thank you, no," Smokey responded. Sunny wanted to scream. She had heard that American women were bold, but this was ridiculous. She was on the verge of giving up and telling them goodbye when Brandon walked in. Sunny was so relieved she nearly sat down. She watched in amazement as her husband, immediately sizing up the situation, walked directly to Smokey and addressed only her.

"Is there a problem?"

"Not really," Smokey replied, growing weary of the conversation. "Darsey and I need to return to London. I hope you won't find us ungrateful, but we really must go."

"I know that Dallas expects to find you here when he returns," Brandon told her honestly, and watched her chin rise into the air. It was a gesture so like his wife would affect that he had to hide a smile.

"Dallas has obviously misled you. I do not answer to him concerning my whereabouts."

"I understand that, and I'm sorry I intimated otherwise. What I meant to say was that he told me he had wanted to talk to you this morning, but you did not come downstairs. He considered leaving you a note, but decided against it. I know he'll be bitterly disappointed to find you gone."

Smokey stared at him in uncertainty. She wanted to

believe Dallas wanted to see her, but she could not take being tossed around for one moment longer.

"When Dallas returns and you find you still want to leave for London, I'll take you there myself. For the time being, please stay, rest, and enjoy yourself."

"Darsey and I do not want to be any trouble."

"You'll be no trouble at all. Dallas and I have been friends for years. Any friend of his is a friend of mine." Brandon paused for just a moment. "Will you stay?"

"All right," Smokey agreed softly and wondered what in the world had prompted her.

"Wonderful," Brandon said. "I'll call Parks to have your bags returned to your rooms."

"We can take them up," Smokey told him, not completely comfortable with the way they were waited on here.

"Fine," Brandon accommodated her. "You'll be back down to join us for tea?"

"Yes."

Husband and wife watched her leave.

"Will you please tell me," Sunny spoke softly when the door was closed, "what that was all about?"

Brandon moved forward and kissed her before he spoke. "I'm sorry I never explained. *She* is the captain of the *Aramis*, and *he* is her first mate."

Sunny's mouth dropped open, and Brandon laughed.

"I really think the two of you will like each other," he told her, "if you get a chance to talk. She's probably one of the few women in the world who could actually rival you for independence."

"She is actually the captain of the ship?" Sunny asked in disbelief.

"That's right."

"Does she own it?"

"Yes. It's said to be one of the fastest ships on the sea, and she, one of the finest captains."

"But she's so petite and unassuming. I just..." Sunny

shrugged, and Brandon hugged her. Sunny was right, Smokey did not look like she held the position she did.

What Brandon didn't know was that there was far more to Smokey Simmons than even he could imagine, and that he and Sunny would both grow to think the world of her before Dallas returned.

≈ Twenty~Seven ≈

THE REST OF THE DAY was a bit strained for Smokey and Darsey, but the next morning Sunny asked Smokey if she wanted to see her baby. It turned out to be the perfect ice-breaker.

Lord Sterling Hawkesbury, future Duke of Briscoe, was nearly eight months old and able to crawl all over the nursery His face split with a huge grin on sighting his mother, and Smokey's heart melted the moment she laid eyes on him.

Both women sat down, and Sterling's nurse put him on the floor. He made a beeline for his mother until he spotted Smokey. In midcrawl he paused and stared at her. Smokey could not wipe the smile from her face, and when he saw her friendly countenance he changed direction.

She waited only until he was at arm's length before reaching for him. It had been years since she'd held a baby, and this one was a cuddler. He snuggled against her and popped a thumb into his mouth, the picture of contentment.

"He's beautiful," Smokey told Sterling's mother over the top of his head.

"We think so," Sunny responded with pleasure. "His grandmother tells me that Brandon looked just like him at that age."

"My friend Jenny, Dallas' sister," Smokey said to her hostess, who nodded, "is going to have a baby this summer. I was hoping to get home in time, but I'm not sure if I'll make it."

"I'm sure you will. Brandon was telling me last night that they need you to testify, but he hopes they have enough other evidence to convict the pirate." Sunny paused and went on. "Dallas told him you had a pretty rough time of it."

Smokey nodded. "I know it could have been much worse, but it's such a helpless feeling to be powerless against a captor."

The conversation was broken momentarily as Sterling's nurse returned, saw the child was asleep in Smokey's arms, and came to retrieve him. Sunny dropped a kiss on her young son's head, and the women exited the room.

"You're not afraid to testify, are you?" Sunny asked, fairly certain what the answer would be.

"No," Smokey told her emphatically as they walked down the stairs. "I want to see him put away. He's never hit my ship before, but I grow furious when I think of the hard hours we put in and then men like him who come along and help themselves without even breaking a sweat."

"Brandon's been boarded four times," Sunny told her guest.

"I didn't know that. He must be anxious to see this over."

"Yes, he is. I know he'd like to talk to you before the trial, just to get an idea of what you know."

"I'd be glad to tell him anything that might help."

"I was quite certain you would feel that way," Sunny told her with a smile. "By the way, I like to go riding about this time each day. Would you care to join me?"

"Horseback riding?"

"That's right."

"I've never been," Smokey admitted.

"Never?" Sunny was astounded and then grinned. "Well, I've never captained a ship, so I guess that makes us about even."

Smokey laughed, and before she knew it, Sunny had

steered her in the direction of her bedroom to find a riding habit that could be shortened quickly.

"It's not at all as I imagined," Smokey told Sunny just two hours later as she sat on the back of a well-behaved gelding. "I mean, he really goes where he's told."

"What did you expect?"

"I don't know," Smokey confessed. "A ship can't operate on its own, but a horse has a will. I think there are verses in the Bible, the New Testament, about that."

"I know the ones you mean; they're in James three, and they talk about the rudder of a ship or the bit in a horse's mouth, and then about how powerful our tongues are."

"Those were the ones I was thinking of. I always love it when God uses illustrations I can see so well."

Suddenly both women smiled at each other. It was wonderful and precious to find that they were sisters in Christ. Smokey's heart became very full at the knowledge.

Sunny couldn't help thinking that Brandon had been right, she liked Smokey immensely. She was so easy to be with, and they never ran out of things to talk about.

They rode on, and Sunny had to squelch laughter every time she remembered that Smokey was five years older than she was. Not 24 hours ago, she stood opposite Smokey, thinking she was very young and acting out of place with Darsey standing beside her. What a woman! No wonder Dallas was fascinated.

"You mean to tell me that she actually fenced with Haamich Wynn?" Brandon asked Darsey in disbelief.

Darsey grinned before he answered. "She holds her own very well, sir."

"Who taught her?"

"Her father and I."

"You were his mate also?"

"Yes, sir. For years before Smokey was even born."

"Simmons," Brandon said the name softly and then shook his head. "I don't believe I knew him."

Darsey hesitated before speaking. "He never used the name Simmons. Most knew him only as Clancy; to Smokey he was Papa."

Brandon grew absolutely still and stared at Darsey as he sat opposite him in his study. The women were out riding, or he would have looked for Smokey right on the spot. A well of amazement and then deep respect for Smokey and Darsey rose up within Brandon. He knew there was something different about this man and his captain.

"Smokey doesn't like to talk of it, sir," Darsey told him bluntly, wanting to be honest, but also wanting to protect his girl. "She prefers to be accepted on her own, for who she is."

"I understand completely, Darsey. I won't mention it, but I will tell you this, I knew there was something special about that woman the moment I saw her."

Darsey grinned. "I'll have to tell her that, sir. I think it would do her good. We're a bit intimidated in surroundings like these."

Brandon laughed outright. "You tell her she has nothing to worry about, Darsey. She's doing just fine."

"How are you holding up?" Brandon asked Smokey the next day during lunch. Dallas had been gone for three days. Even though Brandon thought Smokey looked well rested and lovely, he knew she might be getting a bit anxious.

"I'm well. A little sore since your wife decided that I needed to go riding yesterday *and* today."

Sunny laughed unrepentantly.

"Just wait, Sunny," Smokey warned her. "One of these days I'll shanghai you and make you scrub the deck of my ship."

Sunny, who had always been fascinated with ships, rather liked the idea.

"As you can see, that was no serious threat," Brandon said dryly as he watched his wife's face. "Sunny and I met on a ship, and I've always thought she might have a bit of the sea in her veins."

Husband and wife grinned at each other, and the meal progressed in high humor. When Sunny asked for tea at the end of the meal, Brandon looked across the table at Smokey, his dark eyes intent on her face.

"Darsey tells me that you fence."

To his surprise, Smokey only smiled and said, "Did he now?"

Brandon inclined his handsome head and failed to notice the look of astonishment on his wife's face. Sunny had told herself she was beyond surprises, but it just wasn't so.

"He tells me," Brandon went on smoothly, "that you hold your own very nicely."

Again Smokey only smiled. Brandon waited, but still she said nothing. Smokey's teacup was halfway to her mouth when he asked the question.

"Will you fence with me?"

Brandon's respect for her doubled as she calmly raised the cup to her mouth, drank, and just as calmly placed it back in her saucer.

"I'd have to change my clothes."

"So would I," Brandon informed her, and Smokey nodded.

"In the den, in one hour?"

"I'll be there," Smokey told him. She thanked Sunny for the delicious lunch. When she exited a moment later, Darsey went with her.

"You can't be serious," Sunny spoke as soon as the door closed. Brandon chuckled at her look of horror.

"I'm not going to hurt her, love."

"Are you sure?"

"Quite sure. I've never known a woman who fenced, and I must admit I'm more than a little curious. Chelsea wanted to learn for years. When she finally badgered Rand into showing her, she cut herself. Now there's nothing clumsy about my sister, and I just wonder how proficient Smokey will be."

Sunny raised one eyebrow in the direction of her mate. "If you're thinking of telling me I can't watch, don't waste your breath."

Brandon laughed. "I wouldn't dream of it, sweetheart, but let me warn you not to get too settled in. I sincerely doubt it will take long to prove the better swordsman."

Twenty~Eight

SMOKEY'S SMALL-BOOTED FEET were muffled by the carpet as she walked into the den. Parks closed the door behind her, and Smokey was glad for the few minutes of privacy. She had changed into her work clothing and stood comfortably gazing around the room, waiting for Brandon. She knew he would be along any minute, but in the meantime she studied her surroundings.

The den was as masculine a room as she had ever seen, done in navy and gold with hunting trophies everywhere. It was easy to see why Brandon chose this room for their match. All the furniture sat back against the walls, leaving the middle of the room wide and clear. Huge windows on three of the four walls made the light ideal.

Smokey was studying an embroidered hunting scene when the door opened. Sunny walked in, followed by Darsey and then Brandon. Smokey stood calmly, her hands clasped behind her back. She watched both Brandon and Sunny study her and smiled at their expressions.

Sunny, whose look was almost envious, was thinking how well suited Smokey would look at the helm of a ship. Brandon on the other hand, thought she looked ten years old. His face gave nothing away, however, as he opened a case and invited Smokey to select a foil. She chose a sleek weapon with an

Italian grip. Carefully weighing it in her hand, she walked confidently to the center of the room.

Darsey had seated himself in a comfortable chair, and Sunny stood in indecision. Smokey's first mate looked settled in for the afternoon, but if Brandon's predictions proved accurate, it would be awkward to sit down, only to have to rise again in a few minutes. After another moment of hesitation, she took the sofa.

Smokey stood still and watched as Brandon moved toward her. As he came forward, Smokey read something in his gaze. Her own lit with amusement.

"Is that doubt I see in your eyes, Lord Hawkesbury?"

"I must confess that it is," he told her with a grin.

"I'll have to see if I can put your doubts to rest," Smokey responded easily, and just held her laughter.

Fighting his own mirth, Brandon bowed low and straightened.

"*En garde*," he said, and their swords clashed.

Only moments into the match, Smokey sliced one of the buttons from his vest, and Brandon's demeanor, much as the pirate's, changed in an instant. His every sense was alert as his small but worthy opponent parried every thrust. As with Haamich Wynn, Brandon found himself to be stronger, but Smokey was faster.

He also found her gaze unnerving. Her eyes rarely left his. Brandon began to believe she could anticipate his moves before he made them. He feigned moves, tried the offense and then the defense, but to no avail. She was with him every step of the way.

Had he not needed every ounce of concentration, he would have laughed at his own conceit in the matter. Darsey's comment that she could hold her own was turning out to be a gross understatement.

As time passed in the most intense fencing either of them had ever done, each participant began to think of an end. Brandon was drenched with sweat, and his arm was screaming at him. Smokey's own face was beaded with perspiration, and her arm ached as well. She was tiring fast and about to cry truce when Brandon surprised her with a fast lunge and flick of his wrist. He flipped the foil right out of her grasp. They all watched as it spiraled neatly through the air to land beneath the north windows.

Smokey sighed with relief and bowed to Brandon, whose chest was heaving.

"I thank you, Lord Hawkesbury," she said. "You are a worthy opponent."

"As are you," Brandon gasped. "Allow me to apologize to you, Miss Simmons, for ever doubting your skill."

The two smiled at each other, and Sunny let out a small sigh of relieved laughter. She felt completely wrung out, and all she had done was watch. Darsey stared at Smokey like a proud father. Everyone began talking at once until Brandon, who had been facing the door, spoke.

"Well, Dallas, welcome back."

The other three turned in surprise. Smokey immediately felt apprehension rise within her. Dallas' face appeared to be set in stone, and she knew in an instant he had seen the match. Embarrassment flooded her, and she wondered if he thought she was out to prove something. She didn't know how to tell him that this was the farthest thing from her mind.

They all watched as Dallas came forward, unaware of how badly he wanted to take Smokey out to talk with her. The way she kept her head down and eyes averted, stopped him, however.

Brandon began to question him about his trip. Dallas did not comment on the fencing. Some minutes passed before Smokey slipped soundlessly away. Everyone noticed her departure, but no one commented.

Many hours later, Sunny knocked on Smokey's bedroom

door, a note in her hand. Smokey opened the door but did not immediately ask her in.

"Are you really not hungry?"

"I didn't say that in the note, Sunny. I said I didn't feel well."

The younger woman stared at her, and Smokey stood back to give her entrance. Garbed in a pale silk creation that perfectly suited her dark hair and gray eyes, Smokey looked lovely. To Sunny's gaze she looked completely ready to join them downstairs, but she had obviously made up her mind otherwise.

"You look wonderful. Are you pleased with the way Kendra did your hair?"

"Yes, thank you."

The conversation died then, and the silence became uncomfortable. Smokey took a small walk around the room. Sunny watched her intently.

"Are you wishing right now that you'd gone back to London on the first day?"

"No," Smokey told her after a moment. "I wouldn't have wanted to miss these days with you, Brandon, and the baby, but I'm afraid I never dreamed Dallas would return right then, and in a rage to boot."

"I don't know Dallas the way you do, Smokey, but I'm not really sure he was angry. Surprised maybe, but not angry."

Smokey sighed. "I don't know him all that well myself, but I'm embarrassed, and the thought of facing him makes my stomach hurt. So rather than come down and sit at the same table with him and pick at my food, I felt it best that I stay away."

"Why would you be embarrassed? Certainly not because of your fencing. You should be proud of your skill."

"It's not that really, although it didn't help."

"What is it then?"

Again Smokey sighed. "I'm just afraid that he'll feel obligated toward me since he brought us here. I fear that he'll force himself to be witty and entertaining when he really wants nothing to do with me."

Sunny didn't think there was any bigger fairy tale in all of England than the story of Dallas Knight wanting nothing to do with Smokey Simmons, but Smokey wasn't up to hearing that at the moment. Smokey was feeling hurt and vulnerable, and on the off chance that Sunny was wrong about Dallas' feelings, she refused to push Smokey. Instead she prayed. Moments later, someone knocked.

"It's probably Darsey," Smokey commented as Sunny went to answer it. Dallas, in dark suit and white shirt, stood in the hall.

"I've come to escort Smokey to dinner. Is she ready?"

Feeling like an anxious mother at her daughter's coming out, Sunny backed away from the door to allow Dallas a view of the woman within. When Dallas stepped across the threshold, Sunny quietly made her way from the room. Smokey, wishing Sunny hadn't gone, licked her suddenly dry lips as Dallas' eyes met hers.

"May I have the pleasure of escorting you downstairs?"

Smokey told herself to say no, but she couldn't follow through. With just the slightest nod of her head, Dallas came forward and offered his arm. Smokey placed her hand within the crook of his arm and walked with him from the room.

Not a word was said as they descended the stairs. Although Smokey didn't look at him, she was aware that Dallas seemed to be looking all around them as they walked. When Smokey thought they would be headed into the dining room, she suddenly found herself whisked behind the stairs, into the picture gallery at the rear of the entryway, and into Dallas' arms.

Smokey blinked as she looked up with wide eyes into his face. He bent close to speak to her and forced himself not to kiss her. With one arm snugly around her, he reached with the back of his free hand to stroke the soft skin of her cheek, his eyes warming as they held hers.

"I missed you," he finally said.

"You did?" Smokey was truly surprised.

"How could you think that I wouldn't?"

Smokey shrugged, feeling helpless and uncertain.

"Oh, Smokey, what have I done? You didn't wake up before I left, and I hated the thought of leaving you a note." Dallas stopped. There was so much to be said and no time right now.

"We're going to talk after dinner, do you hear me?"

Smokey could only nod.

"And one more thing," Dallas' voice dropped to an intimate whisper. "I'm going to kiss you tonight, so if my attention is unwanted, Smokey, you had better make yourself scarce."

Smokey couldn't have replied if she had wanted to. Dallas held her for a moment more before he released her, took her hand within his own, and led her in to dine.

Twenty~Nine

DALLAS HEARD VERY LITTLE of the evening's conversation. His mind and eyes were so centered on Smokey that someone could have set his boot on fire and he wouldn't have noticed.

As he had thought many weeks ago while aboard her ship, Smokey was far and away the most fascinating creature he had ever encountered. He now realized he was very much in love with her.

Both Brandon and Sunny, as well as Darsey, saw the change in him that evening and sensed his need to be alone with Smokey. The night was still young when the three made their excuses and Dallas finally found himself alone with Smokey in the parlor. Smokey became rather nervous but tried hard not to show it. She kept thinking about Dallas' words before dinner. The thought of his kissing her was very exciting, but it was also a little scary.

"You're not tired are you? I was rather hoping we could talk," Dallas said from his chair by the fire as he watched Smokey on the sofa. He wanted to join her but knew that for the moment he would need to keep his distance.

"I'm not tired," Smokey replied and licked her lips, a sure sign, as Dallas had come to learn, that she was nervous. As much as he wanted to tell her all that was in his heart, he made a firm resolve not to rush her.

"I was surprised to come in and see you dueling with Hawk," Dallas began.

"You weren't surprised," Smokey countered, her voice calm. "You were angry."

"I wasn't angry, Smokey. I was flabbergasted. I thought you told me at Willa's that you'd never fenced before, and I come in to find you giving Hawk the duel of his life."

Smokey frowned at him, trying to recall what she had said. "I've been fencing since I was a child. What I'd never done before was go for a person's face."

Dallas' eyes slid shut with remembrance. That was what she had said, but she'd been a bit flustered and talking very fast; he had completely misunderstood her.

"No wonder you didn't believe that I'd escaped him."

"You can't know how I've regretted my words and actions that day." Dallas' voice held pain.

"It's all right," Smokey told him before he could berate himself any longer. Dallas stared at her for a quiet moment.

"Did he hurt you, Smokey?"

"Not physically. He planned on it, but I escaped." Dallas watched as she wrapped her arms around herself as though cold, and wished he hadn't asked.

"He was so big; he loomed over me," Smokey continued softly, speaking to the fire. "He said if I didn't put the dress on, he would put it on for me." Smokey shook her head. "I couldn't let him do that, so I felt I had no choice. I felt so cheap in that dress."

Smokey had begun to tremble. Suddenly Dallas, no longer able to keep his distance, was there, his arms lovingly surrounding her. He held her for a moment and spoke gently.

"I'm sorry I asked you. Don't think about it anymore. He can't get you now, and even if he tried, you'd protect us."

Smokey's surprised gaze flew to Dallas' face. He was grinning at her, and Smokey, forgetting the pirate, laughed with delight. Dallas joined her and snuggled her against his chest. The silence in the next few minutes was warm and easy. After just a moment of quiet, Smokey continued to talk.

"I was really anxious on the docks. When you wouldn't let go of me, I pictured Haamich Wynn coming and killing you in his rage. I couldn't stand the thought, and so to save you, I ran away.

"I'm sorry I threw myself at you that way," Smokey went on. She felt Dallas' chest move. "Are you laughing?" Smokey shifted to see his face again.

"Yes, I am. The woman of my dreams comes out of the dark, kisses me in a way that makes my blood boil, and then apologizes for it."

"You didn't feel used?"

"Definitely not. I did wonder, however, where you learned to kiss like that."

"I don't know; it was my first time." Smokey didn't go on to tell him that she thought it was always like that when a woman was in love.

Dallas shifted then and could have easily kissed her. In fact, if either of them moved their heads, their lips would come together.

"You could kiss me again," he told her softly as he caressingly studied every detail of her face.

"You would like that?" Smokey's voice was just as soft. He was the kind of man a girl dreams of. Warm and caring for those he loved and with a deep love for Christ. Smokey was finding it hard to believe that he really cared for her.

"Oh, yes," Dallas told her. "I would like it very much, and if you kiss me, then I'll know I'm not pushing you where you don't want to go."

"And if I don't kiss you?"

"I'll wait until you're ready."

Smokey's smile was so tender that Dallas' heart melted. Smokey reached up and touched the gold loop in his ear before her hand went to the back of his head and she brought his lips to hers.

The kiss was sweet with yearning and passion, and when Dallas could speak, he whispered, "I love you."

"Oh, Dallas," Smokey breathed. "Do you mean that?"

"Every word. I have for a long time, but you're such a will-o'-the-wisp that I could never keep you with me long enough to tell you."

"I love you too," Smokey said before her small hands came up and gently cradled his face. She'd never had someone care for her romantically in the way Dallas seemed to care for her now. She found herself feeling so cherished that it took her breath away. It certainly didn't hurt that Dallas was so handsome. Smokey thought she could stare at his face forever. She was suddenly so overcome with joy that she reached up and kissed his chin.

"You missed," Dallas teased her.

Smokey shook her head. "I never miss; I was aiming for your chin."

"Ah. Then allow me to aim for your mouth."

Smokey chuckled, but the sound was cut off as Dallas kissed her again. Neither one knew it could be like this, so sure and so in love. Wrapped in each other's arms, they continued to talk for the next hour. Smokey was just starting to get sleepy when their host knocked discreetly and came back in. Dallas removed his arms, but took Smokey's hand in his own and stayed beside her on the sofa.

"I can hear Darsey pacing in his room, so I thought I'd better come down in order to rescue him." Brandon had taken a chair by the fire and now sat grinning at the couple on the sofa.

"You look as though you've ironed out your differences."

Dallas and Smokey smiled contentedly in return, and Brandon felt a little surprised that they didn't tell him they were getting married.

"It's not very easy for me, but we've talked some about Haamich Wynn," Smokey told Brandon. "Will I have to tell the magistrate everything that happened?"

"Probably, yes. I know it won't be easy, but we don't want to do anything that will give Lord Lynne a loophole."

"What did you call him?" Smokey wanted to know.

"Lord Lynne. He's the Baron of Farmington, and his English name is Lord Darrell Lynne. Why do you ask?"

"During the second capture I heard one of his men say his name, but I thought he said Lordlin and was referring to someone else. It never occurred to me that Haamich Wynn wasn't his real name."

Brandon's look was grim. "We've known for some time that he was a peer of the realm with an assumed name."

"So you've known all along who he was, you just couldn't catch him?" Smokey asked.

"Not really. But it was coming quickly. You see, he hung himself with his own method. A group of us met together about six weeks ago in order to compare notes. Lynne hit only ships owned by someone against whom he had a personal vendetta. He's never liked me, although I'm not sure why, and it was the same with everyone else who'd had ships attacked.

"When a few names were mentioned and investigated, it didn't take long for Lord Lynne to stand out. He's been sloppy lately; he hasn't even been pirating, just roaming the seas.'

"He was looking for me," Smokey put in and both men stared at her.

"He told you this?"

"Yes. He said he'd been following me for quite some time." She shivered a little, and Dallas put his arm back around her.

"Can you tell me what he wanted?" Brandon asked carefully.

"Me." Smokey told him simply, although her eyes were pained.

Brandon stared at her and nodded slowly. "The magistrate may ask you all of this. It might be easier if you tell me now."

After a moment's hesitation, Smokey did as he suggested. She left out nothing this time, although a few times she spoke with her flushed face averted, so as not to look at the men.

Brandon's jaw was clenched in anger over some of what she revealed. It sounded as though Lynne planned to make her a permanent part of his life. Brandon told Smokey that the pirate had been married for years. If rumors could be believed, his wife was a bedridden shrew, but he was married nonetheless.

Suddenly Smokey was very tired. The day had been so full. As much as she wanted to stay and be with Dallas, she knew she had to get to bed. With a soft-spoken word, she excused herself, thinking that the men would want to talk. Dallas surprised her.

"I'll walk you to your room," he offered, and Brandon rose as they left, taking note of the fact that Dallas rested his hand tenderly on Smokey's back.

He was about to follow when he spotted his wife's shoes on the floor. Sunny was forever taking them off and leaving them wherever she had been sitting. Brandon liked to tease her that he could track her anywhere just by following her trail of shoes. He bent low and scooped them up in one hand. Only then did he make his way to the door and upstairs for the night.

Thirty

"I DIDN'T KNOW YOU COULD RIDE," Dallas said to Smokey the next morning as she and Sunny returned from an early morning jaunt.

"A woman likes to keep some things a mystery," Smokey told him with a cheeky smile, and Dallas started toward her, his eyes watching her intently.

Without so much as a by-your-leave, he reached for her waist and swung her off the horse's back. As her feet touched ground, Smokey smiled up at him and Dallas dropped a kiss on her nose. He knew they weren't alone, but he couldn't help himself. Her hair was coming out of its chignon, her face was flushed, and her eyes were sparkling with love for him. Dallas glanced up to find Sunny grinning at him.

"Good morning, my lady," he said with a slight inclination of the head, his eyes twinkling with humor.

"Good morning, Mr. Knight. I trust you slept well?"

"I did, indeed."

Dallas said no more because Brandon was suddenly there, doing just as Dallas had, reaching for the woman he loved. When Sunny was on the ground, the four of them made their way to the house. They were nearly to the door when Smokey spotted Darsey in the yard. With just a brief word, she excused herself and walked to see him.

The old friends said nothing for a moment, but studied one another in open honesty. They were both satisfied with what they saw. Smokey saw Darsey's blessing, and Darsey beheld a sweet serenity in Smokey's small face.

"Were you really worried about me last night?"

Darsey grinned. "Just a mite. If the look on Dallas' face during supper was any indication, I knew he was going to declare himself. I didn't have a problem with that, but you're not married yet, and I just didn't know if I should leave you alone."

"Actually," Smokey said, as they began to walk through the gardens, "we haven't spoken of marriage."

"But he loves you?" Darsey pressed her carefully, not wishing to intrude.

"Yes, and I love him. If he does ask me to marry him, I'll accept in a moment, but I don't know if his mind has moved that far. As he said last night, I've been elusive for so long that he never had time to say what was in his heart."

Darsey nodded, satisfied with her words. He was also terribly relieved. He was feeling a need to return to the ship.

"Since you now know where you stand with Dallas, would you object to my returning to the *Aramis*?"

"Why, no, Darsey, not if you want to. Is anything wrong?"

"No," he assured her. "It's just a restlessness that comes over me when I can't smell the ocean and see the waves. I'll be more comfortable on board knowing everything is all right."

"Maybe I should come too," Smokey began, but Darsey cut her off with his hands on her shoulders.

"There's no reason for you to come, lass. Stay here and enjoy yourself; you deserve a rest. After this it's the trial, and then everyone will be back to work. Take this time while you can."

"If you're sure," Smokey began.

"I'm sure. Now let's get into breakfast. I'm about starved."

Darsey would have moved away then, but Smokey suddenly threw her arms around him. She hugged him with all her might, and he hugged her in return for long minutes.

"I love you, Darsey," Smokey finally said.

"And I love you, lass," he answered her, one huge hand tenderly cradling her face.

"It's all right with you about Dallas and me, isn't it?" Smokey had to know.

"Of course. My only concern was not knowing his intentions."

Nodding in contentment, they walked together to the door. After Smokey entered Bracken's huge front door, she ran upstairs to clean up. She was late to the table then, but to come in and find Dallas and Darsey talking amiably and then to have both of them turn and smile at her in love was worth any apology she had to make.

Darsey left for London right after breakfast. For the next few hours, everyone went in his own direction. Dallas didn't seek Smokey out until just before lunch. He found her on the lawn with Sterling. Sterling's nurse was not far away, but only Smokey and the baby occupied a huge quilt where they played and laughed.

Dallas smiled at the sound as he approached. Sterling moved a little closer to Smokey when Dallas dropped down beside them.

"This is Dallas," Smokey told the child. Sterling stared with wide eyes at the tall, unfamiliar figure.

"Can you say Dallas?" Smokey prompted, and watched as he put a thumb in his mouth.

"He can't really talk, can he?" Dallas wanted to know.

"Not the way you and I do, but sometimes he'll try the sounds. You should hear his version of Smokey. Can you say Smokey, Sterling?"

He grinned around the thumb in his mouth but didn't

speak. Smokey laughed at his look, and he laughed with her, all with the thumb firmly planted. The thumb was removed quickly, however, when Sterling glanced behind Smokey to see his father approaching.

The little boy dropped onto all fours and began to crawl toward the edge of the blanket as fast as he could move. Smokey grabbed him before his knees hit the grass, but he struggled until Brandon's hands were there to reach for him.

Both Dallas and Smokey watched as Brandon tossed his small son into the air and caught him in a burst of giggles. Smokey watched them play like this for some time, until she chanced to glance at Dallas. He was looking at her with such an odd expression that the smile died from Smokey's face.

"Dallas, what is it?"

"Nothing," he said, but Smokey was not convinced.

"Have I done something?"

"No, no," Dallas tried to reassure her and reached for her hand. He worked at controlling his expression, realizing he could not let his feelings show until they had time alone to talk.

Seeing Smokey with the baby had put Dallas' thoughts in a whirl. His mind had suddenly pictured Smokey as his wife, his wife to love and hold. He saw her swollen with child as Jenny now was, but the baby was his—theirs—and he was there for the birth. He saw her on a blanket in Maine with their own dark-haired child grinning at her. He saw himself playing with his own baby, not Brandon with Sterling.

Tonight, he told himself. *Tonight I'll ask her. I'll ask her to be my own for as long as we both live. We've been apart so much that I'll ask her to marry me right now so we can begin our life together immediately.*

Dallas' resolve gave him such a feeling of peace that it showed on his face. Smokey found herself staring at him again. She was still coming to know this man, so she wasn't certain, but he suddenly looked very satisfied to her. She told herself that one of these days they would be close enough so she could ask him. One of these days, she found herself hoping, she might even be his wife.

The coach and driver delivering Darsey to London were not due back at Bracken until the following day. Just before dinner, however, there was a sudden commotion when the driver arrived back early.

Parks was there to meet him, and after hearing his story, turned to seek out the family. Within minutes Brandon, Sunny, and Dallas were gathered to hear his account. Smokey, coming quietly downstairs to the entryway, heard also.

"They arrested him almost immediately, sir, as if they'd been waiting." Brandon's coachman was breathless with excitement.

"And you think Haamich Wynn is behind it?"

"I don't know about that, sir, but the talk all over London is that he's been released and the *Aramis* has been confiscated and her crew arrested for piracy."

Something cold ran down Smokey's spine, but she knew what must be done. She turned from where she had been standing on the bottom step to move back up the stairs. Dallas spotted her and caught her wrist just in time.

"Let go of me, Dallas. I've got to go to my ship."

"Smokey, listen to me—" Dallas began, but the young captain cut him off.

"No. You listen to me, Dallas." Her voice was calm, but no one within earshot could have missed the underlying note of steel. "I would love the luxury of sitting back and letting you take care of me, but I'm the captain of that ship and responsible to my men. I *will* go to London, and you'll not talk me out of it."

"I'm not trying to," Dallas began again, tightening his hold on her wrist. "I'm just asking you to wait until morning. We can do nothing tonight."

Smokey hesitated, and Brandon cut in.

"He's right, Smokey. It would be after midnight by the time we arrived. I doubt if even *I* could see anyone of importance at that time of the night."

Smokey stood in indecision, her heart so broken over Darsey's arrest that she thought she might be sick.

"I need to be away before dawn," she told them.

"You realize," Brandon began, "there's a good chance you will be arrested as well."

Smokey had not thought of that, but it changed nothing.

"I still need to leave for London before dawn."

"The carriage will be ready," Brandon promised her.

Smokey nodded. When she would have thanked them and continued up the stairs, Dallas tugged on her arm.

"Come to dinner and try to eat something."

"I have to pack."

"I imagine you'll be up most of the night. You can pack then. You need to eat."

Standing on the first step made Smokey almost level with Dallas, and for a moment she could only look into his eyes.

"Tell me you understand, Dallas."

"I understand completely," he said to her utter relief. "I just didn't want you riding to London tonight with no food or sleep."

Smokey nodded, and Dallas realized they were alone. He stepped near, his arms going around her. Smokey needed his closeness right now in a way she'd never needed it before. When he would have stepped away, she wrapped her arms around his neck. Dallas was more than happy to comply and hugged her again, holding her firmly for some time.

"Come into the dining room, darling," he said when he could speak. "You won't want much, but you need to eat."

Smokey agreed and startled herself by eating a fairly decent meal. She surprised herself again after going to bed. After praying with her whole being, she actually gained a few hours of sleep. She woke to find Brandon good at his word.

His largest carriage, pulled by four horses, left Bracken more than an hour before daybreak, after a tearful farewell with Sunny. Smokey was inside, hair braided and dressed for work. Seated beside her was Dallas. Across from them was Brandon.

The duke's face was calm, but he was a man who clearly needed answers. Looking at his stern visage, Smokey could almost find it in her heart to pity Haamich Wynn.

Thirty-One

SMOKEY'S VIEW OF THE *ARAMIS* from the carriage window was one to make her heart pound. She had halfway hoped to find that this was all a frightful mistake, but not seeing a single familiar face, as well as the heavy guard apparent at the foot of the gangplank, made her heart plummet.

The magnificent carriage stopped, drawing attention from nearly everyone. Dallas alighted to give Smokey a hand. Brandon was directly behind her, but not even he could stop the happenings of the next few minutes.

"Miss Simmons?" a voice spoke, and the three of them turned to see a young officer approach.

"Yes, I'm Miss Simmons. Where is my crew?"

"If you'll come with me, please," the constable said, ignoring her question.

"Where are you taking her?" Brandon spoke calmly, and the officer looked surprised.

"I'm sorry, your lordship, but Miss Simmons is under arrest."

"And what are the charges?"

"Piracy," another, older constable came on the scene and answered. His demeanor was that of one in control, but his voice was respectful. "I'm afraid Miss Simmons will have to come with us, my lord."

Dallas was ready to jump in at Smokey's defense, but Brandon, wearing his position and power like a cape, spoke up.

"I will be handling Miss Simmons' case myself, constable."

"Yes, sir," the other man answered, his face serious.

The younger officer stepped forward then and put a hand on Smokey's arm to lead her away. She looked back over her shoulder at Brandon and Dallas. Her face was a mask of numb surprise.

Dallas shared her shock, but for just an instant. He recovered quickly, and when he started after her, Brandon moved his entire body to block him.

"Don't do it, Dallas," Brandon said as he, with no little effort, held his friend against the side of the carriage.

"I can't let them take her, Hawk! Did you see her face? I've got to do something!" Dallas' eyes were wide with panic, but Brandon only shook his head.

"You can do nothing for her right now. Your interference would only get you arrested as well. Pray, Dallas, and trust God to work this out. I'll do all I can to set her free."

Smokey's mind was in a mass of confusion as she was led to a waiting carriage and then to a part of London that was new to her. The ride seemed very brief. In no time at all, Smokey was being led inside a huge stone structure. Her head craned back to take it in as they moved inside, and Smokey wondered if this was the infamous "Tower."

She was given little time to speculate, but was led immediately inside and to a cell. There was no rough treatment and few words spoken as she was locked inside. Smokey stood for a long moment and just stared.

The room was spacious with a large, barred window, and Smokey was surprised at the cleanliness. It was dry and swept, with a cot in one corner. Smokey's relief was so great that she moved to the room's one chair and sank gratefully down.

She started to pray, giving this nightmarish situation over to the Lord. She committed herself, Dallas, her men, and everyone involved to her heavenly Father. She'd been praying for the better part of two hours when she heard movement and voices in the corridor without.

"Smokey."

Smokey stood quickly, unable to believe her ears, and moved to look at the barred portal in the door.

"Dallas!"

"Are you all right?" His voice was anxious.

"Yes." Smokey felt breathless with relief as she stood on tiptoe in order to be nearer the man she loved. "Have you come to get me?"

"No." Dallas' voice and eyes were pained. "But Brandon is working on it."

"All right. Have you talked to Darsey or the men?" Now Smokey's voice was anxious.

"They're all right; just worried about you," Dallas replied. "They didn't hurt you?"

"No. It's not bad in here at all. It's just that I'm..." she hesitated slightly, "a little frightened."

"No need to be." The surety of Dallas' voice calmed her. "God is with you, and I know He's going to show us the best way to help you."

Smokey nodded, unable to speak. Dallas' fingers were suddenly there through the bars, and Smokey reached her own to touch his. For just an instant they let their eyes and fingers speak for their hearts. The next minute a voice was heard in the corridor, and Dallas' face disappeared from view.

Before Smokey could turn away, Brandon's face appeared beyond the bars. He spoke gently, and Smokey took his words to heart. "Don't give up hope, Smokey. I'll do everything within my power to set you free."

Brandon's "everything" was something to behold. Dallas accompanied Lord Hawkesbury to the office of a private investigator, where he paid the man a huge retainer to immediately go to work on the case.

When they were back in the carriage, Brandon ordered his driver to Parliament. Confidently striding into this building, Brandon moved into offices where Dallas could not follow in order to gain the real news of this case.

The charge against Smokey Simmons, captain of the *Aramis*, was piracy, and the rumors about the actual pirate were all too true—Haamich Wynn was a free man. The problem, as Brandon did more research, stemmed from the fact that Haamich Wynn had an airtight alibi for every charge.

Lord Darrell Lynne had reputable witnesses, one of whom was the prime minister himself, who had seen him at balls, parties, and even on the streets of London each and every time he was supposed to be attacking a ship.

By the evening of the first day, Brandon had gathered enough conflicting information to baffle a genius. He and Dallas retired to Brandon and Sunny's town house in the early evening, both men feeling spent and confused.

They talked over dinner and then for hours afterward before both went to bed exhausted but peaceful. They had formulated a plan. In the morning they would pay a visit to Haamich Wynn.

Neither Brandon nor Dallas would have slept so soundly had they realized that not two hours after they left Smokey, she had a visitor. He was a fat, foul-smelling man who did not use the main entrance to exit the Tower. Fear clawed at Smokey's throat as she was led out of the Tower courtyard and into a back alley to a waiting carriage.

"Where are we going?" she tried to question the man who

seemed to be in charge, but she was simply ignored as the carriage lurched into motion.

Ten minutes later the coach came to a halt in front of London's Klink Prison for women; Smokey could only stare in horror until she was commanded roughly to alight from the carriage and go inside. The smells that assailed her senses nearly caused her to vomit as she was led below street level to a dark, damp cavern.

She could barely see as she was ushered forward to her cell, but as her eyes became accustomed to the dark, she realized that the inmates of Klink Prison were treated like animals. Pale faces beneath layers of dirt were momentarily illuminated as the lantern moved across their cells. The eyes in those faces were nearly lifeless, as hopeless as Smokey had ever seen.

Smokey was taken all the way to the cell at the end. Until that time no one had touched her, but she suddenly found herself pushed forward over the threshold where she heard the door slam behind her. With just two steps she caught herself, but started violently as a weak but irate voice spoke from the corner.

"Put her across the way in an empty. It's my turn, and I don't want her."

"Shut yer trap, ya old hag," the guard snarled, banging on the bars with his stick. Smokey shrank back from both the jailer and her cellmate and then watched as the jailer walked away, taking his light with him.

A few moments passed before Smokey's eyes acclimated once again to the dark and she took in her cell, illuminated only by a small, filthy window, some ten feet off the floor. The cell was a square, Smokey figured perhaps eight by eight feet in size, with two filthy straw ticks on the floor and a chamber pot in the corner.

Her nearly skeletal cellmate lay prone on one of the ticks and spoke when Smokey's eyes met hers.

"You'll not 'ave all that pretty flesh on yer for long," she said in a voice weak from her surroundings as well as her age.

"How long have you been in here?" Smokey asked, although not sure why she did.

"This time? A month, maybe two. Down 'ere, you lose count."

Smokey suddenly felt as if her legs were going to go out from under her. She moved to the edge of the unoccupied tick and sank to her knees. Her pants grew immediately damp, but she couldn't force herself to stand again.

With a shudder that ran over her entire body, she let her shoulder fall against the damp stone wall. The old woman appeared to be sleeping. Smokey let her own eyes slide shut, only she didn't sleep. She silently prayed the only words that would come to mind as her world began to close in to the point that she thought it would suffocate her.

Help me, Father, I beg of You. Help me to believe You never make mistakes.

"I'm sorry, you must be mistaken, my lord," the young footman told Brandon the next morning as he and Dallas tried to gain information from the doorman of a rather seedy club in the heart of London.

"We have not now, nor ever, had a member by the name of Lord Lynne." The servant's air was so superior that Brandon wanted to laugh, but he also felt the man was telling the truth.

That day and into the next had led them to one dead end after another in an effort to speak with Darrell Lynne. A visit to Lord Lynne's London town house had directed them to his club. They had gone to White's, only to come up empty, and finally now to this club, where no one had ever heard of him either. Brandon was beginning to wonder if the agency he had hired was going to offer him anything more than empty leads. He also began to wonder how many aliases the pirate had.

Their choices were quickly narrowing down. Brandon and Dallas would have to ride out into the country where Lynne's wife lived in hopes of tracking the man down. Brandon knew he could damage the case if Lynne could prove harassment, but something was driving him to confront the man himself, and without knowing exactly why, he knew he must carry on.

"Is it routine to starve the prisoners?" Smokey asked her cellmate in a small voice as the second morning of her captivity dawned.

"They say it keeps us weak and easy to 'andle," the other woman told her. Smokey's heart sank.

They had done very little speaking since Smokey had arrived, mainly because the other woman seemed to sleep a great deal of the time.

Even though Smokey was still in a state of shock, she was aware enough to believe that the woman across from her was dying right before her very eyes. There was water every day from a bucket in the corner, but neither she nor Smokey had been given anything to eat since Smokey arrived. Smokey was hungry; the other woman was starving.

"Every other day," the other woman went on in a whisper, as though talking took more energy than she could spare. "They brings bread every other day."

Suddenly the other woman's words became clear. As Smokey had been pushed into the cell, she said it was her turn. Smokey understood now that her cellmate had gone extra days without food since they were not yet ready to feed the newest resident of Klink Prison.

What kind of place is this, Smokey asked herself not for the first time, *that they starve people to death?* Smokey could think of no crime so heinous as to deserve this.

The morning stretched on. Just when she thought she would go mad for want of food, a light appeared from somewhere down the cavern. It hurt her eyes as it neared, but she forced herself to look anyway, hope pounding in her breast.

Two men appeared, one carrying a bucket and cups, the other a basket of loaves. Keys jingled, and the cell door was opened. Two loaves of bread were thrown in, and cups of some type of gruel were scooped up and set just inside the door before it was slammed shut again.

Smokey scrambled for the bread as fast as she could move, cramming it into her mouth in a frenzy, but the other woman stayed her movement.

"Easy, go easy, child, or it'll make ya sick."

Smokey stopped in midchew and forced herself to calm down. She reached for the other loaf and set it beside the other woman's pallet.

The woman's laugh was low and had a rusty sound to it. "Ya must be something special when yer not in 'ere. Anyone else in this 'ole would 'ave eaten 'em both."

Smokey moved to the cups then and ignoring her own, took one to the other pallet. She held it while the old woman took a sip and left it within reach next to the bread.

Her hand shook so violently as she drank from her own cup that she nearly spilled the contents. The gruel was thin and gritty, but Smokey didn't know when anything had tasted so wonderful. After she'd taken a few sips, she looked over to see that the other woman had at least picked up her cup.

"What's your name?" Smokey asked her.

"Aggie."

"Why are you in here?" Smokey asked around a mouthful of bread. Again the older prisoner laughed.

"Now I can really tell that yer new to this. There's two things ya don't ask down 'ere—the first is why yer 'ere, and the second is if yer deserve to be."

"Oh" was all Smokey could think to say as she tried to eat slowly.

"You're an American?" Aggie asked, although it was more a statement than a question.

"Yes" was all Smokey said.

They fell silent after this small exchange, both now working on the food. Smokey was nearly done with her bread when she thought she should save some for later. She didn't want to think about the next two days, but forcing herself to do so, she reached to put the small crust into the pocket of her tunic.

"Don't do it," Aggie said, making Smokey aware of the fact that she'd been watching her. "Eats it all, or the rats'll come lookin' for it."

Smokey's breath left her in a rush, and she couldn't stop the shudder that ran over her frame as her eyes searched the dark corners of the cell and cavern. She took the bread back out and, after eating it, finished her gruel as well.

The older prisoner went back to sleep as soon as she was done, but Smokey only sat on her pallet, a new shudder running over her frame every time she thought of Aggie's words.

≈ Thirty-Two ≈

LYNNE MANOR WAS STRUCTURED in classic Italian architecture and set on grounds that were as grand as any Brandon had ever seen. The landscape was perfect, and both Brandon and Dallas thought they could have used their imaginations and been in any number of small villages in Italy.

The front door was opened without hesitation, and both men were greatly encouraged to at least gain entrance to the grand home. Only seconds passed, however, before their hopes were dashed.

"Lord Lynne is not here at the moment," a stuffy butler informed them, looking down the length of his long, well-shaped nose.

"Can you tell us where he might be?" Dallas questioned politely, just barely holding his temper at being treated like a commoner.

"I'm sorry," the man began, not sounding sorry at all. Before he could go on, a petite but lovely woman appeared on the stairs behind Brandon and Dallas. They turned when she spoke in perfect Italian to the servant.

Brandon, who was fluent in French and German, caught a smattering of her words, but missed whether she was pleased or angry over their presence. She stared at them a moment before moving down to the floor, across the entryway, and into an adjoining room. The butler motioned to the men to join her.

Once inside, the room proved to be a somewhat neglected library. Brandon held every one of the myriad questions running through his mind. He assumed the woman would need an interpreter before they could communicate, but only a moment passed before she put that wrong assumption to rest.

"I wish to know your names, gentlemen," she spoke in English, her accent very subtle.

The men supplied her with the information before she took a seat and asked them to join her. They did so cautiously, thinking this situation felt a little more bizarre with every passing moment.

"I am Lady Constanza Lynne. Mario tells me you were inquiring about my husband."

Brandon's face showed his shock, and Lady Lynne smiled with a bitter twist to her mouth.

"I can see, Lord Hawkesbury, that you have listened to the rumors around London—that I am a bedridden termagant. As you see for yourself, I am not bedridden, and as for the charge of shrew, let us just say that at times I have cause."

"Please excuse my behavior, Lady Lynne," he apologized immediately. "We are looking for your husband. Can you help us find him?"

"Why do you wish to see him?"

Brandon answered without hesitation. "He was arrested just days ago for piracy and has since then been freed. An American woman, a friend of mine, has now been arrested for the same charge. I wish to question your husband myself as to whether or not he had a hand in the matter."

"This woman—she is accused unjustly?"

"Yes, she is."

The regret they saw in her eyes was very real.

"I wish you would tell me everything."

Brandon hesitated then, knowing he could not sugarcoat the truth in any way and wondering if that was fair to her.

"Please," Lady Lynne beseeched him softly when she saw his reluctance.

Brandon nodded and began. He explained the pirating of his own ships and how he had come to meet Smokey. Dallas took over whenever the story moved to the seas and shared his knowledge of Smokey's capture. Brandon recounted a few details of the case he was building and also informed her in no uncertain terms that her husband would answer to the charges.

Constanza listened without comment. Neither man had spared details, and even though they were both calm, she could see that the woman, this American sea captain, meant a great deal to them.

"This Captain Simmons—you say my husband abducted her?"

"That is right," Dallas told her.

"Is she all right?" the woman asked with genuine concern. Both men were amazed that she didn't seem to doubt a single one of the allegations against her husband.

"When we saw her last, yes, she was well, but prison is—" Brandon let the sentence hang and shrugged regretfully. "Can you help us, Lady Lynne?"

She hesitated for only a moment. "I am speaking the truth when I say I do not know the whereabouts of my spouse. I wish that I did."

Brandon's and Dallas' disappointment was obvious. Thinking she would be a lead, they had spent valuable time here only to again encounter another dead end. They both stood, Brandon's voice a bit curt as he excused them.

"I won't ask you to report him should he come home— that might not be fair. We must take our leave now."

Dallas did little more than nod in Lady Lynne's direction as they both started toward the door. Brandon's hand was on the knob when Lady Lynne stopped them with a few words. Brandon turned back and nailed her with a look and one question.

"Can you explain what you just said to me?"

Constanza swallowed hard and nodded. She gestured with a slim hand for the men to be reseated. Brandon and Dallas didn't leave the Lynne library for another two hours.

When they did leave, they talked of nothing but the case all the way back to London. On entering the city, they went directly to the Tower in order to inform Smokey of the newest information. Both men were momentarily silent with shock to learn that she had been moved the night before.

After recovering, Dallas watched once again as Brandon went into action, this time to locate her. Dallas had to fight panic such as he had never experienced before, when, after several hours, Brandon told him that not even he could find out who had moved Smokey or where she had been taken.

The day after Aggie and Smokey had been fed someone else came down the caverns with a light. Smokey's heart leaped with hope that there would be more food, but a darkly cloaked figure, hood pulled completely over his head, stopped outside the cell.

The jailer held his lantern high, and both Aggie and Smokey squinted and turned away from the bright assault. Smokey was still squinting when the keys rattled and the door swung open.

From her place on her pallet, the man looked huge as he entered. Smokey could not think who would be coming to see her. Brandon or Dallas would not have been so mysterious. The big man hung the lantern on a nail and spoke over his shoulder to the guard.

"Leave us."

Smokey stiffened at the sound of his voice and used what was left of her quickly fading strength to come off the pallet and move against the far stone wall. Her breath quickened as fear pounded in her chest.

"This place does not befit a lady of your beauty and talents, my dear. Already I can see it's taking a toll."

The hood came off then, and Smokey stared into the face of her abductor, his smile and scar still in place.

"What do you want?" she asked softly.

"What I've always wanted—you."

"Get out," she ordered him, but he only smiled.

"I should have known a woman of your spirit would need more time, but I hoped."

"Hoped for what?"

"Why, that you would see reason, my dear." He spoke as though addressing a slow child. "My offer still stands. I want you and the *Aramis*. I'll have you out of here in an hour, and we'll be married by the week's end."

Smokey's lip curled in disgust, but Haamich Wynn only smiled.

"Will we live with your wife, or have a home of our own?" Smokey's voice dripped with scorn, and the smile vanished as if by magic. The pirate's face contorted with rage as he came toward her. She tried to move away, but he was too fast and the room too small. He grabbed Smokey and hauled her against him.

"Who have you been talking to?"

"Don't touch me," Smokey nearly spat at him.

With a near growl of rage, Haamich moved and a knife appeared, an evil-looking blade that made the breath catch in Smokey's throat.

Aggie came alive upon seeing that blade, but he ignored the insults and threats she rained on him in her weak voice. Smokey closed her eyes in terror, certain that he was about to slit her throat.

Smokey gasped, and her eyes flew open again when he grabbed her hair and gave a great pull. She stared in horror as he stood back and held all two feet of her braid up before the lantern's light.

"I always get what I want, my dear." The man's voice was so genial that Smokey felt chilled to the bone. "Think about my offer, will you? Next time I might cut something off that won't grow back."

With those words he left, slamming the door behind him and taking the lantern and Smokey's braid back down the cavern. Smokey sank onto the tick, her hand going to the hair that was now falling into her face.

Like a woman in a dream she felt around to the back of her neck. He'd cut her hair off at the nape. Smokey hadn't shed one tear since she had been thrust into this cell, but she now bordered on the edge of hysteria.

As she collapsed face first onto her pallet, the sobs began from deep in her chest and came to the surface as harsh weeping. Smokey cried as she never had before, aware of nothing but the pain of isolation and abuse. Smokey barely noticed when Aggie used what little strength she had left to crawl on her belly from her own flea-infested tick. She came to clumsily pat Smokey's shoulder and offer words of sympathy.

Thirty~Three

BOTH MEN WERE SPENT after their futile search for Smokey. They talked for a long time, or rather Dallas talked and Brandon listened. He shared from his heart concerning the panic he felt when they had found her gone, and then the men took time to pray, turning the evening into a time of spiritual renewal.

Just before the men turned in, Brandon told Dallas of his only remaining worry concerning the case. That was Smokey's ledger books. He knew them to be in the hands of a magistrate, and Brandon worried that they might have been altered. The charge of piracy seemed outrageous, but if Smokey's trading was too good to be true, the judge might sentence her for pirating on her own or as an accomplice.

"Then you'll have to sail the *Aramis*," Dallas told him.

"What was that?" Brandon questioned him, wondering why he had never thought of it.

"I said, sail the *Aramis* yourself. Then you'd understand how she does it. You've never been on a ship so sleek and yare, Hawk. I tell you it's like nothing you've ever seen."

Brandon nodded, his mind going a hundred miles an hour. "I'll do it," he finally said.

The next morning Brandon and Dallas left the town house after breakfast. They visited the home of an old family friend, and not long after he headed with them to the House of Lords.

Once again, Dallas watched with fascination as Brandon's power and position seemed to melt all obstacles and yield him incredible privileges. It took the better part of the day, but with very little fuss he was able to pull the *Aramis* out of confiscation and sail her.

With only a skeleton crew, both men sailed away from London with the late afternoon tide. Dallas played the part of mate and enjoyed watching Brandon's face as he stood on the deck of the *Aramis* for the ride of his life.

It took some time for Brandon to notice Dallas' scrutiny, and when he did, the young duke only grinned like a boy caught in the pantry.

"Smokey doesn't want to sell, does she?" Brandon cheerfully wished to know.

"I doubt it, but even if she did, I somehow think Sunny might have a few things to say about it."

Brandon's brows rose in dismay, and Dallas laughed as a shudder shook his friend's frame. The diversion was pleasant as so much of their time had been spent fighting anxious thoughts of Smokey.

They weren't out for long. Brandon had been given a time limit, and he had seen enough. Dallas had been right about the *Aramis*; Brandon didn't know when he had sailed a finer craft.

They talked about the ship at length on the way back to the town house and were pleasantly surprised to find that Sunny and Sterling had arrived in their absence.

"I got to thinking that this might continue on for some time and just knew I had to see you," Sunny told Brandon as soon as he walked in the door. Brandon, always happy to see his wife, took her in his arms.

Dallas moved into the study to give them a moment's privacy. The door was open, however, so when young Sterling joined his parents, Dallas heard every word of their reunion. Suddenly his thoughts were on his sister.

He had given her little thought in the uproar with Smokey, but as he contemplated the date, he realized she might already be a mother. His musings caused him to pray for her. He asked God to bless her and keep her safe whether she was still waiting, had already given birth, or was even this minute in the process.

Jenny nearly wept from her place on the bed when she saw Tate come back into their room and straight to her side.

"You were gone so long," she gasped.

"I'm sorry, but I couldn't find the doctor. I rode all the way to Willa's and brought her back."

Jenny's eyes widened as she looked around her husband to the older woman near the door. Jenny didn't know Willa beyond Smokey's loving description of her, but the sight of Willa's serene features was enough to cause Jenny to forget some of her fears. She would have told Willa all of this, but another contraction hit.

She gasped as it grew in intensity and was hardly aware of the way Willa came to her side, giving words of instruction and gentle encouragement. When the pain began to ease, Jenny spoke.

"I've never done this before, and I'm afraid something is wrong."

"Nothing is wrong." Willa had already checked her and spoke in confidence. "And you're doing just fine. Your husband, on the other hand, is about to faint. Send him away, Mrs. Pemberton, or I'll have two of you to nurse."

Jenny's eyes met those of the man she loved, and her smile was gentle in her flushed face. Tate's smile, however, was very pained, and try as he might he could not stop sweating.

"Go downstairs, Tate, unless I call you." Jenny released him, feeling calm now that Willa was there.

Thinking his place was with Jenny, Tate hesitated, but just then another contraction hit. With a walk that closely resembled a trot, Tate hit the door. He was shaking so badly when he got to the parlor that he could barely turn the knob. Inside he found Buck and Greer. After greeting them, he collapsed with relief into a chair.

He had sent a servant to tell Buck the news but wasn't sure if he had arrived. Buck told him that Greer had been over for supper, and so he'd brought her along. Tate was glad for all the support he could get.

"How is she?" Buck's voice was slightly anxious, but Greer's face was calm.

"Willa says she's fine, but she's in so much pain that I had to get out of there."

From that point on, Buck and Greer did their best to console and uplift him. Every so often he would go to the door, open it, and look up the stairs. But each time he would come back to his seat.

"Do you want me to go out and look for Doc?" Buck offered after an hour of pacing.

"No," Tate told him. "I've left messages all over town, so if he can come, he will. I think Willa will do fine."

The words were no more out of Tate's mouth than a blood-curdling scream came from the bedroom upstairs. Tate came out of his chair as though jerked up by a rope and ran for the stairs. Buck began to tremble all over as he sat on the sofa. From her place beside him, Greer reached for his hand.

He held onto it like a lifeline. "She's my baby sister, Greer. I can't stand to see her hurt." His breath caught on the last word.

"It does hurt, Buck, but you know that childbirth pains are normal. The doctor has told Jenny she's strong."

Buck let his head fall back against the seat, and Greer did the same, her head turned slightly so she could study his profile. She had just watched him put aside his own feelings in the last hour to be a comfort to Tate. Now that Tate was out of the room, he let down to the point of shaking all over. Greer thought he was wonderful. She didn't know exactly when it had happened, but she had finally fallen for Buck Knight.

"I hope you haven't given up on marrying me, Mr. Knight," she said softly and watched Buck freeze. Like a man in a dream, his head came off the seat and he turned to stare at her.

"What did you say?"

"I said, I hope you haven't given up on me."

Buck looked so stunned that Greer smiled. She reached with gentle fingers and brushed the hair from his forehead, her eyes full of love as she watched him.

"Am I to believe that if I asked again, your answer might be different?"

Greer nodded serenely, her eyes warm with love. Buck suddenly found himself with nothing to say. They leaned simultaneously toward each other, and their lips touched. When Greer would have pulled away, Buck's arms went around her. She laughed in delight before his lips met hers once again.

"Will you marry me, Greer?" Buck asked when he could speak.

"Yes, I will," Greer answered without the slightest hesitation. Buck had to refrain from shouting his joy to the room at large. Instead, he kissed her again. They were still wrapped in each other's arms when the door burst open 20 minutes later.

"It's a girl!" Tate shouted, and Buck jumped from the sofa to hug him. Greer was next in line, and Tate nearly broke her ribs, so exuberant was his embrace.

"A girl," he repeated as though they had not heard. "And she's beautiful. We're going to name her Victoria. Isn't that beautiful? Victoria Jennifer." Tate's smile was so triumphant that Buck and Greer laughed.

Upstairs a much quieter scene was taking place. Willa, now washed up and needing a seat, came to sit next to Jenny's bed. Tears poured down the old's woman cheeks as she looked at the tiny infant in Jenny's arms.

"I've always dreamed of being there for Smokey when she had a baby; you're the next best thing."

"Oh, Willa, I don't know what I would have done without you," Jenny said, her own eyes filling with tears.

Willa grinned. "Won't Smokey be surprised when she hears the name?"

"I can hardly wait. I wonder where she is now?"

"I don't know," Willa admitted. "But I sure hope she's on her way home."

"Yes," Jenny agreed. "And bringing my brother with her."

"Are you going to continue to search for Smokey?" a distressed Sunny wanted to know as they talked after supper.

"No," Brandon told her regretfully. "It might seem heartless of me, but we've tried every avenue and now we need to concentrate on the case. All we can do is hope and pray that she's all right."

"And this new information?" Sunny went on. "What will you do about that?"

"Keep it to myself for the time being. I've still got men looking everywhere for him. If they can beat him out into the open, that's going to be the best way to free Smokey, wherever she is."

Dallas was about to put a word in when a footman knocked on the door to announce a visitor. Brandon and Dallas stood as Brandon's private investigator walked into the room. Brandon, who was beginning to doubt the man's ability, did not greet him cordially.

"I can't stay," the man began without preamble, "but I've got to tell you, it's not good. He seems to have disappeared from the face of the earth."

"You're searching the docks?"

"No. I've had two of my men jumped and one killed and—"

the man cut his words off when he spotted the distressed look on Sunny's face and the anger in both men.

A muscle jumped in Brandon's cheek, not only over the man's refusal to do the job, but over his careless words in his wife's presence. His voice was curt and dismissive. "I'll be in your office in the morning. Until then, goodnight."

The room was strangely quiet after he left, and when the silence was broken, it was by Dallas. Both Sunny and Brandon knew he meant every word.

"I'll find him and bring him in. The trial starts in five days and I won't be back until I've got him. You stall or do whatever you have to do, Hawk, but don't let them pass sentence until I get there. I won't let Smokey down."

This said, Dallas bid them goodnight. He knew they needed to be alone, and so did he.

I can't stand the thought of her in jail, Dallas told the Lord of lords as soon as he climbed into bed and turned down the lantern. *I ache each time I think of it. Please take care of her, and give her Your peace and comfort.*

Tears came to Dallas' eyes and slid down his temples onto the pillows. He knew he had to get his mind off of Smokey, so he began to silently name God's attributes. He was halfway between "holy" and "righteous" when sleep came to claim him, something he would be thankful for in the morning. He would be heading out early to find the man who would save Smokey from death.

Smokey squinted against the light but could see enough to reach for the food thrown in to her. She passed Aggie's over with trembling hands and then frowned at the light when it didn't go away.

"My offer still stands, Smokey. Have you changed your mind?" a voice asked from somewhere behind the light.

Smokey started. She tried to see him in the cavern, but could only make out a dark shape.

Weak as she was in body, she was strong in spirit. With a deliberate move she turned her head away and continued to eat. She even asked Aggie to pass the salt, which brought a cackle of laughter from the old woman.

Smokey made herself ignore the low curse that emanated from the cavern just before the light went away. This time trembling did not come with the darkness as it had so many times before. The women finished eating in silence and when Smokey thought Aggie had gone to sleep, she surprised her by speaking.

"Somethin's different 'bout you."

Smokey smiled. "Yes, it is," she agreed. "Want to hear about it?"

"Well, A've an appointment with the dressmaker in an hour, but let's 'ear it anyway."

The comment brought a small laugh out of Smokey, but she went on. "Do you believe in God, Aggie?"

"Yeah," the old woman answered briefly.

"Well, I believe in the one true God, Aggie, and His Son, Jesus Christ, even when it wouldn't be logical to do so. Like right now, when it feels like I've been deserted, I know that God is with me.

"The last time that man was here and cut my hair, I was devastated. But then I got to thinking about all the stories I've read in the Bible. I thought of Joseph. He was in jail because his own family sold him, but he trusted God and believed it was for the best.

"And then I got to considering all the people walking around in the world who are in their own little prisons. I've been in a prison about my hair. I wish he hadn't cut it, but I still have so much to praise God about. He could have cut my throat. It doesn't matter what they do to my body; my spirit can always be free if I choose to obey God. I'm telling you, Aggie, I can be in this cell and still be free as a bird."

"It's all gettin' to you, ain't it, girl?" Aggie voice was compassionate, and Smokey wanted to laugh.

"No, Aggie, I am really free. I'm free to know that God loves me and sent His Son to die in my place. I'm free from the sins of the past and from the bondage of sin in the future. It doesn't matter where I am—I can be free in Christ, and so can you."

Aggie stared at her as if she had gone around the bend. "If God loves us, why are we starving to death down 'ere?"

"It is awful down here, Aggie." Smokey's voice was sad. "But I know of someplace that's worse, and that's a lost eternity, an eternity in hell. I don't know if I'm going to die down here or not, but I do know that I've a better home after I die. I'm talking about heaven, Aggie, and it can be your eternal home as well."

Aggie only stared at her.

"Have you heard of Jesus Christ?" Smokey's heart pounded in her chest. She had never done this before and desperately wanted to say the right words. She saw Aggie nod and continued.

"Jesus Christ is God's Son, and He came hundreds of years ago to die for our sins, but He didn't stay dead, Aggie. He rose again, and He lives today to save people like you and me, and to give us hope.

"I don't know why you're down here, but it doesn't matter what you've done. God is waiting to forgive you and save you from your sins. I trusted Him when I was just a little girl. You can trust Him too."

"I ain't never prayed before," Aggie murmured softly when Smokey paused.

"The words don't have to be fancy. I remember that I told God I was a sinner and that I believed His Son died for my sins. Then I asked Him to live in my heart, and I know He did because He's never left me."

"Until ya came down 'ere," Aggie said with soft regret.

"You're wrong, Aggie. It's awful down here, but God is

with me," Smokey repeated herself. "As long as I've got breath
in my body, I'm going to praise Him."

Smokey stretched out on her pallet, praying that she had
made sense to Aggie.

The older woman watched Smokey fall asleep, her heart
thoughtful. For the first time in nearly two months, her mind
was too busy for sleep.

Dallas stood against the wall of a dockside tavern and
scanned the room's occupants. In the four days he had been
out searching, he had found his height to be a hindrance. It
made him more conspicuous than he cared to be. Since he
was not a regular in these places, it was easier to stand in the
shadows against the wall than to take a table and be watched.

Four days and he'd come up with nothing. The detective
had mentioned that their prey seemed to have disappeared.
Dallas was beginning to believe he had been right.

With another scan of the smoke-filled room, Dallas pushed
away from the wall. He was meeting someone at midnight in
yet another tavern. Maybe this one would be of more help
than the others. With Smokey on his mind, he prayed this
would be the lead he needed as he walked back out into the
foggy London night.

Thirty-Four

THE MORNING OF THE TRIAL the jailer came for Smokey without warning. Giving her no time to even speak to Aggie, she was cuffed and led slowly back up to the streets of London. The sun nearly blinded her as she was led to a waiting wagon. She stumbled repeatedly from her blindness and the weakened physical state of her body.

By the time she was pushed onto a seat in the prison wagon, her legs were ready to buckle. The ride was rough, and her stomach started to turn. She prayed with confidence though, telling the Lord she simply had to be freed if she was going to help her men and Aggie.

Brandon stood inside one of the small anterooms outside the courtroom and waited. He had pulled a few more strings and was granted permission to meet with Smokey prior to her going before the magistrate.

He'd told himself to expect the worst, but he hadn't fully reckoned with how tiny Smokey had been before her captivity. Brandon was so stunned by her appearance that for a full ten seconds he didn't move.

She was a walking skeleton. Huge dark circles ringed eyes that were sunk deep in her head. Her skin had a frightening pallor to it and her clothing hung on her emaciated frame. Brandon's heart pounded, and he praised God that Sunny had not argued with him over coming to the trial.

"Sit down, Smokey," Brandon said, finally finding his voice. It sounded hoarse even to his own ears. He watched Smokey lick her lips, but beyond that she didn't seem able to move.

"It was a long walk from the wagon," she said cryptically, and Brandon knew then that she was barely staying on her feet.

He moved forward swiftly and positioned a chair so that she had only to bend her legs. She did so. When she sat, Brandon noticed a look of peace amid the fatigue in her eyes. Again she licked her lips, and for the first time Brandon saw how dry they were.

He pressed a glass into her hands and watched as her whole frame shook with exertion. She raised it to her mouth and found it fresh-tasting, unlike the water in prison that tasted strongly of iron, and she nearly choked as she tried to swallow it all at once.

"Easy, easy," Brandon warned her, but she didn't notice his words or the tears that had formed in his eyes. *Please, Father*, he silently begged. *Please don't make her go back to that place. I don't know if she can take much more.*

"Here, Smokey." Brandon finally had to step in and take the cup from her before she made herself sick. She looked at him with vague, wounded eyes that cleared after just a moment.

"They don't give you that much to eat inside. For a moment I forgot where I was."

"Smokey," Brandon spoke softly. "It's almost time to go in. Are you going to be all right?

"Where are my men?" she asked, ignoring the question.

"They were released just this morning and all taken back to the ship. Darsey said none of them had been mistreated."

Smokey eyes slid shut with relief. It simply didn't matter what they did to her, as long as her men were safe. She opened her eyes when Brandon spoke.

"You're going before Judge Pinkerton. He's a complete eccentric and loves a show, so be prepared for anything."

"Where is Dallas?" Smokey asked as though she hadn't heard Brandon's words.

"He'll be here." Brandon spoke with confidence even though he hadn't seen him in nearly five days.

The door opened then, and the guard outside came for Smokey. She was led into the courtroom and onto a bench. Another trial was in session, but Smokey didn't really catch the gist of it. Praying all the while, she half dozed until her name was called.

When she did hear the sound of her name, Smokey opened her eyes and was directed to stand in the criminal box called a dock. The magistrate appeared to be hundreds of feet above her, but in truth it was only six or seven. She looked up into his frowning face and had to catch herself when the room tilted.

"Has this woman been drinking?" Judge Pinkerton's voice sounded outraged, and Brandon spoke.

"No, your worship. She was in the Tower and then moved without my knowledge. I've just learned within the last hour that she'd been taken to Klink Prison, where I believe she was mistreated."

"You've no proof of that," the jailer stood and began to protest.

"As you can see," Brandon cut him off in anger, "she can barely stand for lack of nourishment, and when she was taken into custody, her hair was long. Heaven knows what else she's been through."

The judge's gavel hit its pad at that moment, and his voice was dry as it rang out over the courtroom. "Is the jailer on trial here, Lord Hawkesbury?"

Spectators laughed, but Brandon didn't join them.

"No, your worship, I'm sorry," he apologized. "I was only trying to prove my client innocent of drinking."

"Very well, carry on. No!" he said, suddenly changing his mind. "Don't carry on. I wish to know from the girl, who *did* cut your hair?"

Smokey blinked, not fully understanding that she was expected to answer.

"Does this woman have the proper faculties to come to her own defense?" Judge Pinkerton asked, frowning again.

"Miss Simmons," Brandon addressed her from his own box, his voice all business. "Tell the judge what he wants to know."

"What does he want to know?" Smokey was feeling completely disoriented. She could tell that the room was full of people because she heard constant whispering and some laughter, but she was too tired to even turn around.

"Just answer the questions he asks of you," Brandon instructed her. As Smokey looked to the white-wigged judge, Brandon prayed.

"What is your name, young woman?"

"Victoria Simmons."

"And you are an American?"

"Yes, sir."

"Do you know why you were arrested?"

"Yes, the charge was piracy." Smokey was feeling a bit better with something specific to think about.

"Now, why would you be charged with piracy?" The judge was again scowling.

"I own and captain my own ship, but I've never stolen anything."

"How did you come to own your own vessel?"

"It was left to me by my father."

"His name?"

"Clancy," she said, and a murmur went through the crowd.

The judge's scowl intensified. He studied her silently until Smokey thought she wouldn't be able to stand it. Trying to be as subtle as possible, she moved her hands to the railing of the dock and held on for her life.

"Did they feed you in prison?"

"One time, every other day," Smokey admitted and saw the judge visually spear someone standing behind her.

"Tell me your story, Miss Simmons," the judge continued. Smokey watched as he settled back in his chair. She took a deep breath, tried to settle her thoughts, and began.

"Some weeks ago when I was docked here with my men, I was grabbed, drugged, and abducted. I was taken aboard a ship, and when I woke the pirate Haamich Wynn admitted that he'd taken me. I escaped him and—"

"How did you escape?"

"We fenced—" Smokey had to cut off when the room exploded with laughter. The judge himself was looking incredulous, but he shouted for order.

"You fenced with Haamich Wynn," the judged asked, "and won?"

"Yes. I cut his face, and he fainted at the sight of his own blood." Again the room exploded, and Smokey had to stop. The judge watched as she began to wilt. His heart was unaccustomed to compassion toward Americans, but for some reason this small woman touched him. She was clearly not going to stand up against this crowd for much longer.

He rapped for silence once more and threatened to clear the court if there were any more outbursts.

"Please go on, Miss Simmons."

Smokey stared at him for a moment and then continued, her voice a bit stronger.

"He came aboard my ship some weeks after I'd escaped him the first time and tried to take over. He tried to push his unwanted attentions on me and steal my ship. A friend of mine sneaked aboard, and I was again able to escape him.

"We came directly here to turn him over to the authorities. I went to stay with some friends. When I returned it was to find that Haamich Wynn, who I'm told is really Lord Darrell Lynne, had been released. My ship was commandeered, and I was charged with piracy. I was put into the Tower immediately, and then taken to Klink Prison.

"While imprisoned, Haamich Wynn came to see me." Smokey, whose eyes were intent on the magistrate, missed Brandon's scowl. "When I would not agree to marry him," she went on, "he grew furious and cut my hair off at the neck."

Although the crowd was quieter now, everyone seemed to be talking. Smokey could not read the judge's face, so she waited, still gripping the railing with all her strength.

"What have you to say to these charges, Lord Lynne?"

Smokey's whole body stiffened on these words. He was here; he was actually here! Smokey's gaze flew to Brandon's, whose eyes, amazingly enough, seemed to be telling her to trust him. She prayed again and tried to stay calm, but her heart pounded in her chest.

"As you can see," a mocking voice spoke, "I have no such cut on my face."

Smokey turned slowly at the sound of the familiar voice. She stared into the pirate's face and felt stunned. He was the same in every way; handsome, arrogant, and seemingly bigger than life, except that his scar was missing. Smokey stared at him, but he ignored her. She turned back to the judge after just a moment, wondering if she might be losing her mind.

"So you deny all such allegations that you have been a pirate?"

Darrell Lynne laughed expansively. "I guarantee you, I have no need to steal from anyone, and as for pressing my attentions on this woman," the huge man's face was sneering as he looked at the back of Smokey, "I assure you my tastes run to women of beauty and grace—English women!" he emphasized at the end.

Smokey felt utterly defeated. Why wasn't Brandon saying anything? She tried to read his face as he too looked at the pirate, but it gave nothing away.

"Do you hold to your story, Miss Simmons?"

"Yes, sir, I do. I don't know why he doesn't have a scar, but I did fight him and I did cut his face."

"Would you be willing to prove that?" the judge asked her.

This time it was Brandon's turn to stiffen. He feared something outrageous like this would occur, but to refuse the idea would surely hang her. Brandon stayed quiet long enough to pray for Dallas' swift arrival and then spoke.

"What did you have in mind, your worship?"

"Why, a duel, of course. If Miss Simmons is as adept as she says, she will surely be willing to display her skill."

Brandon glanced at Smokey to find she did not seem as stunned as he felt, and wondered if she understood what was about to happen. Brandon knew he had to keep control of this.

"My client accepts on one condition, sir—that I be allowed to fight her."

"So that you can go easy on her, Lord Hawkesbury?"

"The duel will commence before his worship's very eyes, and you alone will be the judge."

"Done!" Judge Pinkerton announced with satisfaction. "This court will recess for 15 minutes so foils can be gathered."

Brandon came for Smokey then, leading her though the noisy crowd and back to the anteroom. Once inside he said only one thing.

"Resign yourself to the truth, Smokey. I wish it were otherwise, but the duel we fought at Bracken will feel like child-play after today. Dallas is not yet here, and I'm afraid that nothing else will save you."

Thirty-Five

"TELL ME ABOUT MY MEN," Smokey asked Brandon, who blinked at her in surprise.

He had just warned her how difficult their duel was going to be, and she asked about her men. Brandon stalled by giving her some more water, frustrated that he hadn't thought to bring her some food. She was still very shaky.

"You did say they were released, didn't you?"

Brandon was brought abruptly back to the present. "Yes. I'd been working for a couple of days on their case, and it was finally decided that you were the one they were after.

"I couldn't get comfortable until they were out. It wouldn't do much good to have you released without your crew."

"And you believe I'll be released?"

"Yes."

Smokey sighed. "Where was his scar, Brandon?"

Brandon opened his mouth, but the guarding constable knocked and entered. Just minutes later Smokey found herself back in the courtroom. Her eyes met the seething gaze of Haamich Wynn, and Smokey began to tremble as she had done when she'd been locked in the cell.

She was still shaking when the guard led her to the open area of the courtroom and held the foil for her hand. Her heart sank when she grasped the weapon. It felt as if it weighed a hundred pounds.

Smokey suddenly realized the room was deathly still. She glanced up to find every eye in the court upon her, and she hadn't even lifted her sword. Brandon was in place opposite her, and she met his eyes, ready to tell him she couldn't do it.

"Is that doubt I see in your eyes, Miss Simmons?"

From where the strength came, Smokey knew not, but her chin lifted and so did her foil. Brandon cried *"en garde,"* and their foils met.

Occupants of the room barely breathed as they watched Lord Hawkesbury's immediate attack. He came at Smokey without mercy. She countered every move, years of training overcoming her weakness. Judge Pinkerton came to his feet, absentmindedly dragging the wig from his head as the opponents danced around each other, both trying to gain the advantage.

Using the move that had wiped the smile from Brandon's face the first time they dueled, Smokey cut his coat. It was to be her undoing. She couldn't recover, and in a merciless downward stroke, Brandon flipped the foil right out of Smokey's grasp. The move left Smokey's arm tingling from shoulder to fingertips.

Smokey was so spent at that point that she couldn't move. Only seconds passed before the room erupted in pandemonium. Everyone seemed to be talking at once, and over the pounding of the gavel, Haamich Wynn could be heard shouting.

"This proves nothing! You could see how easy he was with her!"

Brandon turned to the man in fury, but the door burst open and a commotion ensued from the rear. The occupants of the room finally heeded the judge's call for silence as Dallas Knight marched in. Wrists tied behind his back and preceding Dallas at the point of his sword was Haamich Wynn, scar and all.

Smokey stared at the man's face in shock. His eye was blackened and his lip was bloody, but the resemblance to the man already in the room was remarkable.

Suddenly the first Haamich Wynn panicked. With no warning whatsoever, he vaulted over the railing and grabbed Smokey. With an arm around her throat in a choke hold, he dragged her back toward the judge.

"I'll break her neck," he shouted in desperation, his eyes wide with panic. Smokey clawed at the arm that was cutting off her air, but it did no good.

"Stay back or she's dead." He continued to back toward the judge's podium. He was about to shout again when he stopped dead in his tracks. The judge, his wig in place once again, was holding the point of one foil in Wynn's ear. The impostor had never noticed as Brandon set the foils up on the stand.

"Now release her," Pinkerton's voice was calm, "or the entire room will watch what we do with pirates."

With the point pressed against his ear, the first Haamich Wynn grudgingly released Smokey and stood frozen in place; in fact everything seemed to freeze outside of Smokey, who crawled to safety and stayed were she was as Brandon began to speak.

"The man you see before you is *not* Haamich Wynn. This man is Lawrence Lynne. The man in the rear, however, is Lord Darrell Lynne, alias Haamich Wynn." The crowd began to buzz, but Brandon continued.

"Darrell and Lawrence are cousins who have been robbing us blind for nearly a year. When Darrell is in London, Lawrence goes into seclusion. Only when Darrell is headed out to sea does he contact his nearly identical cousin to cover for him on the streets of London. The split is 50–50 from what I understand, and with the success they've enjoyed, there have been no plans to quit."

"Take them away," Judge Pinkerton said softly. "The case against Victoria Simmons is dismissed." The room exploded with noise and confusion.

The guards started toward Lawrence, but with a swift move he leaped away from the judge's box and tried to run. The guards fell on him.

It seemed to Smokey that a fight was breaking out in every corner of the room, forcing her to hold her position on the floor. Just seconds passed before Brandon appeared before her. As he reached to pull her to her feet, she saw the judge shouting to be heard above the fray.

"The press will be pitiless. Bring her out through my chamber."

Brandon followed without question and began to move Smokey forward. Her head whipped back just before they left the courtroom, hoping for a final glimpse of Dallas. Smokey spotted him amid the commotion, struggling with a man on either side. Then just moments later, before Smokey could find her bearings, she was outside, lifted into a carriage, and headed onto the streets of London.

"Where to, Smokey?" Brandon asked her from his place across the coach.

"The docks," she said wearily, praying as she did that Dallas would be all right.

"Are you sure? I know Dallas wants to see you. Sunny is at our town house here in London."

Smokey nodded. "I appreciate the offer, Brandon. I would like to see Sunny and especially Dallas, but I need to get to the *Aramis*."

"As you wish," Brandon told her, seeing that she was fading fast. He gave orders to his driver and settled back against the squabs.

"Brandon," Smokey's voice came weakly from her seat. Her senses were beginning to dull, but this had to be said. "In Klink Prison I had a cellmate. Her name is Aggie. I told her about Christ," Smokey's head had fallen back against the seat, but she forced the words from her mouth.

"Please check on her. I didn't even get to say goodbye. Please go to her, pray with her. Please—"

"I'll take care of it," Brandon told her, and Smokey let her eyes slide shut with a sigh. She wasn't aware of the way the driver used back streets to avoid being followed or of Brandon himself, who was determined to get her to her ship safely, even if he had to lay down his own life.

They stopped 30 minutes later. Smokey had been sound asleep for most of that time and was not aware that her ship was finally in sight. Not until someone called her name did she come out of the dream she had been having about sitting at Willa's kitchen table.

"Smokey," the voice grew louder. When someone shook her by the shoulder, she opened her eyes.

"Darsey?"

"It's me, lass."

"Is Willa here?"

"No, but if you come aboard the *Aramis*, we can sail home and see her."

"I can go home?" Smokey asked with childish wonder, just before she began to sob. Her hands covered her face, and amid her harsh weeping she was hardly aware of the way Brandon lifted her from the carriage and tenderly handed her to her first mate.

A crowd that included newsmongers who had been keeping an eye on the *Aramis* was swiftly converging upon them. Smokey's crew was there to surround her and to take care of anyone overly zealous for a story. In an effort to see them safely up the gangplank, Brandon's own coachmen climbed down and assisted in the fray.

With no time wasted, Darsey carried Smokey to her cabin. He knew that Scully was already preparing a bath, but when he got to the cabin, he saw it would have to wait. Smokey was asleep once again. Darsey stayed below only long enough to cover her with a blanket before going topside to cast off.

Lord Hawkesbury's coach was gone, and Darsey was glad that he'd already said his thanks. They cast off, leaving the docks teeming with frustrated journalists and spectators. By nightfall, they were out at sea.

Darsey held a cup of strong broth to Smokey's mouth, and she drank greedily. Her hands came up to hold the mug, but they were shaking so badly that Darsey did not relinquish his hold. After just a few swallows, Smokey lay back as though the effort was too much for her.

She had managed to bathe and even wash her hair. Darsey had changed the sheets for her, since she had lain on them before her bath and couldn't stand the thought of touching them after she was clean. After washing she had put on a nightgown and crawled into bed, ready to sleep for weeks, but Darsey had other ideas.

"You've got to eat something."

"I'm too tired," she told him, but he ignored her.

"I'll help you," he said and did, holding the broth and letting her take all she could. Then she was asleep again, and this time Darsey allowed it. She hadn't taken much in, but Darsey knew they were going to have to take things slowly.

Truly, "slow" would be the operative word where Smokey was concerned. As long as he was in charge, they were in no hurry. If it took weeks to gain their home port, then weeks it would be. And if it took weeks for Smokey to tell him all she'd been through, he would wait.

He found himself making these promises in his heart as he gazed at her sleeping form. Like the last time they had been separated, the tears poured down his face, tears for all the pain she'd known, and tears of thanksgiving that God had brought her back to him.

≈ Thirty~Six ≈

"I DIDN'T THANK BRANDON," Smokey told Darsey when they had been at sea for five days.

"He'll understand."

"Or Dallas," she went on.

"He'll understand."

"He didn't last time I left in such a hurry."

Darsey stared at his skipper. "This was nothing like last time, mainly because this time Dallas knows that you love him."

Smokey nodded from her place on the deck, desperately wanting to believe Darsey's words.

She had barely been able to climb the stairs, but she was sick to death of her cabin and insistent on going topside. She was wrapped in a blanket against the wind, but the sun felt wonderful on her face. The men had all come one at a time to sit and visit with her, and she could see that although they were a bit thinner, they were all right. Her heart overflowed each time she looked at them and saw that they were safe and well.

"Dars, can you tell Scully that I'm hungry?"

"Sure," Darsey forced himself to answer calmly and rose slowly from his seat. What he wanted to do was shout and to run for the galley as fast as his legs could carry him. She had wanted so little to eat since they had set sail. And even though her color was good, the skin of her face was still stretched tightly across her cheekbones.

That, along with the change in her hair, made her look like a completely different person. Her eyes were still just as big and just as gray, but there was a new maturity there. Darsey mourned the lack of innocence, but understood that God's way was always best.

The days flowed one into another as the *Aramis* made good speed west. Smokey slowly regained her strength, and a week outside of Maine was fully back in command of her ship. She even raced another vessel and won adroitly.

Outside of her regular duties, Smokey spent a lot of time sitting on deck and thinking. Dallas was constantly in her thoughts, and she prayed for him every day. She also remembered Brandon, Sunny, Sterling, and Aggie. Whenever she thought of Aggie, she remembered how true it was that a person could walk around in a prison of his or her own making and never be behind bars.

It wasn't easy to dispel the image of that cell. At times it was so real to Smokey that she could smell the stench of it, even in the wind. But she never allowed her mind to rest there. She would always push onward to God's grace and protection. Then the black clouds of memory would be rolled away to reveal the glorious sunshine of God's love, and Smokey would ask God for her heart's desire—to be Dallas Knight's wife.

Almost hourly she prayed for him, his well-being, both physical and spiritual, his ship, and his crew. She prayed that he would soon realize his dream to stay in Maine and build ships, and that he would want her at his side when he launched his first Knight Craft.

It was during these prayers that Smokey would tell the Lord all the things she loved about Dallas—his convictions and tenderness, his beliefs and compassion. But even amid Smokey's desire to be with Dallas for always, she never failed to end her prayer by telling the Lord that as much as she wanted this, she wanted Him more. She always asked God to help her accept His will above her own, no matter what.

It was because of this commitment concerning God's will that Smokey's gray eyes shone with joy and inner peace—a peace so deep that Willa did not believe she had been through all she said. When Darsey was finally able to convince her, the older woman sobbed like a baby.

But true to form, when the weeping was over, she rose and took care of her loved ones once again. In the first week of Smokey's homecoming, Willa fed her constantly. She also sat Smokey down at the kitchen table and trimmed her hair into an adorable style. It had grown ever so slightly on the voyage home, and Willa was able to make the front hang over her forehead in wispy little bangs and the back and sides to curl under, giving a lovely frame to her face. The effect was darling, and Willa said they should have cut it years ago.

Smokey was not so convinced. All she could think about was what Dallas might have to say. She knew he had loved her long hair. When such thoughts crowded in, she told herself that it didn't matter, that as soon as Dallas returned he would come looking for her and they would pick up right where they had left off at Bracken. But the weeks began to drag, and this didn't happen.

"Why haven't you been to see Jenny?" Willa asked her pointedly one day.

Smokey hesitated. It was tempting to tell Willa that she wasn't up to it, but that would have been a lie.

"I think I'm afraid," Smokey finally admitted.

"Of?"

"Of Dallas being there and not coming to see me. Of my realizing that his feelings might have changed when mine are stronger than ever."

Willa didn't believe for one minute that Dallas had changed his mind about Smokey, but she was not going to make any promises.

"It's not like you to be afraid of anything. You'll never find out the truth by sitting around here. Not to mention that Jenny is your friend and you've got a lovely little baby named after you that you've never even seen. If I were Jenny, which I'm not, I'd be a mite hurt by your indifference."

"I don't feel indifferent," Smokey protested.

"I know that, but Jenny doesn't."

This gave Smokey pause, and she realized she was being very selfish. Dallas was probably still at sea, leaving Tate and Jenny in the dark as to why their friend would stay away after all these weeks. In the morning Smokey packed her bag and asked Darsey to take her to Kennebunkport.

Smokey stared down into the cradle at Victoria Jennifer Pemberton and wondered if she had ever seen anyone so tiny and sweet. Jenny lifted her tiny daughter and passed her into Smokey's waiting arms. Smokey sat down on the edge of the settee and just stared into the tiny dark eyes that seemed to be gazing right at her.

"She's precious."

"We think so," Jenny said softly. The two friends smiled at each other.

After another look at Victoria's round face, Smokey's eyes skimmed down the front of her friend's dress and then twinkled with suppressed laughter.

"I can see you've traded fullness in one area for another."

Jenny really laughed at this and put her hand to her milk-swelled bosom. "I think I could have fed twins."

"So all I have to do to gain a fuller figure is become a mother."

"That's all," Jenny said with a nonchalant shrug, and the two women shared another laugh.

Smokey looked down at that point to see that Victoria had fallen asleep. She gently laid her back in the cradle. The women silently left the nursery. Neither one spoke until they were downstairs in the parlor.

"You look wonderful, Smokey," Jenny told her sincerely. Smokey's hand went self-consciously to her hair.

"I guess I should have explained."

"There is no need; Dallas was here."

"Dallas was here?" Smokey asked, trying to keep her voice light.

"Yes, and I'm sorry about everything you had to go through." Jenny's eyes filled with tears.

"It's all right, Jen," Smokey told her. "I'm going to be all right." Smokey was not sure she believed her own words at the moment, but she was trying.

They fell silent for just a few moments, a silence that bordered on discomfort until Jenny's face lit.

"I have some good news—Buck and Greer are married!"

"Oh, Jenny!" Smokey exclaimed as she tried to put aside her feelings of loss. "That's wonderful! When did this happen?"

"Just a month ago. They wanted to wait until you were back, but they just didn't know when that would be."

"That's all right. I'll have to go and see them. How does Buck like living in Greer's house?"

"He doesn't; I mean, they live at Buck's. Greer loves it."

Smokey's whole frame tensed. "And Greer's house?"

"It's sold," Jenny told her softly, wanting to say more. She wished at the moment that she had never promised Dallas she would stay as quiet as possible about the sale.

Smokey nodded, her face full of calm acceptance. Jenny went on to fill her in on the goings-on of a few more folks, and then Victoria began to cry.

"I'll have to feed her," Jenny said. "You can stay if you like."

"Thanks, Jen, but I think I'll take a walk on the beach. I'll be back before supper."

The women went their separate ways then, but Smokey might have come back to the house if she could have seen Jenny in the second-story nursery window, tears pouring down her face, even as her baby fussed in her bed.

"Please, Lord," she whispered against the glass, begging God with every fiber of her being, "Smokey has been through so much, and so has Dallas. Please help them to find each other and work things out very, very soon."

Thirty~Seven

IT FELT WONDERFUL TO SMOKEY to be able to stretch her legs and feel the sand beneath her shoes and the wind on her face as she prayed. Her voice was carried away on the wind, but still heard by her heavenly Father.

"You just want it to be You and me, don't You, Lord? You didn't want me to have Dallas or the house. Help me to accept that. Help me to see that having You is enough."

Smokey stopped at that point and looked out to sea. It was a sight of which she never grew weary. For a time it had seemed that she would be giving up the sea and the *Aramis*, but now she thought she'd best reconsider. Sailing was all she really knew how to do, and she was used to being her own boss.

"I want to face that pain of loss, Lord, and not just busy myself to avoid it, but I can't sit around Willa's and be underfoot there. Show me if You have a new path. Show me where I can best be used."

The tears came then, not a torrent, but they did flow down her face as she mourned the loss of her dreams. Smokey went on asking God to give her new dreams, dreams to reach for and realize.

Although her heart was heavy, she felt much better after she cried. For the moment she couldn't think about Dallas. He was not attainable, and she would only cry again if she allowed her mind to dwell on his face. Smokey was about to turn back to Jenny's when she glanced up the beach and saw Greer's house. Telling herself she wanted just one more look, Smokey moved toward it.

It really was the most spectacular home she'd ever seen. She felt there was little point in telling the new owners to keep her in mind if they decided to sell—she'd probably be an old woman by then—but she was tempted to rap on their door anyway.

Smokey gazed at the house in wonder for some time before she realized a man had come outside and was looking down at her on the beach. It was Dallas! Smokey watched in frozen amazement as he took the cliff steps to the sand and walked toward her. She didn't move a muscle, not even when he stopped less than two feet in front of her.

Smokey's eyes met his and then flicked to the house. Understanding dawned like a light out of the sky.

"You bought it," she said slowly.

"I bought it," Dallas agreed, his voice as deep and wonderful as she recalled.

Smokey took a deep breath and nodded. Dallas' face gave nothing away, and Smokey summoned a smile.

"I'm glad, Dallas," she spoke sincerely. "Buck told me a long time ago that you loved that house, and Greer told me she hoped whoever owned it after her would care for it the way she did."

Dallas simply didn't know what to reply, so he just stood quietly and gazed at the women he loved. The silence was too much for Smokey.

"Are you all settled in?" Her voice sounded too cheerful, even to her own ears, but Dallas didn't seem to notice.

"I'm getting settled. I have a few additions to make, but that may take some time. Would you like to come inside?" Dallas asked, thinking that if she refused, he would follow her all the way back to Jenny's. Anything to be near her.

Smokey told herself that going in with him was the worst thing she could do, and at the same time nodded her head and began to follow him back up the steps.

Even with slightly less furniture the house was as wonderful inside as she remembered. Smokey noticed it was spotlessly clean, and every windowpane gleamed in the afternoon sun.

"It's a beautiful home, isn't it?"

"Beautiful," Dallas agreed with her. Smokey didn't notice that he never took his eyes from her face.

When she could find nothing else to gaze at, she let her eyes meet his and could not pull away. Dallas whispered to her from his place some ten feet away, but Smokey caught every word.

"I've missed you, Smokey."

Smokey drew in a shuddering breath on those words. If he missed her, why hadn't he come? When Smokey voiced the question, her voice was tight with anger. "Why didn't you come to Willa's?"

"I thought you needed time," he told her, his eyes so full of pain that the spark of anger that had ignited in Smokey was quickly snuffed out.

"God has asked me to trust Him many times over the years," Dallas went on, his voice still soft, his look intense. "I've trusted Him when I thought the sea was going to take my ship down, and I trusted Him when it seemed that I would never gain the money for my company, but never has He asked for so much.

"I thought my insides were being torn in half, when I found that you'd been moved from the Tower. And then when I saw you in that courtroom, so pale and fragile, again I thought someone had thrust a knife into my side."

His words were heartbreaking to Smokey and she didn't think she could take much more. "You risked your life to bring Lord Lynne in. I'm sorry I didn't stay and thank you for all you did."

"It's all right. I understood. Brandon told me you were with Darsey, and I was fine as long as I knew you were safe."

"Why did you think I needed time?" Smokey had to know.

"Because you'd been through so much. I didn't know if my

presence would complicate things or help them. *And* I wanted to get things ready," he added.

Smokey looked a little confused and he went on.

"This is no passing fling for me, Smokey. The night that Brandon's coachman came back to say Darsey had been arrested was the night I planned to ask you to be my wife."

Smokey was utterly speechless as Dallas slowly covered the distance between them. When his hands held her upper arms, he went on.

"You did understand about the additions to this house, Smokey, didn't you? The first is you, as my wife, and then as God blesses, a bunch of little people who strongly resemble Dallas and Smokey Knight."

Smokey's eyes slid shut, and Dallas pulled her into his arms. Dallas loved her! God had given her all her dreams and more.

"I was in such pain when you didn't come." Smokey's voice was broken.

"I'm sorry. I thought it was the right thing, and I wanted this house, our house, to be so perfect."

He stopped speaking when Smokey moved and grasped the front of his shirt with both small fists.

"The house is wonderful, Dallas," she told him, her eyes pleading with him to understand. "But it's *you* I wanted, only you. Outside of that, nothing you could give me would mean a thing." The tears came then, and Dallas wrapped her in his arms once again.

"I'm so sorry," Dallas whispered as she sobbed, "so very sorry. I'm here now, and you don't need to cry anymore."

His words did little. He led her to the parlor then, and to the sofa to sit beside him. It was some time before she let her head fall against his shoulder and tried to control her tears.

"You know," she heard him say, his voice gentle, "I may never want your hair long again."

Smokey raised her head. "Do you mean that?"

"Of course. Why?"

"I thought you would hate it," she wailed. Dallas only laughed.

"I can't think of any hairstyle I would hate on you," Dallas told her, punctuating his words with a soft kiss. When he drew away, Smokey's eyes were thoughtful on his face.

"You've lost weight," she said as the backs of her fingers stroked his lean cheek.

"I haven't felt very hungry," Dallas admitted before hesitating and going on. "Was it awful?"

"Yes," Smokey told him without pause. "I know it could have been far worse, but it was the worst thing I've ever known. To keep us controlled, they fed us very little."

Now it was Dallas' turn to close his eyes. He wondered if he would ever forget the sight of Smokey's frail frame in that courtroom. From what Brandon told him afterward, he was almost relieved not to have seen the duel.

"You didn't answer my question," Dallas said when he had reined in his wild thoughts.

"You haven't asked a question," Smokey reminded him and then bit her lip when he slipped off the sofa, took her hand, and went down on one knee before her.

If Smokey had read such a scene in the pages of a book, she would have laughed. There was no laughter in her right now, however. The man she loved was fixedly gazing at her, his eyes telling her in ways he could never verbally express how deeply she was loved.

"Will you marry me, Miss Simmons?"

"Yes, Mr. Knight, I will."

No other words were necessary for quite some time. Smokey and Dallas sat wrapped in each other's arms and talked about their dreams. Not until Dallas mentioned a possible wedding date just a few weeks down the road did some of the sparkle die in Smokey's eyes. Dallas would have questioned her had he noticed, but someone knocked on the door just then and he rose to answer it.

It was Tate, looking for Smokey to come to supper. Smokey

was so amazed at the lateness of the hour that she laughed, the joyful sparkle back on her face.

"I'm sorry, Tate, but I had other things on my mind."

Tate looked between the two and grinned a slow grin. "May I be the first to offer my congratulations?"

The two men shook hands, and Tate grabbed Smokey in a fierce hug. "I've got to bring you home right now with this announcement, or Jen will have my head."

Dallas, whose appetite suddenly seemed to increase, was more than ready to comply. The three of them walked together, but only Tate and Smokey talked. Dallas felt as if he were stepping on a cloud—Smokey was going to be his wife!

Thirty~Eight

LESS THAN A WEEK LATER, Dallas rode a borrowed horse toward the port where Smokey usually docked the *Aramis*. His animal was already lathered and flagging with exertion, but still he drove him on.

In Dallas' front pocket was a note, delivered earlier and from Smokey. It was brief, and in Dallas' estimation, said nothing.

> Dallas—
>
> I need time to think, so I'm headed out on the *Aramis*. I'll come see you when I return.
>
> Yours, Smokey

Desperate to talk to the woman he loved, Dallas rode like a man possessed. He hadn't stopped to pack a bag or say goodbye to anyone. Smokey was on her way out to sea, and he had to have some answers.

They'd parted just two days earlier, when Smokey had decided she needed to get back to Willa's. All had seemed fine when she left. Smokey had grown rather quiet at different intervals, but considering her life in the last weeks, Dallas felt this understandable. Right now he was terrified that he had missed something important and was driving Smokey away from him. He simply had to see her to find out.

Darsey moved like an old man as he prepared the *Aramis* to cast off. Never had he made it take so long. He knew that if he carried on too long, Smokey would come up and ask questions, but if he moved any faster, Dallas would miss them. Darsey was as certain as any man could be that he was riding to find Smokey right now.

To most people, Smokey seemed to be a very controlled woman. But she also struggled with fears, fears that plagued her because she would not stop thinking. Just yesterday morning, Darsey had stared at Smokey in dumbfounded amazement when she asked him a question.

"Do you really think I should marry Dallas?"

Darsey blinked. "Don't you?"

Smokey shrugged. "I've been thinking that he doesn't really know who I am."

"So tell him. It's not as if he won't want to listen." Darsey stopped because she was clearly not convinced. "He's not going to change his mind," Darsey added flatly.

"You never saw his girlfriend, did you Darsey? Kathleen is beautiful."

"I see," Darsey said when he didn't see at all. "I don't think you're giving him a bit of credit."

"I don't know what you mean."

"I mean, you assume he's not sincere or has some hidden motive. It's not as if he were marrying you for your money." Smokey's face showed surprise, and Darsey instantly regretted his words.

"You know he's not, Smokey," the mate reasoned. "He doesn't even know how much you have."

"That's just it," Smokey spoke with sad logic. "That's just one more thing he doesn't know about me."

Darsey looked at her in despair. He honestly didn't know what to say, but then he wasn't really given time. Before the day was out, Smokey had gathered her crew, sent Dallas a note that said she would be away, and gone to the *Aramis*.

Now Darsey had begun to give up and put them underway when he caught sight of a rider. He squinted up the docks and noticed a tall man leaping from a horse. He watched as Dallas pressed a coin and the horse's reins into a young man's hands and ran for the ship.

Darsey continued to put them off while Dallas came aboard and labored to catch his breath. He then handed the ropes over to Robby and moved toward Dallas, who was still breathing hard.

"I didn't think you were going to make it, lad. I couldn't have stalled much longer."

Dallas nodded. "What's going on?"

"I'll let her tell you."

"Is she in her cabin?"

"Yes, but I'd wait until you're sure she can't swim for shore."

"That bad, is it?"

"Well, it's not good. I only pray that you'll be able to convince her."

"Convince her of what?" Dallas was completely in the dark.

"That you'll love her no matter what. You best go below and clean up so she doesn't see you."

Darsey didn't wait for an answer, and a rather bewildered Dallas made his way to the crew's quarters. After washing up and using Scully's brush on his hair, he sat on a bunk to wait, praying all the while that Smokey would believe and accept his love.

"You're being ridiculous." Smokey threw herself on her

bed and spoke to her empty cabin, but felt no better. No matter what she said, she could not convince herself that all was going to be well with her and Dallas.

She knew the best way to clear the matter was to talk with him, but what if her worst fears proved to be true? She had wanted to get away to prepare her heart for what might be. Yet she hadn't done a bit of preparing, only fretting and stewing. She felt the Lord calling her to trust Him, but at the moment she was too worked up, and choosing not to listen.

Smokey hated the jumble her thoughts were in and dozed for a time. When her thoughts began moving to Dallas and the last time he'd kissed her and held her close, she jumped up and reached for her brush.

Wanting to dispel any and all thoughts of Dallas Knight, she gave her hair a ruthless brushing and then tied it in a small ponytail at the back of her neck. She didn't bother to fuss with anything else because she was going topside into the wind.

They had been at sea for over an hour, but Darsey had taken forever to cast off and Smokey wanted to check on everything. She didn't have the foggiest idea where they were headed, something for which her father would have given her a tongue-lashing, but she planned to go up now and act as if she were in control.

Her short legs climbed the stairs quickly, and she stormed onto the deck like a woman with a mission. She saw a tangle of rope that needed attention and was about to yell for Pete, but something stopped her. Leaning against the mainmast, legs stretched out seemingly for miles, was Dallas. His face was expressionless, but his eyes were intent as they studied her.

"How did you get here?" Smokey asked after a moment.

"It wasn't easy," Dallas answered cryptically.

Smokey couldn't take his intense stare, and she turned her gaze to sea. "I had to get away and think."

"About?"

"You and me. I can't think straight when I'm with you." Smokey had given Dallas her profile as she said all of this, but he asked her a question that brought her eyes back to his.

"Do you love me, Smokey?"

"Yes," she answered without a drop of uncertainty.

"Do you know that I love you?"

"I know you love the person you think me to be," Smokey told him. Dallas was more confused than ever. "Dallas," she now went on, frustration rising within her. "There is so much you don't know about me. Take my family, for instance."

"I didn't think you had any family." Dallas' voice was calm even as he attempted to piece together what was going on.

"I don't, not now, but I did. You've never even asked me about my father or mother."

"You've never asked me about my mother or father either," Dallas replied, trying to reason with her.

"I didn't need to," Smokey retorted. "Jenny told me all about them."

They fell silent for just an instant, and Dallas' mind raced.

"Your mother died having you?" he finally tried and watched Smokey nod.

"Yes," she said, glad that he knew that much.

"And this was your father's ship at one time?"

"Yes."

"But you want me to know more before you'll believe that I love you?"

Smokey nodded, calming somewhat. "Do you remember the first time we met?"

"I think so; at Jenny's wasn't it?"

"Yes. You had just come into port and stopped for a few minutes to see your family. You told a story that night about seeing another young sailor. He'd raced through the coral reefs, and you thought he was trying to rival Clancy for daring acts. The way you spoke that night made me think you saw Clancy as a fool."

"Are you trying to tell me that because I ridiculed a legend that you admire, I don't love you?" The question sounded absolutely absurd even to his own ears, and Dallas saw in an instant that he should have kept it to himself. He watched rather helplessly as Smokey turned and walked toward the bow.

Dallas followed slowly, but for her sake kept his distance. There was something far wrong here, and he had to keep his head if he was going to find out what it was. If he followed his first impulse, he would grab Smokey and hold her until there was no doubt in her mind that he was a man in love.

"I was a little girl when I learned who my father was." Smokey spoke softly as she looked out over the sea, her small-booted feet planted perfectly to balance her body against the waves. Dallas watched her profile and listened intently.

"He told me he never wanted to be a hero to me, just a loving father." This said, Smokey turned to look at Dallas, her heart in her eyes. "It seems silly to be bothered about your opinion of Clancy, but I am. He was my father."

Smokey could see that she had thoroughly stunned him, but she went on.

"I started thinking about the fact that you didn't even know that. Here we are planning to spend the rest of our lives together and you didn't even know Clancy was my papa. How much does it cost to build one ship, Dallas?" Smokey's change in topics so floored Dallas that he stuttered when he spoke. He named an approximate figure, and Smokey went on.

"I could build you ten ships on just what I have in the Kennebunk bank alone."

Again Dallas felt as if he'd received a hard blow to the gut. He was surprised over these things, but he still couldn't believe they made Smokey doubt his love. He spoke carefully, hoping he had the right words.

"I am surprised that Clancy is your father, but I also think it's wonderful. And I wouldn't care if you had one dollar or one million, I would love you just the same. I believe with all my heart that we love each other, Smokey, and knowing that, I also believe we can talk all of this out."

"I also want a white dress and a fancy wedding," Smokey told him as if this would be the final straw. Tears began to puddle in her eyes.

"Well, you can have both." Dallas told her with a smile.

"Not if we get married in two weeks," she said, and Dallas watched a single tear roll down her cheek. She looked so forlorn that Dallas wanted to cry himself. All this was very important to her, and she hadn't known how to tell him. As he gazed at her, she turned back to the railing and stood still. She didn't move or speak even when she felt Dallas come to stand behind her.

He reached with long arms and grasped the railing on either side of her, effectively locking Smokey between his arms. He bent and placed a kiss on the top of her head and then one below her right ear.

"I never meant to rush you," he began softly, his chin resting on her hair. "In the future all you have to do is come to me, and we'll talk the problem out."

"Will there really be a future?" Smokey wanted to know.

"Definitely. In fact, it's starting right now."

Smokey turned in the circle of his arms, and looked up into his beloved face.

"From this point forward," Dallas told her, "I'm not going to rush you. Whatever is important to you is important to me. You're going to have the wedding you want; I will see to it myself. We're going to talk every day and not let any upset or anger go undiscussed.

"I don't know of any other woman who could survive what you have this past year, and your self-sufficiency sometimes makes me forget how much tender care you need. I'm telling you now that I'm here to give you that, and I'm going to be more sensitive in the very near future."

Smokey's heart melted at his words, and Dallas could wait no longer to kiss her. He held her tenderly for long moments and kissed her with all the love and desire he had kept stored inside. When Smokey could finally breathe, she nearly laughed at the sight behind Dallas.

"My men are watching." It was literally the whole crew.

"What do they see?" Dallas asked without turning around.

"A man and woman in love," Smokey told him contentedly.

"Do they also see a man and woman who are going to become husband and wife?"

Smokey nodded. "Yes, but I won't promise not to be overcome with fears again."

"I can deal with that as long as you promise to come to me."

"I promise."

Dallas kissed her again, and then stared down at her with childish wonder in his eyes.

"He was really your father?"

Smokey smiled in return. "Really."

"Wow," Dallas said in deep admiration, before he kissed her once again. When he raised his head, it was Smokey's turn.

"Wow," was all she could get out before he kissed her anew.

Epilogue

FOURTEEN MONTHS LATER

DALLAS PACED THE SMALL CONFINES of the captain's cabin, imploring the ceiling in frustration as he moved.

"'Just a quick trip down the coast, Dallas,' she says to me. 'We haven't seen your folks since the wedding, and I miss them,' she says. 'The baby's not due for ages,' were her words."

He stopped and turned quickly toward the bunk, his expression going from frustration to worry until a small moan escaped his wife.

"I'm sorry," he spoke breathlessly as he knelt by the bunk and brushed the hair from Smokey's damp face. "I didn't mean any of that. I'll never say another sarcastic word as long as I live if you'll just wait until we get home to have this baby."

Smokey panted as the contraction died down. "I can't help it, Dallas. He's coming, and I can't help it."

"*She's* coming," Dallas automatically corrected her as he had done for six months. "We'll be there in less than an hour," he continued pleadingly, as though she could control the demands of her body.

Smokey opened her mouth to tell him she was trying, but another contraction hit. Dallas watched his wife's agony as the pain of seeing her suffer racked his own body. Smokey moaned low in her throat at that moment but said nothing; Dallas didn't think he could take any more.

I don't know the first thing about delivering a baby, Lord. Please help us, Dallas began to pray. He continued to pray for the next hour.

Smokey didn't seem any more comfortable, but she was wonderful as each pain came and went. An hour later they had docked at Kennebunk, but not left the ship. Darsey had gone for help. Just when Dallas didn't think he could go on much longer, someone knocked on the door and entered. He breathed a great sigh of relief at the sight of Willa. The older woman checked Smokey with swift, practiced movements and pronounced her too far along to be moved.

Dallas would have groaned at the news, but there was no time. The next 40 minutes passed in a blur for the young husband, as Willa coaxed and coached and then presented Dallas and Smokey with a large baby boy. He was red and screaming and the enamored father thought him beautiful.

Smokey, in a state of near exhaustion, commented that he was rather wrinkly. Willa told her in a huff that he was the most beautiful baby on the earth, but Smokey only chuckled and closed her eyes.

Five hours later, after much careful maneuvering, Dallas had his wife and son at home. Smokey was tucked up neatly in their big bed, and the baby, who had just eaten, was sleeping beside her. Dallas sat down gingerly on the bed and looked into Smokey's eyes.

"Have I thanked you for my beautiful son?" Dallas asked her.

"I think you just did," Smokey told him, a tender smile on her lips. "Are you terribly disappointed that I got my boy?"

Dallas grinned. "No. We'll have that girl next time."

Smokey groaned, and Dallas leaned to kiss her.

"What are we going to name this little person?" Smokey asked, even though she had already decided she wanted another Dallas.

"Well, I think it's rather obvious," Dallas told her. Smokey sighed with pleasure, knowing he was going to agree with her.

"This," Dallas spoke as he lifted his sleeping son from the crook of Smokey's arm, "is Clancy Knight."

Smokey's eyes rounded, and her pretty mouth dropped open. Dallas, who was kissing his son, grinned in delight over the top of his silky head.

"Clancy?" Smokey whispered.

"Of course." Dallas' voice was low as well. "I didn't need to know your father to believe that he would have been thrilled with his grandson."

Smokey bit her lip, but tears still filled her eyes.

"And," Dallas continued, "it won't be long at all before our little Clancy understands what a special man his grandfather was, and he'll be proud to share his name."

"Oh, Dallas," Smokey sighed. "I think you're wonderful."

"Thank you, my love," he said simply, and he placed Clancy back in Smokey's arms. "I think you're pretty special yourself."

Fatigue was swiftly crowding in on Smokey, and she could only manage a contented smile before her eyes closed.

Dallas quietly took a chair near the bed and watched his family sleep. A letter had come from Sunny, telling Smokey that Aggie, who had been working at Bracken for some months, had come to a saving knowledge of Jesus Christ. Dallas knew that Smokey would be thrilled with the news.

Tate, Jenny, Victoria, and their new little Carol had all come with a gift, but hadn't stayed when they'd learned that Smokey had just been settled in.

Dallas had forgotten to tell Smokey any of this, and now she was asleep. At the moment, however, none of it seemed to matter. God had given them a son so perfect and wonderful that Dallas couldn't, as yet, find the words to thank Him. He felt tears sting at the back of his throat every time he tried.

As Dallas watched them sleep, he suddenly chuckled to himself when he thought about how closely Clancy had come to being born at sea, and how fitting it was that he had been born aboard the *Aramis*. The laughter quieted when his mind unexpectedly turned back to the last weeks, months, and years in which he had known Smokey. So much had happened, and God's love and provision had been so faithful.

Smokey's favorite verses from Psalm 139 jumped to mind at that moment. Dallas was feeling very tired himself, but before he drifted off to sleep in the chair, these were the verses in his heart:

> *Whither shall I go from thy Spirit? Or whither shall I flee from thy presence? If I ascend up into heaven, thou art there; if I make my bed in hell, behold, thou art there. If I take the wings of the morning, and dwell in the uttermost parts of the sea, even there shall thy hand lead me, and thy right hand shall hold me.*

Books by Lori Wick

A Place Called Home Series
A Place Called Home
A Song for Silas
The Long Road Home
A Gathering of Memories

The Californians
Whatever Tomorrow Brings
As Time Goes By
Sean Donovan
Donovan's Daughter

Kensington Chronicles
The Hawk and the Jewel
Wings of the Morning
Who Brings Forth the Wind
The Knight and the Dove

Rocky Mountain Memories
Where the Wild Rose Blooms
Whispers of Moonlight
To Know Her by Name
Promise Me Tomorrow

The Yellow Rose Trilogy
Every Little Thing About You
A Texas Sky
City Girl

English Garden Series
The Proposal
The Rescue
The Visitor
The Pursuit

The Tucker Mills Trilogy
Moonlight on the Millpond
Just Above a Whisper
Leave a Candle Burning

Contemporary Fiction
Sophie's Heart
Pretense
The Princess
Bamboo & Lace
Every Storm
White Chocolate Moments